A SLIGHTLY BITTER TASTE

On the night when Quinn of the *Morning Post* began his holiday, he strayed into a late party. When he got drunk, a girl called Carole made herself responsible for him. Next day, she took him off for a quiet weekend with friends in Dorset. But Carole's friends turn out to be very strange people. Within a few hours, death joins the guests at Elm Lodge. Inevitably, Quinn gets caught up in the smouldering passions that govern this house of secrets.

HARRY CARMICHAEL

A SLIGHTLY BITTER TASTE

Complete and Unabridged

LINFORD
Leicester

First published in Great Britain

First Linford Edition
published 1997

British Library CIP Data

Carmichael, Harry, *1908 –*
    A slightly bitter taste.—Large print ed.—
Linford mystery library
1. Detective and mystery stories
2. Large type books
I. Title
823.9′14 [F]

ISBN 0–7089–5160–0

Published by
F. A. Thorpe (Publishing) Ltd.
Anstey, Leicestershire

Set by Words & Graphics Ltd.
Anstey, Leicestershire
Printed and bound in Great Britain by
T. J. International Ltd., Padstow, Cornwall

This book is printed on acid-free paper

To my wife — with love
' . . . Give her of the fruit
of her hands.'

Yet she must die, else she'll betray more men,
Put out the light, and then put out the light :

Othello
Act V, Sc. ii

1

IT was a good party. At the end of an hour Quinn was enjoying himself immensely. From the very start they hadn't treated him as a stranger. He was one of them as soon as he walked in.

During the next hour he decided that he hadn't enjoyed anything so much in a long time. Everybody was very friendly, everybody laughed at everybody else's jokes. There was plenty to eat and plenty to drink and plenty of ready listeners.

They laughed extravagantly at everything Quinn said. They kept saying he was the last word. As the evening wore on he told himself this was one of those nights to remember.

Afterwards he didn't remember very much. From one a.m. onwards he had only a hazy recollection of noise and

1

laughter and a never-empty glass.

They were all such nice people — warm, hospitable people who made him feel at home. Come to think of it, home was never like this. Anyone would've imagined they were all old friends. A few drinks later he wondered how he could ever have thought they were strangers.

Later still he found himself in the company of a little dark girl with a husky voice. She was fun. Not especially good-looking but attractive enough to feed his vanity.

Her sharp wit amused him, too. The longer they were together the more he liked her. They were two of a kind, except that she drank tomato juice — plain, undiluted tomato juice without even a dash of Worcester Sauce.

That made her different from all the rest. He liked her even better for not drinking like the others. They certainly knew how to knock it back.

Not that they weren't nice people . . . real friendly lot . . . the sort of company that was all too rare these days. Funny why he hadn't met them before. On the other hand the world must be full of people he'd never met . . .

This little dark girl, for instance. She was cute.

. . . No wedding ring . . . no rings on her left hand. Don't suppose she'd mind if I kissed her. There's a couple over in that corner who look as if they're making a meal of each other. No harm in a kiss between friends. If she objects she's only got to say so. I can't imagine her screaming the place down . . .

The dark girl didn't scream. She didn't do anything. She just stood quite still, her eyes wide and distant, her mouth unresponsive.

As the moments passed he began to feel rather foolish. It was like kissing a dummy made of sponge rubber.

She went on looking up at him as he drew back and tried desperately to think of something funny to say — anything

3

that would get him over this awkward silence. The way he felt was absurd. He had no reason to be embarrassed just because she didn't fancy him.

. . . So you're not her type. So you made a mistake — that's all. It's not the first time and it won't be the last. No need to apologise. You'll only make an idiot of yourself . . .

With the same remote look in her eyes, the dark girl asked, "Satisfied?"

Quinn didn't know what kind of answer she expected. If he hadn't had too much to drink he'd have been more sure of himself. In a situation like this there was always a right thing and a wrong thing to say. He had to think of something to salvage his dignity.

Common sense told him to keep his mouth shut but his befuddled wits wouldn't let him. He said, "Hardly. Of all the girls I've ever kissed you give the least satisfaction. Are you like that with everybody — or do I smell?"

She gave him a quick smile, her white even teeth just showing. In a

4

barbed voice, she said, "That's a double question so I'll give you a double answer: I'm not and you do. Your breath could be bottled and sold back to the distillery at a profit."

"You don't have to be rude," Quinn said. "If you took a drink like everybody else — "

"Why should I? Alcohol doesn't agree with me. It makes my bones ache. What's more, I can have a perfectly good time without it. I don't need anything to help me run away."

"Meaning what?"

"You know quite well. Most people get drunk to escape from their inhibitions."

"And you haven't got any," Quinn said.

"Well" — her eyes were suddenly laughing at him — "let's say I don't put them on display."

He wanted to be angry with her. She had no right to treat him like a small boy.

Yet if he hadn't kissed her this would

5

never have happened . . . so maybe it was his own fault. They'd been having fun until he did something he shouldn't have done. No use denying it.

Pity . . . Now he'd spoiled everything. Best thing he could do was go and get lost.

Helluva start to a holiday. They might've spent a little time together . . . just the two of them . . . that would've been fun . . . no monkey business . . . she wasn't that sort of a girl . . . although you never could tell . . . not many nowadays who didn't do a spot of hopping in and out of bed . . .

He had got as far as that when she asked, "Have you forgotten I'm here?" Her mouth was still smiling but her eyes were serious.

Quinn said, "That's what I don't understand. It's obvious you don't like me and — "

"Because I didn't swoon in your arms?" Once again her voice had a bite.

6

"Not at all. Now you're being silly."

"All right. Then what made you think I'd enjoy being pawed by someone I met less than an hour ago?"

Resentment prodded Quinn into hot protest. "That's damned unfair. I never did any pawing. The amount of fuss you make just because I kissed you . . . "

The dark girl asked, "Why?"

"And that's another thing," Quinn said. "All these questions are enough to drive a fellow round the bend. How do I know why you made a fuss? Maybe it's got something to do with your upbringing. Maybe you should see a psychiatrist. I once read — "

"Never mind what you read. I'm just curious to know why you wanted to kiss me."

Quinn retired into the confused depths of his own mind and searched for an answer. After a while he discovered that he had forgotten what she'd asked him.

So he said, "I need time to think

that over. It's rather difficult . . . "

"No, it isn't. You must've had a reason."

"For doing what?"

She studied him with her sleek dark head tilted a little on one side. Then she said, "You have had a few, haven't you? Guess you'd better go somewhere and lie down."

"I'm fine," Quinn said. "Don't change the subject. You were saying I must've had a reason for doing something or other. Now go on from there."

"If you insist — although it doesn't seem important any more. Why did you kiss me?"

"Ah, now you're being ridiculous. Why does anybody kiss anybody?"

"But I'm not the kissable type. My best friend wouldn't say I was beautiful . . . and you must admit I don't act sexy. Yet you suddenly wanted to kiss me. What I'd like to know is why."

Quinn came to the conclusion she wasn't nearly as intelligent as he had

8

imagined. He said, "I'm beginning to think you ask questions for the sake of asking them. I kissed you because — well, because I thought it would be nice."

"For you — or for me?"

"There you go again," he said. "For both of us. Kissing is a two-way affair . . . or it was until now. You're a brand-new experience that I'd hate to repeat. Remind me never to kiss you again."

He liked that. As he walked off and left her he told himself it served her damn' well right. These clever-clever types deserved all they got. Anybody would think she had the looks that could afford to pick and choose.

. . . Might not know it but she's lucky any fellow would want to kiss her. Don't suppose I'd have dreamed of doing it if I hadn't had one too many. Still . . . she's cute. In spite of all her nonsense she has got something. Pity she insists on analysing motives . . .

In the next room he was welcomed by

a back-slapping, jocular group. Within a couple of minutes he had forgotten the little dark girl who asked too many questions.

Someone brought him another drink . . . someone told him a funny story that had no point and no end . . . someone filled up his glass again . . . and again . . . and again.

He lost count of time. Once when he looked at his watch he couldn't tell whether it was half past two or ten past six.

While he was trying to get the hands into focus, a man with an exaggerated moustache tapped him on the shoulder and said, "Forget the time, old boy, and have another drop of Scotch. The night is but a pup. Sad, isn't it, to think we won't be lapping it up like this for months and months and months?"

Through the tumult of noise and light rotating inside his head Quinn groped for a thought that kept eluding him. When at last he caught hold of it, he asked, "Why not? Why can't we do it again to-morrow night . . . or the next night . . . or the next night . . . or any night we like?"

The man with the moustache said, "Silly question, old boy, damn' silly question . . . if you don't mind me saying so."

He swayed closer and peered into Quinn's face. "You don't mind, do you . . . old boy?"

Quinn said, "Not in the least. As I always say, it's a free country and — "

"Don't you believe it, old boy. Nobody's free any more. Presidential system, that's what we've got. Parliamentary government's dead as the bloody dodo . . . take it from me."

"But I don't see how — "

"We're ruled by the executive . . . no independence of opinion . . . M.P.s are like sheep herded into whatever pen the Cabinet think fit . . . three-line Whips and all that sort of rot . . . "

Dimly Quinn realised the conversation had gone astray. What this fellow was talking about might be interesting some other time but it was hardly relevant right then.

He said, "Hate to change the subject just when you're getting warmed up, Mister . . . Afraid I don't know your name."

"Reg, old boy, just plain Reg. Cut out the mister. We're all pals here. No need for fancy titles. What's your name?"

"Quinn."

"Come again, old boy?"

"Q-U-I-N-N . . . Quinn."

"Is that so?" The man with the lavish moustache looked owlishly surprised. "Funny name. Don't think I've ever met anyone before who was called Quinn. No offence, mind you."

He emptied his glass and stood blinking thoughtfully. Then he said, "Once heard of a Jewish bloke who called himself Quinn . . . You're not a Jew, by any chance?"

"Neither by chance nor design," Quinn said.

That was quite good, he thought.

Quite good. He must remember it. Difficult to remember anything, of course. Too much of a row going on . . .

Reg was saying "Noisy bastards, aren't they? Can't hear yourself think. However, I was telling you about this Jewish character. Somebody asked him how he got the name Quinn and he said it used to be Cohen but when you said Cohen quickly and went on saying it faster and faster it eventually sounded just like Quinn. Get the point, old boy?"

Quinn was searching his mind for a missing thought. When at last he managed to grasp it, he said, "There's something I'd like to know . . . if it's all right with you."

"Sure, old boy. All you gotta do is ask." Reg tapped his head with a wavering forefinger. "Lifetime's experience up there. Been everywhere, seen everything. If I told you — "

"Yes . . . but this isn't anything like that."

13

" — only half of what I've learned about people and places and the depravity of human nature you could write a book — two books, more likely. You might not believe me but it's gospel truth — "

"I believe you," Quinn said. "I've been around quite a lot myself. But what I want to know is what you meant when you said I'd asked you a damn' silly question."

Reg tried to get another drink out of his emtpy glass. Then he gave Quinn a bleary look. "I'm not with you, old boy. What question?"

The elusive thought finally crystallised. Quinn said, "I asked you why there won't be another party like this for months and months and months."

"Did you?"

"Yes. Don't you remember?"

"No recollection at all, old boy. Mind's a complete blank. I suppose it's *anno Domini* and all that. But if you say so . . . "

He held back his head and stuck

14

out his tongue and turned the glass upside down to extract the last drop of gin. Then he went on, "I shouldn't have to tell you that nobody — but nobody — can put on a party like Charlie Hinchcliffe, God bless him. So if old Charlie's going abroad and won't be back before the end of the year — well, I ask you. Things can't very well be the same, can they?"

Quinn said, "No, I suppose not."

"You're damn' right. Aren't many like Charlie Hinchcliffe. Heart of gold, that's old Charlie. Hasn't got an enemy in the world. Give you his shirt if you asked him. Everybody knows that."

"Oh, sure. But the funny thing is — "

"'Course, he can afford to push the boat out in a big way. Charlie isn't short of the old folding money, you know. His wife left him pretty well fixed. D'you ever meet her, old boy?"

"Not that I'm aware of," Quinn said.

His head was spinning and his legs

seemed to be made of jelly. The room had suddenly become unbearably hot. He knew if he didn't sit down soon he would fall down.

Reg had carried on without waiting for an answer. " . . . very considerate woman. Went and snuffed it while old Charlie was in the prime of life. Ever since then he's been having himself a helluva time. Makes you think, doesn't it?"

"It certainly does," Quinn said.

"Take my old ball-and-chain, for example . . . and she's a lousy example at that. Doesn't possess tuppence and strong as a horse. Looks like one, as well. If I'm any judge she'll live long enough to shovel the old clay on top of me when I retire to the country. But Charlie got rid of his handicap and came into a packet of money at the same time. Some fellows have all the luck, don't they?"

"Seems like it," Quinn said.

"Not that I grudge Charlie anything he's got. Don't get me wrong. Salt of

16

the earth — that's what he is. Take it from me."

With his empty glass held up to the light, Reg repeated, "Salt of the earth . . . I'll go and get another drop of mother's ruin and we'll drink old Charlie's health. Won't be long, so stay right there. I'm enjoying our little conversation. You're an interesting fellow, Quinn, damned interesting fellow . . . Where the hell's that bar gone?"

He went away and never came back. Quinn loitered around for a while and then he squeezed through the crush and wandered here and there until he came to an unoccupied room where the only light came from a small shaded lamp beside a bed.

After he had closed the door to shut out most of the din he pulled a chair up to the open window. It was a hot, still night and there was scarcely a breath of air. With his head resting against the wall he fell asleep.

The dark girl found him there. He

woke up in time to hear her saying " . . . looking for you. I had an idea you'd eventually want to crawl into a hole and die."

When Quinn recovered the use of his voice, he said, "I was doing all right until you disturbed me. Why don't you go away? I'm trying to get some sleep."

"You can't sleep here. This is Jacqueline's bedroom."

"Who's Jacqueline?"

"Well, Charlie Hinchcliffe calls her his secretary. And I understand she's listed in the firm's books as an employee. In a way, I suppose, that's true enough. He has kept her regularly employed since his wife died . . . and I mean employed."

The words spattered on Quinn's mind like a shower of gravel. From a long way off he heard himself ask, "Who's Charlie Hinchcliffe?"

The dark girl said, "It's easy to see you've had a skinful. Everyone knows Charlie."

18

"Well, I don't," Quinn said. "What does he look like?"

"Short, tubby and bald as a hard-boiled egg without the shell. Considering that it's his liquor you've been drinking all night, I'd have thought . . . "

Sleep kept dragging Quinn down below the level of her voice. It took a considerable effort to keep his eyes open.

When he had forced himself awake, he said, "Let's get this thing straight. I was in a pub and I met a man I knew from somewhere. This man introduced me to another man and the other man said a friend of his was throwing a party and any newspaper man who cared to go along would be welcome."

"What was this friend's name?"

"Haven't the foggiest idea."

"But it wasn't Charlie Hinchcliffe?"

The mist was thickening in Quinn's mind. He had to hold on to his dwindling consciousness.

He said, "I don't know anyone called Hinchcliffe, I've never known anyone called Hinchcliffe, and I don't want to know anyone called Hinchcliffe. Does that make me a criminal?"

The dark girl said, "No, only a gatecrasher. You're at the wrong party."

Quinn thought that was funny. He leaned his head against the wall again and began to laugh. And as he laughed his wits spun like water rushing down a waste pipe . . . down . . . and down . . . and down . . .

It didn't last long. Through the darkness came pinpoints of light . . . and the pinpoints were splintered words . . . and the words were in many voices from above and below, from near and far.

Then the myriad voices became one. He knew that voice. It reminded him of a girl with dark hair and a cheeky smile — the girl he had met at a party in Muswell Hill.

Something funny about that party. He couldn't remember whether he had gone or not. Yet if he hadn't gone he wouldn't have met her. That was logical. And you couldn't get anywhere without logic.

But she wasn't just anywhere. He could hear her close beside him.

She was saying " . . . come on. It's time you went home."

That was silly for a start. Nobody who lived in digs ever looked on the place as home. Once upon a time . . . but that was long ago.

Somebody shook him into reluctant awareness of the present. Somebody said, "If you've got a car you're not fit to drive. If you haven't you're not fit to walk. Looks as if I'll have to act the Good Samaritan."

Quinn said, "Don't do me any favours. I can manage quite well by myself."

"In your present condition you'd finish up sleeping in the gutter. So don't argue. Someone's got to look after you . . . and it seems I'm the lucky one."

From then on he had only fragmentary

impressions of movement and half light, a background of noise receding behind him, a long flight of steps leading down to a street. In the pale light of a June dawn the street lay empty and silent.

Cool sweet air . . . trees growing out of pools of shadow . . . that familiar voice urging him to keep going. He knew he was being helped into a car, he could hear the dark girl asking him, "Where do you live?"

The queer thing was that she didn't seem able to hear him. He told her twice but she went on asking him each time he woke up. Eventually he decided he wasn't the only one who'd had a few drinks.

Through the jolting noise of a car he heard her say, "O.K. I've asked for this so I've no one to blame but myself now that I'm stuck with it. Why don't I learn to mind my own business?"

2

THE echo of that question roused him from a long, deep sleep. As he came up to the surface, a hand shook him and a voice he well remembered began talking to him.

" . . . If you're dead, just say so and I'll drink this coffee myself. After looking at something like you I need it. You remind me of the corpse of Marat in Tussaud's Chamber of Horrors."

There was bright light shining in his face — a cruel light that seemed to be trying to prise open his eyelids with sharp little knives. He turned his face away and groaned.

The voice said, "Be sure your sin will find you out . . . May I be the first to say it serves you right?"

He took a quick peek at her and then he shut his eyes tight. When the pounding in his temples subsided, he asked, "What time is it?"

"Five fifteen — p.m., not a.m. You've slept like a child — a snoring alcoholic child — for more than twelve hours. How's your poor head?"

Quinn said, "As ill as can be expected. Give me that coffee and see if you can keep quiet for a while."

The coffee was hot and strong. He kept his eyes closed while he sipped it, one small mouthful at a time, until the feeling of nausea left him. Then he took a chance and peered up at her.

She looked fresh, well-groomed and youthfully attractive in a dark-red trouser suit that flattered the slim lines of her figure. Late hours didn't seem to leave any effects on her.

He wondered if she'd been seen helping him up to his room . . . or going downstairs . . . or coming back up again in daylight. It would give his fellow-boarders plenty to talk about.

Then he realised something was very far wrong. This wasn't his room: this wasn't anything like his room. He didn't have a big, comfortable settee and bright curtains and a vase of pretty flowers on a spindly-legged table. He didn't have an Indian carpet, either.

Through an open door he could see a bed and a dressing-table with bottles and jars standing in front of the mirror. The bed was as smooth and neat as a well-made bed in a hospital. On the dressing table stool lay a handbag and a pair of gloves.

What he guessed didn't make sense. When he'd gulped down the last of the coffee, he asked, "Where am I?"

She took the cup from him. With a smile in her dark eyes, she said, "That's what they always say on television when the goody wakes up after being slugged by the baddy and — "

"Oh, to hell with television! Where am I?"

"The one place where you shouldn't be. I've still got a reputation for respectability — even if it is somewhat tarnished."

"You mean this is where you live?"

25

"Well, it isn't the British Museum."

He pushed himself upright and held on to the back of the settee long enough to take a look out of the window. When he slumped back again, he said, "I'm beginning to feel like Rip Van Winkle. Whereabouts is this?"

"A mile and a half outside Basingstoke. It's the cottage where I stay when I want to get away from the rat race. Pleasant change from the non-stop rushing about that you do in town with everybody — "

"Stop talking like a guide book," Quinn said. "Do you mean you brought me all the way from London and I didn't even know it?"

With a laugh bubbling in her throat, she said, "That's right. You were like a lump of meat the whole time — all forty-nine miles of our journey into the dawn. May as well tell you I stopped twice to see if you were still alive."

"Why don't I remember anything about it?"

"Don't ask me. But I can assure you

that you crawled out of the car — with a little assistance, of course — staggered up the path and through the door, and got as far as here."

"Damn' funny why the whole thing's a blank."

She stared at him with the eyes of a school-teacher. "All I did was give you a little push and you collapsed on to the settee." She laughed again. "If you'd fallen down before you reached it I'd have had to let you sleep on the floor."

"It might be a joke to you but I don't see anything to laugh about," Quinn said. "Why in heaven's name did you bring me here?"

Her smile vanished. She said, "So that there's no misunderstanding let me assure you it wasn't because I was in desperate need of a man. The choice was either here or a straw mattress in the lock-up at Muswell Hill. You were drunk and incapable, my dear Mr. Quinn — but incapable."

Quinn said, "You could've taken

me home to my digs ... although I don't want you to get the idea I'm not grateful."

She gave him a razor-edged grin. "Too late. I'd already got that idea. Just to keep things straight, how could I take you home if I didn't know where you lived?"

"But I remember giving you the address."

"Oh, sure. What you mean is that you remember thinking you'd given me the address. As it happens that was about the only thing you didn't tell me."

The change in her voice made him feel uncomfortable. He said, "What are you talking about now?"

"Your confidences. I got it all, a complete life story, an autobiography that left nothing to the imagination."

With a look in her eyes which reminded him of the night before, she added, "You wouldn't make a good spy, Mr. Quinn. When you've had a couple — if you'll pardon

28

the understatement — you reveal all your secrets to the first sympathetic listener."

His head was throbbing, his eyes hurt. Thinking was difficult. He only knew he'd made a fool of himself.

Best thing would be to get out and never see her again. Then it wouldn't matter how much he'd blabbed . . .

He asked, "What did I say?"

"Oh, nothing you could call very juicy. I was rather disappointed."

"Don't be facetious. I'm not in the mood."

"All right. You're a reporter, unmarried, and you run a crime column in the *Morning Post*. Seems you enjoy your work but you'd enjoy it even more if your news editor wasn't quite such a bastard."

She passed the empty coffee cup from one hand to the other while she studied him with an expressionless face. "Have I got it right so far?"

"It's right," Quinn said. "What else?"

For a moment she hesitated. "I don't think I should repeat any more."

"Why not? Embarrassed?"

"No, not at all. It just wouldn't be fair."

"That's for me to decide. Go on. What else did I say?"

She looked down at the cup and took a long time to answer. At last, she said, "Very well — if you insist. I gather that you spend most of your spare time in pubs because you're lonely; you envy many of your colleagues who are married; compared with other people you think you're a louse; you blame your parents for making you what you are and hate yourself in consequence because you suspect they're merely an excuse for what you call the failure you've made of your life — "

She broke off. Then she looked at Quinn with a trace of compassion in her eyes.

In an abrupt voice, she said, "And that's enough for one sitting. Would you like some aspirin for your headache?"

Quinn said, "Yes, please — if it's not too much trouble."

Her eyes lit up with laughter. "Trouble! After last night that is a joke."

If anyone else had laughed at him like that he'd have resented it. But she was different. Being with her — even if there was a gong beating inside his head — made him feel good.

He said, "I'm sorry if I caused you a lot of bother. Afraid I kind of let myself go at that party. I haven't had a proper break in a long time . . . and to-day I begin a two weeks' holiday."

"Yes, I know. That was another thing you told me while I was unfastening your tie and removing your shoes. You kept adding bits of information about yourself even after you fell asleep."

With an underlying query in her voice, she added, "I gather you've no idea where to go for this long-awaited holiday."

"Too many places to choose from," Quinn said.

31

"Everywhere's the same if" — she reached out and put the empty cup down on a small table near the settee — "if you take the wrong half of your personality along with you."

Quinn said, "Makes me sound like a schizophrenic. Maybe you ran a bigger risk than you knew when you let me spend the night here. After all, we were alone together and I might have — "

"Oh, no, you wouldn't." She was still laughing at him. "Two minutes after I lugged you on to that settee you departed this life. I'd have been quite safe even if we'd shared the same bed. For twelve hours you were insentient, incompetent and entirely impotent."

There didn't seem anything that Quinn could usefully say. But when she went on looking at him as though trying to read his thoughts, he said, "I'm sorry I was such poor company. If you'd care to invite me back some time when I'm sober I'll endeavour to make amends."

The dark girl shrugged. As she turned

away, she said, "I'll ignore that. When you've had a couple of aspirins maybe you'll feel well enough to apologise."

He told himself he was a louse. After she came back with the aspirins and a tumbler of water, he said, "I didn't mean what you thought I meant."

"No . . . ? You could've fooled me. Still, never mind. Swallow these . . . Now shut your eyes for a while and you'll feel better. If you shut your mouth at the same time" — the sting had gone from her voice — "I'll feel better, too."

The thumping in his head gradually slackened as he lay quiet and listened to the tap-tap of her heels moving here and there . . . the gushing of a tap . . . the squeak of a door opening and closing again. He had no wish and no energy to think. It was pleasant just to relax and let the aspirins do their work.

Wonderful what a few little tablets could do for a headache. Aspirin was supposed to have been discovered by a German research chemist before the turn of the century . . . man should have been given the Iron Cross and the V.C. and the Croix de Guerre . . . no, that wasn't right. They were for bravery in time of war . . . a knighthood would have been better.

Be a change to see an order of gallantry given to people who hadn't merely amassed fame and fortune in pursuit of their own personal interests . . . like a pop group . . . Wonder why it was called knighthood?

He must have dozed off. Next thing he knew the dark girl was asking him if he'd like another cup of coffee.

" . . . I think you've slept enough for one day. What you want now is a cold shower. You'll find clean towels in the bathroom and everything else you need — including a razor. No, I don't shave. It belonged to a man who used to live here. I went into Basingstoke and bought some blades while you were playing Old Macdonald's Pig."

Quinn said, "Thanks. You've been

more than kind. If there's ever anything I can do in return — "

"Don't worry. I won't hesitate to ask. And while we're on the subject" — she shook her head lightly — "if you're thinking of buying me some flowers or a box of chocolates, forget it. I'd have done the same for anybody."

"That's a pity," Quinn said. "I've been hoping you did it because you liked me."

She studied him carefully, her head tilted first to one side and then to the other. At last, she said, "Unless you've got a pure and shining soul under that debauched exterior, I don't see what there is to like."

"Looks aren't everything," Quinn said.

"Lucky for you, isn't it?"

Her eyes travelled slowly over his face as she went on, "Your hair's the colour of dried grass, you've got a sandy complexion, your eyes are bloodshot . . . and you need a shave. What's more, if I'd been designing your

35

features I wouldn't have given you a sharp nose and that chin. They don't go together."

"They've been going together for thirty-odd years," Quinn said. "Meeting you looks like making this the oddest year so far."

She nodded thoughtfully. "I must be crazy, but in spite of everything, there is something about you that I like."

He combed back his lank hair with both hands and asked, "Should I be flattered?"

"Not really. There are so many things I don't like. If we saw a lot of each other I think it would be easy for me to go off you."

"That cuts both ways. But it might be fun while it lasted."

Once again she was thoughtful. "I'm not so sure."

Quinn said, "There's nothing sure in this life. If you've got any time to spare during the next two weeks let's see who goes off whom first."

"You mean" — she held her lower

lip between her teeth for a moment — "you want me to go away with you?"

"Yes — but not as Mr. and Mrs. Smith. My offer has no strings attached."

She glanced at her watch as though it helped her to make up her mind. Then she said, "Just good friends?"

"That's all. Of course, in the words of the Victorian novel, there's always the chance that our friendship may ripen into something deeper."

"Don't count on it."

"No, but I can hope. And it might be a good start if you told me your name."

"Oh, I thought you knew." She held out her hand. "I'm Carole Stewart."

He liked the touch of her skin, the soft pressure of her fingers. It lasted only a moment but it was very pleasant.

As she took her hand away, he said, "I'm still waiting for your answer. What do you say?"

"I'll think about it. Now do you want another cup of coffee before you have a shave and a shower?"

Quinn said, "Yes, please."

He lay back again when she went into the tiny kitchenette. She left the door open and he could hear the rattle of cups and saucers, the opening and closing of a drawer.

Then from somewhere in the kitchen, she asked, "Ever been to a place called Castle Lammering?"

"No, can't say I have. Where is it?"

"In Dorset . . . not far from Blandford."

"Don't know Blandford, either."

"It's twenty miles or so from Salisbury. Right in the heart of the country. The village — Castle Lammering, I mean — has only got a couple of hundred people, two pubs, no betting shops or bingo halls or juke-boxes. And the nearest main road is miles away."

"Sounds good," Quinn said. "You been there?"

"Oh, quite often. I've got friends

who live just outside the village. It's a biggish house called Elm Lodge. They've plenty of money and entertain a lot."

"Nice for your friends," Quinn said.

"They've invited me to spend a long week-end with them whenever I can get away. In actual fact I thought of setting off this afternoon and staying, perhaps, until Tuesday morning."

"Nice for you," Quinn said.

The rattle of dishes stopped and Carole Stewart came out of the kitchenette. She was carrying a tray with a plate of biscuits and a cup of steaming coffee.

She said, "Treatment as before: black coffee without sugar . . . and drink it down hot."

In the same tone she went on, "You've got time on your hands and nowhere to go right now. A few days at Castle Lammering might do you good. How would you like to come with me?"

He'd had a tantalising feeling that

this might be what she was going to say but it had been too much to hope for. Now that she had asked him he was afraid she didn't mean it seriously.

He said, "I'd like that very much. But how would your friends feel if you brought along a stranger?"

"They wouldn't mind at all. In fact they'd probably be quite pleased. A new face would be like a change of scenery."

"You're sure?"

"I wouldn't have invited you if I weren't sure."

"Then I accept with thanks," Quinn said. "Funny, isn't it?"

"What's funny?"

"Well, they say justice is supposed to be blind . . . and it's true."

"Why?"

"Because if I'd received my proper deserts for getting disgustingly drunk last night I'd be in gaol. Instead I'm going to spend the week-end in your company at a charming country house. How lucky can I get?"

Carole gave him one of her cheeky grins. "There are two kinds of luck . . . so don't start crowing too soon. You may be bored to death. Nothing ever happens in Castle Lammering."

Quinn said, "It sounds too good to be true. A place where nothing ever happens is the very place I've been looking for."

3

HE felt a lot better when he'd had a shave and a shower. While he was getting dressed, Carole rapped on the bedroom door.

She said, "I've just been thinking . . . "

It had been too good to be true. He'd known all along she didn't really mean it. Some women get a kick out of dangling a carrot in front of the donkey's nose and then whipping it away.

He said, "Thinking about what? That your friends won't take to someone like me?"

"No, don't be a fool. I merely wondered why you had to go back to town. Anything special you have to do there?"

"Well, I've got to pick up some things — clothes and so on. Haven't even got a toothbrush."

"If you look in the bathroom cabinet you'll find a new one still in its original sealed wrapper . . . and I'll let you borrow that razor as well if you want."

In a voice that was a little too flippant, she added, "The man who owned it won't object."

Quinn said, "That's very obliging of him. But if I'm going away until Tuesday I'll need more than just a razor and a toothbrush. Among other things, I can't wear the same shirt for six days on the trot . . . especially after sleeping in it all last night and the best part of to-day."

Through the bathroom door, Carole asked, "What size do you take?"

"Fifteen collar. Why?"

"Because there are half a dozen shirts in an unopened parcel on the top shelf of the airing cupboard — just as they were when they came back from the laundry. If I'm not mistaken, they're your size. You'll also find two sets of pyjamas, some underwear, and several pairs of socks."

Quinn said, "I'm willing to bet you're not mistaken. But how about the man who owns all this gear? If I help myself to his property, what's he going to say when he comes back?"

For ten seconds there was no sound outside the door. Then Carole said, "Behind those two questions I detect a third one. And the answer is that he won't be coming back. So you can borrow anything you like . . . unless you'd rather pick up your own stuff and come on to Castle Lammering later."

"That would waste part of the weekend," Quinn said. "I don't see why I shouldn't accept your offer — with thanks. Mind if I ask you one more question?"

"Yes, I do mind. So skip it."

As her voice receded from the other side of the door, she added, "Now get ready and I'll give you a case to put your things in . . . "

★ ★ ★

They didn't set off until nearly six o'clock. When Quinn was stowing the two cases in the back of the car, Carole said, "You've still got time to change your mind." Her mood had changed in the past half-hour.

Quinn asked, "Why should I?"

"Well, you never know what you might be letting yourself in for."

"I'll risk it . . . unless you're sorry you invited me."

"No, I never turn back. When I decide to do something I go through with it. And if things don't work out right" — she swung her legs into the car, looked up at the mirror, and smoothed a hand over her dark, shining hair — "no regrets. That's the kind of person I am."

"Then we're complete opposites," Quinn said. "Whatever I do I always think afterwards I should've done something different. I suppose you gathered that much from my maudlin confidences."

"More or less."

"That's the worst of not keeping my big mouth shut."

"You aren't unique." As the car moved off, she said, "Once in a while I can say the wrong thing at the right time."

The look on her face told him what she meant. He said, "Look, Carole, let's clear the air before we go any farther. If you're talking about the man whose shirt I'm wearing, forget it. So far as I'm concerned, he's your brother."

She glanced at him briefly and then she concentrated on the road. She said, "I haven't got a brother."

"O.K. So he's your uncle or your nephew or your grandfather. It's no business of mine."

Without any expression, she said, "That's why I shouldn't have involved you."

"No, it was my fault. I shouldn't have asked personal questions. There's an old saying: 'Never look a borrowed shirt in the laundry mark'."

Carole went on looking straight ahead but now he could see that she was smiling. After a while, she said, "I'm glad I asked you to come with me to Castle Lammering. I have a feeling that someone like you might be just what I can do with right now."

Quinn said, "We aim to serve."

Without looking at him she took one hand off the wheel and gave his arm a little pat. "Don't let your ideas of gallantry or gratitude run away with you. It might turn out that you're serving an unworthy cause."

"Possibly. But as I said before" — Quinn stretched out his legs and sighed — "I'll risk it. And while we're on the subject of gallantry shouldn't I buy something for the lady of the house so that I don't walk in both uninvited and empty-handed?"

"No, you shouldn't. You'd only embarrass her. Adele doesn't need anything you can afford to buy. Remember that."

47

"I'll try," Quinn said. "Not having had any experience in dealing with a rich man's wife — "

"She isn't a rich man's wife. It's her money that pays for everything. I don't think Michael's contributed a penny to the household since they got married."

In a tone of indifference, Carole went on, "You may as well know the set-up before we get there. Of course, I'm relying on you to keep it to yourself . . . "

Quinn said, "Of course."

"Not that all their friends aren't aware of the situation. But naturally I wouldn't like Adele to think I went around gossiping about her and her husband."

Quinn said, "Naturally."

"Well, to start with, Michael Parry drinks too much."

"He's not the only one."

Carole shrugged. She said, "If you're talking about yourself, there's no comparison. You may take one

48

too many now and again but you do a useful job of work. Michael does nothing."

"How does he pass the time?"

"He professes to be a writer. You know the type . . . always slugging away at the book, the *opus magnus*, the epic novel that'll put him right at the top."

"I've met them," Quinn said.

"Haven't we all? We know that books aren't created by talk or by wishful thinking."

"They have to be written," Quinn said.

"Of course. And that means work — even if you're a genius. I'm prepared to believe that Michael has talent but he doesn't use it. To him, work is a dirty word."

Quinn said, "A man can get like that if he marries someone with too much cash."

In a harder voice, Carole said, "Or if he hasn't got enough guts. Michael's what he is because he was born that way. Adele's money just made it easier for him to give in. Now when things get him down — which is pretty often — he crawls inside a bottle and pulls in the cork."

"I'm glad you don't like him," Quinn said. "One drunk in your life is enough."

"Don't be facetious. In any case you're wrong. He can be quite pleasant. It's just that I can't tolerate a moral coward. Adele deserved someone better."

"Maybe she's happy with him the way he is."

Carole turned her head briefly and gave Quinn an irritable look. She asked, "Can you imagine anyone being happy with a man who depends on her for every penny he spends, every single thing he's got?"

"Perhaps not. But he can't be so happy, either. That's why he drinks."

"Yes, I know that. Half the time I'm sorry for him. When he acts the jovial host and everybody knows he's being generous at his wife's expense, he's really pathetic. But what upsets me most is the look in her eyes — "

Carole broke off. With another shrug, she said, "If I go on like this you'll be sorry you came. Let's change the subject. Tell me about yourself instead."

"You already know all about me," Quinn said. "I don't even know what you do for a living. Whatever it is — judging by your cottage and this almost new car — it must be profitable."

"Not in the sense of big money . . . but it keeps me in reasonable comfort. I'm a freelance TV producer."

"Must be an interesting life."

"No. What you see on the small screen may look glamorous but the production side is just another job. There's more romance in what you do."

Quinn said, "The grass is always greener on the other side of the hill . . . until you get there."

"Probably. I don't suppose we'd be

content for long if we all swapped jobs."

In an absent voice, she added, "Still, I'd like to try it some time . . . but I doubt if I'll ever get the chance."

She went very quiet after that and seemed to withdraw into herself. Quinn wondered why she'd invited him to spend the week-end at Castle Lammering, why she wanted his company. She was bound to know plenty of men, any one of whom would make a more suitable guest at a country house.

. . . Like that fellow who went off without his laundry. Must admit he wears nice shirts. Smart line in pyjamas, too. Wonder what it feels like to wear silk next to your skin . . .

That made Quinn think of Carole going to bed with the man who wasn't coming back — the man who was still able to make her subdued when she thought of him. He must've had a wife somewhere or he and Carole would've got married.

And yet, maybe not. She could've been in love with him but he might only have been after a bit of fun. Cottage in the country — all found — a cute girl to provide entertainment whenever he felt in the mood — until she hankered after a more permanent relationship.

Then he'd gone off one day without taking his laundry so that she wouldn't suspect he wasn't coming back. Now she knew it was all over . . . but she'd still kept a parcel of shirts and socks and underwear . . . in case . . . just in case.

Or at least she'd kept them until now. But times might've changed. Now they were maybe for the use of anyone who escorted her home and got invited in for a drink . . . and stayed the night. With women it was difficult to tell.

Quinn hated to think she was the kind who picked up a man and took him home to bed. It seemed all wrong for a woman somehow — a decent woman, as they used to say.

53

Of course, that was an old-fashioned concept. Chastity had become an ugly word . . . Then he told himself not to be a damned hypocrite. If she gave him enough encouragement he wouldn't have any scruples. And she might, at that. Peculiar why she'd picked on him to share her week-end at Castle Lammering.

. . . Can't be because you're dashing and debonair. Maybe she feels sorry for you and this is her good deed for the week. She doesn't like Michael Parry but she says she feels sorry for him, so that lets you know how you stand . . .

Vagrant thoughts came and went without any pattern. He felt drowsy and at peace.

. . . Better leave her alone for a while and not try to make conversation. When she wants to talk, she'll talk. Meantime it's a lovely day and you can relax. In weather like this the country must be superb. You're going to be staying with rich people and living off

the fat of the land . . .

It was a hot sunlit evening without a cloud in the sky and they had all the windows of the car open as they headed south-west from Basingstoke. Quinn sprawled in his seat and let his mind wander in a half-sleep.

They were approaching Sutton Scotney when Carole asked him, "How's your poorly head?"

He roused himself. "Not bad — taking all things into consideration."

"Like to stop for a cup of coffee?"

"No, thanks . . . unless you want to."

"I'm not fussy. It was you I was thinking of. Maybe you'd prefer a hair of the dog that bit you? We can stop at the next pub."

Quinn said, "In my time I've plucked so many hairs off that dog he must be damn' near bald. Thanks all the same but I don't want to be smelling of drink when we arrive at your friends' house."

She laughed without any pretence of

humour. "If you did, Michael would welcome you as a new member of the lodge."

A little later when Lopcombe Corner lay behind them she roused Quinn again. She said, "Aren't you hungry? As far as I know you haven't eaten all day."

"I'm giving my stomach a chance to get over last night's orgy. We'll have a meal when we get there, I suppose?"

"Oh, yes. Probably something cold ... but I can promise you won't starve while you're at Elm Lodge. In fact, if you're not careful you'll put on weight."

Quinn said, "That'll be the day. I've weighed the same ten stone ten for the past dozen years. How far have we to go?"

"Well, it's about six miles to Salisbury. From there Blandford is another twenty-two or -three. Then it's approximately eight miles to Castle Lammering. If we don't get held up too often" — she looked at her watch — "we should arrive not much after seven."

They drove on into the westering sun. Carole put on a pair of dark glasses, Quinn closed his eyes and slid lower in his seat and let the drone of the car lull him to sleep again until they got to Salisbury.

They didn't do any talking until they were on the A354 and some miles beyond Coombe Bissett. There they caught up with the tail of a line of cars and trailer trucks and caravans all travelling at the lumbering pace of a twenty-ton wagon half a mile ahead.

As they slowed to the same speed, Carole said, "We'll probably be stuck in this queue until we get to Blandford. I've known it happen before. Be nearer seven-thirty than seven o'clock by the time we reach the village."

She was right. It was a quarter past seven when they turned off the A354 south of Blandford where a signpost pointed due west: *Castle Lammering — 8 mls.*

The narrow, winding road was barely wide enough for two cars. It ran between grassy banks, straggling over-grown hedges, and briar bushes lush with pink and red blossom. When they reached higher ground Quinn could see wooded country to the south and west.

Carole said, "Not long now. The village is just beyond those trees. We'll be at Elm Lodge in three or four minutes."

The road swung past a stand of old timber, curved sharply left, and then straightened out. Less than a quarter of a mile ahead lay Castle Lammering.

It was set in a hollow between two low hills — just a cluster of houses, some half-timbered, others with thatched roofs and whitewashed stone walls. On rising ground to the north the spire of a church reached up to the sunlit blue of the sky.

Above the village isolated houses nestled among clumps of trees. Where the main village street ran on and lost itself in open country one or two cottages marked the line of the road leading west. Farther on there was a farm, fields of grain ripening in the sun, pasture land carpeted in summer green.

Carole pointed. She said, "See the house behind those elm trees up there to the left? That's it."

Two old men stared after them as they drove through the village. A small boy on a tricycle waved both hands vigorously. A woman in the doorway of the village store turned and shielded her eyes from the sun to look at them.

Quinn said, "I bet they don't see many strangers in these parts."

"No, it's well off the beaten track. Over yonder past those red-roofed cottages you come to an unclassified road that'll take you to Milborne St. Andrews . . . but it would be a crazy way to get there when all you have to do is follow the main Blandford-Dorchester road instead of making a fifteen-miles detour . . ."

She went on talking about places a few miles north of Castle Lammering: places with names like Bishop's Caundle, Bagber, Sturminster Newton.

" . . . Beautiful country around here if you're fond of walking. Lots of little pubs where you can stop for a sandwich and a drink."

Quinn said, "There are a couple of cosy looking spots in Castle Lammering itself."

"Well, the Bird-in-Hand is all right but the Treacle Pot's a bit too much like the old sawdust and spittoon affair for my taste."

With no inflexion, she added, "The Bird-in-Hand is Michael's favourite haunt. Slips in for a quick one most mornings and you'll generally find him there in the afternoons, too, when the Parrys haven't got guests."

A road no wider than the car climbed in a long slope up from the village, passed under an avenue of trees that met overhead, and skirted some gnarled and ancient elms whose branches spread across the road in full leaf. Beyond them curved a low wall, a gateway without any gates, and then the lawns and the flower beds of Elm Lodge.

It was a long, two-storied house of grey limestone with a wide entrance and small-paned sash windows. The pebbled drive ran past a built-on garage big enough for three cars.

Carole said, "We're here. How do you like it?"

With its tyres crunching over the pebbles the car pulled up. As Quinn got out, a colony of rooks took flight on startled wings and spiralled high above the trees.

He watched them settle again, one by one, and then he stretched and looked around. He said, "Home was never like this. Do your friends live here all the time?"

"Mostly. Michael seldom goes away. He says he's got everything he wants right here. Adele goes up to town for

61

a few days now and again to do some shopping . . . or she spends a week or so at a place called Wood Lake where people with enough money can pretend to diet."

"What does she want to diet for?"

"She doesn't. But she likes the baths and the massage and the skin treatment and all that goes with it. Makes a habit of going there every two or three months."

"Sounds as if she has a very hard life," Quinn said.

They went into the entrance and Carole touched the bellpush once. When the soft double chime died away, she said, "I'll bet you're starving."

"Well, yes, I am kind of peckish. My stomach's forgiven me for the way I treated it last night."

She pressed the bell again. She said, "Must be somebody at home . . . "

After her third attempt she gave Quinn a wry smile. He said, "You could be wrong."

"No, don't get worried. Wherever

they are they'll be back soon. They know I'm coming. Let's see if the car's there."

They walked to the garage and Carole pulled back one of the sliding doors. Quinn saw a maroon Rover 2000, a littered workbench, and an assortment of tools hanging on the rear wall. The boot of the car was not properly shut.

He said, "I can hear a radio playing somewhere in the house . . . so they may not have gone out after all. Try the bell again."

Carole walked back ahead of him. With more than a hint of impatience she pressed the bellpush several times, listened for a moment, and then used her knuckles on the door.

She said, "Come on, for goodness' sake! You must've heard that . . . Oh, at last."

The distant music of the radio had stopped. Footsteps trotted downstairs . . . over a stretch of bare floor . . . across a rug . . . on wooden flooring again . . . another rug . . . Then the door opened.

He was of average height with a gingery flamboyant moustache, pale blue eyes and fair hair touched with silver at the sides. His nose and his eyes had the look of the habitual drinker. At one time he must have been a good-looking man but now his features were puffy and he had a double roll of loose flesh under his chin.

With a bemused expression he stared at Carole as though unable to recognise her. Then he fumbled at his unbuttoned collar, realised he wasn't wearing a tie, and smiled weakly.

Like a man pulling himself together he cleared his throat and said, "Hallo, Carole. This is a nice surprise. I wasn't expecting you — at least, not quite so early."

Carole said, "Half past seven isn't early."

"Is that the time?"

He looked down at his left wrist and discovered he wasn't wearing a

64

watch, either. In an apologetic voice, he said, "I've been having a nap and must've overslept. Had a busy morning . . . between this and that. Thought I'd put my feet up. Nothing to beat it on a hot day like this . . ."

His voice tailed off as though he had just remembered something. He glanced at Quinn, turned to Carole again, and asked, "Don't you think you ought to introduce me to your friend?"

She said, "I haven't had a chance yet. This is Mr. Quinn . . . Michael Parry. Adele told me I should bring someone next time I came and . . . by the way, where is Adele?"

Parry shook hands with Quinn and told him he was more than welcome. " . . . Any friend of Carole is a friend of ours. Better come in, old man, and have a drink. You've got a thirsty look in your eye."

They went inside. The wide entrance doors led directly into a room that filled most of the ground floor — a room with a wrought-iron staircase spiralling up to the floor above and a central hearth over which hung a cone-shaped canopy of beaten brass. There were half a dozen arm-chairs and a couple of long settees and lots of loose rugs.

An open-plan divider with shelves of books and ornaments partly split the room in two. One half formed a dining section with a circular table ringed by chairs which fitted snugly into it like the petals of a tulip. In the nearer wall there was a serving-hatch and door leading into the kitchen.

Across a corner in the other half stood a well-appointed bar of bamboo and glass. Parry walked over and leaned his back against it and said, "What'll you have, boys and girls? You name it, we got it."

"It's food we want, more than drink," Carole said. "Have you eaten?"

"Eaten? Yes, I had a very good lunch."

He went behind the bar and brought

out several bottles from underneath and stood them on the glass top. He said, "Don't worry about food. There's plenty in the fridge — chicken and tongue and ham and coleslaw and salad and lots of other things. But first have a drink. Sharpens the old appetite."

"If I must, I'll have a tomato juice."

"No sooner said than done. What about the boy friend?"

Quinn said, "Whisky and pep for me, please. After last night I'd better keep my stomach placated."

Parry put out three glasses. Then he looked at Quinn and asked, "What happened last night? Special occasion?"

"Well, yes, you might call it that. First time I've ever had a skinful at a party I wasn't invited to."

"No kidding?" Parry threw back his head and laughed with all his teeth showing. It was a synthetic laugh. It meant nothing.

When he had switched it off, he said, "You are a bit of a lad, aren't you?"

With clumsy fingers he used an

opener on the bottle of tomato juice. The crinkle top sprang off and rolled along the floor into a corner.

He grumbled "Damn . . . " as he bent down and groped for it. When he stood up again, Quinn noticed that his hands were shaking.

Carole took her glass from him, murmured, "Thanks . . . " and then asked, "Are there just the three of us?"

"Yes. Why?"

"What about Adele? Isn't she joining us for a drink?"

When he had poured out a generous whisky for Quinn and screwed the stopper on again, Parry looked at her. He said, "Didn't I tell you? She's at Wood Lake. I'm picking her up in Blandford very shortly. Her bus is due in about twenty past eight. Soon's I've had a spot of brandy and washed the sleep out of my eyes I'll be off."

Carole asked, "Anyone else coming for the weekend?"

"Maybe Irene and Neil. I'm not sure."

He pushed Quinn's glass across the top of the bar and put a bottle of peppermint cordial down beside it. He said, "Help yourself, old boy . . . oh, and if you two are hungry take whatever you want from the fridge. You know where things are, Carole, so don't stand on ceremony. Irene and Neil can join you when they arrive."

"Aren't you having anything before you meet the bus?"

"No time, dear girl. Must be in Blandford before the seven twenty-five from Salisbury gets there or little wifie will think I've forgotten her . . . and that would never do."

He was fussing with the brandy bottle as he asked, "What's the hour?"

Quinn said, "Just turned twenty-five minutes to eight . . . Your good health."

"And yours . . . cheers." Very carefully he poured no more than a tablespoonful of brandy into a crystal goblet, swilled it round, and then raised the glass to his lips.

As he tilted back his head he gave Quinn a wink and added, "Welcome . . . While you're here make yourself thoroughly at home."

Quinn said, "Thanks. I'll do my best."

The brandy went down in one quick gulp. Parry smacked his lips and asked, "What do you do for a living, old boy? Same racket as Carole here?"

"No, I'm on a newspaper."

"Are you, by jove? Which one?"

"The *Morning Post*."

"Editorial?"

"Yes. Mostly crime stuff."

"Is that so?"

Parry put down his glass and came round to the front of the bar. With a throaty chuckle, he said, "Well met, my friend. I'm a writer, too. Not in your field, of course. Nothing to do with journalism. Straight novels. I'm working on a new one right now."

Quinn asked, "Do you write under

your own name?"

"Oh, sure. But I don't suppose you've read anything of mine. Haven't produced a best-seller yet. One of these days . . . maybe. Who knows?"

He walked towards the staircase, turned to smile at both of them, and went on, "Talking about names, I remember where I've come across yours before. Saw it in the *Morning Post*. You're the bloke who writes Quinn's Column on Crime, aren't you?"

"That's right."

"Jolly good stuff, too. We must have a natter about it later. But meantime you'll have to excuse me. If I'm not there to meet the bus the little woman'll tear off a proper strip."

As he went up the stairs he looked back again and told Carole, "Take care of the boy friend, sweetheart, and see he gets plenty to eat. Remember your Shakespeare."

He trotted up a few steps, glanced round once more, and gave them a wave. Then he went on up out of sight.

A door opened and closed on the floor above. Quinn looked at Carole and asked, "What's he talking about? Why Shakespeare?"

She revolved her glass of tomato juice between both hands as though she needed time to think. At last, she said, "I wonder how often I've heard him say that same damn' silly thing. I'll swear it's the only quotation he knows."

"Which quotation?"

"From *Julius Caesar*: Yond' Cassius has a lean and hungry look."

Quinn said, "Shakespeare's the great stand-by of the literary phoneys ... especially when they're in their cups, if I may coin a phrase. To me our host seems half cut."

"Oh, he's been drinking, all right. Whenever Adele's away he spends all his afternoons in the Bird-in-Hand." Carole shook her head. "I've no doubt he came rolling home the worse for wear, threw himself down on a bed, and hoped he'd sleep it off before he had to go and collect her."

"Lucky we roused him or she'd have been stranded in Blandford."

"Wouldn't be the first time. She's had to take a taxi more than once when she's come back from Wood Lake."

"Where is the place?"

"It's a few miles from Woking, near Chobham. She goes by bus from Blandford to Salisbury, takes the train to Woking, and phones the people at Wood Lake when she gets there. They send a car for her."

"Sounds like a lot of chopping and changing. With all the money you say she's got why doesn't she go in her own car?"

Carole put down the untouched tomato juice. She said, "I'm glad you asked that when Adele wasn't around. It might've been embarrassing."

"Why?"

"Well, you see, she used to drive . . . but one day there was an accident near Chobham and a man was killed. Although the coroner stated no blame could be attached to her she hasn't driven since."

"Once you lose your nerve there's not much you can do about it," Quinn said. He finished his whisky. "Do you think we might eat now before those other people arrive?"

"Of course. I'm sorry you've had to wait so long. Mind eating in the kitchen?"

Quinn said, "I don't mind if you feed me in the garage . . . so long as I get fed."

On the floor above, footsteps clumped here and there hurriedly. As Carole opened the kitchen door, Michael Parry came downstairs.

He gave them a hasty wave and called out, "Enjoy yourselves. The house is all yours. Back soon." Then he rushed outside.

While Carole was setting the table, Quinn listened to the noise of a car reversing out of the garage. He heard its brakes squeal . . . the grunt of a mishandled gearbox . . . the roar of the engine as the car shot off in a flying start, its wheels skittering on the gravel.

When he could no longer hear the car, Quinn said, "I hope your friend Michael doesn't meet someone in the same condition on the same stretch of road at the same time. Has he ever been had up for drunk driving?"

"No, but that's more by good luck than anything else. One of these days it's bound to happen — if he doesn't kill himself first. Would you like chicken or tongue or cold ham with your salad?"

Quinn said, "Yes, please."

She laughed. She said, "I don't suppose you'd say no to a bottle of iced lager? There's some in the fridge."

"I wouldn't say no to two bottles."

"Evidently you've recovered from last night."

"Oh, yes. It always affects me like this. Drinking gives me an appetite and eating makes me thirsty and when I'm thirsty I like to drink and when I've had a few drinks I get hungry and so on . . . *ad infinitum*, ad alcoholicus anonymous. It's called the cycle of nature."

Carole said, "You talk more nonsense than anyone I've ever met."

"Sure. But the difference between me and all the others is that I know it's nonsense."

She shut the fridge door and pulled a chair up to the table. She said, "That's one of the few intelligent things I've heard you say . . . but don't let it go to your head. Sit down and eat before you overstrain yourself . . . "

★ ★ ★

When he had taken the edge off his appetite, Quinn asked, "Who are the people he mentioned were coming — this Irene and Neil?"

"Oh, they're family — Irene and Neil Ford. She's Adele's sister-in-law. Her husband's got a shop in

76

Ringwood — about thirty miles from here. They come for the week-end every month or so."

"What kind of people are they?"

"Not what I'd call the ebullient type. She's one of those negative women who sap your vitality. I always say that when she goes into an empty room there's less in it than there was before."

"Sounds as if we're going to have a rip-roaring time," Quinn said. "Is he the same?"

"No, compared with her he's quite lively. The only fault I find with him is that he's got a roving eye."

"In general?"

"I can't say how he behaves at home but I don't like the sly look he keeps giving me. Makes me afraid he'll do something one day that'll cause unpleasantness all round."

As she began clearing away the dishes, Carole added, "No risk of him making a fool of himself this weekend, of course — not with you around."

"What have I got to do with it?"

"Well, he'll think you're a special friend of mine."

"And two of us know I'm not," Quinn said.

She looked at him steadily, her lower lip held between her teeth. Then she said, "How could you be? Friendship is like good wine. It takes years to mature."

Quinn said, "That should be a Thought for To-day on my calendar."

He had an urge to get up and leave. No one had ever treated him like this before. One moment he would have sworn she liked him; the next, she had shut him out in the cold. All the time there was a barrier between them.

This playing hot and cold was the kind of thing he could never tolerate. If there had been any form of transport to get him to the nearest bus stop he would have told her what she could do with her week-end in the country.

But the thought of lugging his bag

from Elm Lodge down to the village . . . and taking the chance that buses ran from there to Blandford . . . and looking pretty stupid if they didn't . . .

He knew in spite of everything that Carole wouldn't refuse to run him wherever he wanted to go. The galling thing was that she wouldn't persuade him to stay. If he wished to leave it would be up to him.

Either way he'd be left a fool. He should never have accepted her invitation. If he had known she meant to use him as a shield between herself and someone else she couldn't forget . . .

Carole said, "I've never liked to pretend. Anything that's worth having you've got to work for. Friendship's one of them. No reason why you and I can't be friendly — but that's as far as we can go after knowing each other for only a few hours."

"Let us then be grateful for small blessings," Quinn said. "Including Mister Neil Ford with the roving eye. But for him I wouldn't have been asked to spend the week-end at a charming country house."

She carried the dishes over to the sink and stacked them neatly on the draining board. Then she turned round and gave Quinn a frosty look.

She said, "You're behaving like a spoiled brat. I didn't invite you because I needed someone to protect my virtue. Adele's all right — if she weren't I wouldn't come to Castle Lammering at all — but the others can be pretty deadly. I just thought you might be more entertaining."

Quinn said, "Thanks for using 'might be.' That's what I call damning with faint praise."

"Oh, now you're being tiresome. You know perfectly well what I mean. And if you think I'm going to lean over backwards to placate your feeling of inferiority then you're very much mistaken. I like you as much as I could like anybody after knowing him for only five or six hours — including a semi-conscious hour or so last night — but that's all."

"Take it or leave it," Quinn said.

"Yes." She shrugged. "That's exactly the position. So what are you going to do?"

He knew it might be a mistake but he still thought she was cute. He said, "I'll take it. Can't see I've got anything to lose by staying on until — "

The door-bell chimed. Carole said, "That'll be the Fords. Don't let them suspect you were enticed here by a confidence trick."

Quinn said, "Now who's behaving like a spoiled brat? If you really want to know, I'm glad I'm here."

She gave him a wicked smile. She said, "Then you'd better tell your face."

The bell chimed again while she was on her way to the front door. A man's voice asked, "Anyone at home?"

Quinn followed her as far as the kitchen doorway. He remained there while she let the Fords in.

They were not quite what he had expected. Neil Ford was a round-faced man with grey hair, grey eyes and a pinkish complexion. He had plump hands and a mouth like a woman and he looked as though he spent too much of his time indoors.

Irene Ford was fair, thin, negative. She had a transparent skin, an air of self-effacement. While Quinn was being introduced to her she smiled nervously and gave a little giggle before she said how d'you do.

He didn't like the cold touch of her fingers. Neil Ford's clammy hand felt equally unpleasant. But his manner was sociable enough until he learned that Quinn was Carole's guest. After that he more or less ignored him.

Irene sat down primly on the edge of an arm-chair with her knees close together. When she was satisfied that her skirt hadn't climbed up, she said, "Oh, dear. Traffic gets worse all the time. It's exasperating" — she giggled again — "isn't it? Almost makes it not worth while coming all this way . . . if you know what I mean."

Ford said, "You like coming here. You always have. Wouldn't matter to you if it took twice as long."

"Oh, yes, of course I do. I didn't mean . . . " Her colourless voice faded away and she flicked a nervous look at Quinn while she tried to decide what she had meant.

Then she giggled once more. She said, "Well, it makes a change . . . doesn't it?"

Quinn didn't think she cared whether he agreed or disagreed or just remained quiet. But he disliked being pushed into the background by a man like Neil Ford.

So he said, "Certainly makes a very pleasant change for me."

She brightened as though he had paid her a compliment. With a self-conscious wriggle of her thin shoulders, she said, "Nice here . . . isn't it?"

He told himself that everything she said had an unnecessary question tacked on to it because she had a pathological need to be reassured . . . like so many of those people interviewed on TV who couldn't talk without inserting kind of and sort of and you know into every second phrase. Only the indefinite type of person used the word definitely so often.

Another part of his mind kept asking him if she had noticed how her husband was looking at Carole, his eyes straying down to her legs time and time again. Maybe Irene didn't know or didn't care. Maybe she'd learned long ago that there was nothing she could do about it.

Through his thoughts he heard Carole saying " . . . Are you people hungry? If you are, don't wait until Adele gets home. Mr. Quinn and I have already had something to eat."

Irene wriggled and said, "You know what? I've just realised that she and Michael aren't here. Isn't that funny?"

Neil Ford said, "No. Your mind's always a million miles away."

He looked at Carole and asked, "Has

Michael gone to meet the bus?"

"Yes. He should be back any time now . . . well, in about fifteen minutes unless the bus happens to be late."

As though continuing the same trend of conversation, Irene got up and said, "I think I'll go and spend a penny — "

She broke off short and gave Quinn an embarrassed look. She said, "Oh, how awful. I completely forgot there was a strange man in the room. Please excuse me."

With that same wriggle of her thin shoulders, she walked primly to the foot of the staircase. Then she looked round at her husband and said, "Don't forget to bring in our things from the car . . . will you, dear?"

Neil said, "No, I won't forget . . . dear."

He watched her go upstairs, her head bent as though she were counting each step she took. Then he went outside.

Quinn looked at Carole and said, "Happy families . . ."

She made a face. She said, "They've

85

had a row. I can always tell. He behaves as if he's got a hair down his back and she keeps calling him dear."

"You're quite the little student of character, aren't you?"

"There isn't much to study in those two."

With a trace of apology in her voice, she added, "I shouldn't have got you into this. If I'd known . . . "

"Known what?"

"Well, the situation might be kind of prickly. Maybe it wasn't such a good thing to invite you. Between this and that it's not going to be much of a weekend."

"Not to worry. I won't ask for my money back."

"No . . . but you must be thinking this is a crazy household. Adele isn't here when we arrive; soon's we walk in, Michael goes off and leaves us to fend for ourselves; then you get a sample of Neil and Irene. Not a good start, is it?"

"Sunshine, good food, plenty to drink," Quinn said. "With you thrown in as a bonus what have I got to complain about?"

Carole came over and stood looking down into his eyes. After a little silence, she said, "I'm beginning to think you are nice." With a look on her face that he hadn't seen before she stooped and kissed him swiftly on the cheek.

Neil Ford came back. He was carrying a small suitcase and he had a folded raincoat slung over his arm.

He said, "I think I'll have a drink before I take this stuff upstairs."

"I'll get it for you," Carole said. "What would you like?"

"Oh, anything that'll buck up my appetite. A dry sherry will do. I never seem able to eat when the weather gets hot."

"Most people eat less when it's like this," Carole said.

She brought out several bottles before she found the right one. While she was pouring out his sherry he walked across to the bar and stood there with his back towards Quinn.

It could have been an unintentional slight but Quinn didn't think so. Ford had already made his attitude quite obvious.

He drank his sherry, murmured something to Carole, and laughed as though they shared some private joke. Then he picked up his case. Without looking at Quinn he went upstairs.

Carole put the bottle of sherry away and looked at Quinn with a smile that he knew was meant to pacify him. She said, "I can understand how you feel but don't pay any attention."

"How did you guess what I was thinking?"

"It's written all over you. If you want my advice don't let him see he's succeeded in getting your back up. He likes nothing better. Imagines it makes him look big in other people's eyes."

"Yours, for instance?"

"Don't ask silly questions. I'm not interested in Neil Ford."

"Just as well, isn't it? After all, he's married."

"If you go on like this you'll become a bore," Carole said. "And I can stand anything except being bored. For your information, Neil's the kind of man I don't like, married or single."

Quinn said, "Before this week-end's over maybe I'll find out the kind of man you do like. What was the big joke?"

She looked momentarily puzzled. Then her face cleared and she said, "Oh, that . . . Believe it or not, I don't know. I didn't quite catch what he said . . . but it wasn't anything about you. So you don't need to start — "

The phone bell cut her off. As it rang again footsteps sounded on the floor above.

Before she had time to come out from behind the bar Ford came trotting downstairs. He said, "O.K. I'll take it. Might be for me."

The phone was on the other side of the open-plan divider. Through a gap in the upper shelves, Quinn saw Ford pick up the receiver.

He said, "Yes . . . yes . . . oh, hallo, where are you? . . . This is Neil."

As he listened to the voice at the other end a bank of cloud drifted over the face of the sun and the windows darkened in sudden twilight. South of Castle Lammering the sky had become black across the whole expanse of the horizon.

Carole glanced at Quinn and said, "Looks as if we're in for a storm."

"They forecast outbreaks of thundery rain by evening," Quinn said. "We can do with some wet after such a long spell of dry weather."

The elm trees threshed in a gust of wind that whipped past the house and went rushing on over the uplands. Then everything was still again — an oppressive stillness in which nothing moved.

Quinn wondered if the rooks thought night had come or if they knew there was going to be a downpour and had taken refuge. Their lifespan was only a few years but they lived long enough to know the difference between normal dusk and an approaching storm. The feeling in the air would tell them — a clammy pressure as though sky and earth were about to meet, increasing static that made his skin creep.

Far off to the south a pale light winked twice . . . and then again. He remembered reading long, long ago that if you counted the number of seconds between the flash and the following thunder you could tell how far away you were from the source of the lightning.

. . . *Something to do with the speed of sound through the air. I've forgotten whether it's eleven hundred or twelve hundred feet per second. Anyway, I can't hear any thunder. Maybe the storm's got to be within a certain range . . .*

Neil Ford was saying " . . . No, not to my knowledge. If there had been I'm sure Carole would've mentioned it. Perhaps you got the time wrong . . . well, don't get irritable. It was only a suggestion."

He listened again. Then he said, "If you ask me there isn't much point in hanging about . . . O.K. O.K. You do just what you like. I'm not trying to stop you . . . right . . . yes, I'll tell the others . . . but if she does how are we going to get in touch with you? I can't see . . . all right, as you wish . . . so long. Keep sober."

He hung up and stood cracking his knuckles thoughtfully. Then he looked out through the window and said, "Gone very dark all of a sudden, hasn't it? Start chucking it down any minute, I'd say."

Carole asked, "Was that Michael?"

With a slight raising of his eyebrows, Ford said, "Yes."

"What did he want?"

"Just to say he'll be delayed. Adele wasn't on the eight-ten. Probably missed it because her train got in late. Michael thinks she'll be on the next one and so he's going to stay in Blandford to save trailing here and back again. It's due about a quarter to nine."

Carole looked at her watch and said, "He's got fully an hour to wait. If she missed the bus I'd have thought she'd phone. After all, she knew Michael would be meeting her at eight-ten."

"Don't suppose she cares a damn if he has to hang around all night," Ford said.

As though not expecting to be taken seriously, he added, "Could be she doesn't intend to come back at all."

Then he turned his head and looked straight at Quinn. For the first time since they had met he spoke to him directly.

In a biting voice, he asked, "As an outsider what do you think?"

The sneer on his pink-and-white face left no room for doubt. He meant to be offensive.

Quinn said, "As an outsider it's none of my business."

"Really? I'd have thought you were in the right kind of job to make it your business."

"Then you'd have thought wrong. What do you know about my kind of job, anyway?"

"Merely that you're a reporter. Or am I mistaken?"

Carole said, "Stop it before you go too far . . . both of you. It isn't funny."

"I'm not amused either," Quinn said. "And don't blame me. This isn't any of my seeking. He's made his attitude obvious from the moment he set eyes on me. I wish I knew what's eating him."

In an overbearing tone, Ford said, "Oh, nothing personal. But I hope you won't be offended if I say that Miss Stewart seems to choose most peculiar friends."

Quinn said, "And I hope you will be offended if I say that Mrs. Parry seems to go in for even more peculiar relations that she couldn't possibly have

94

chosen unless all her taste was in her mouth."

Carole stepped between them and waved her arms in the style of a referee. "I'm stopping this contest right now. Both of you are disqualified for hitting low."

She was trying to sound flippant but her eyes were angry. Quinn knew she was holding herself in with an effort.

He said, "I didn't come here to quarrel with anybody. This situation was forced on me . . . but I'm evidently odd man out so if you wouldn't mind running me to the nearest bus stop I'll leave you all — "

"You'll do nothing of the kind! This is Adele's house and anyone I bring is treated as Adele's guest. There's no question of leaving."

She swung round on Ford and asked him sharply, "What's wrong with you? Why are you behaving like this?"

He spread out his plump hands and looked at her with bland, innocent eyes. He said, "I detest reporters — that's all."

"Pretty sweeping," Quinn said. "As people are fond of saying about those of a different religion or a different colour, there's good and bad alike wherever you go. Have you some special reason for lumping all newspaper men together and hating the lot?"

"Well, if you must know I had an unfortunate experience with the local Press some time ago — and once was enough."

"I've got no connection with the local Press. I'm crime correspondent for a national paper. Unless you're engaged in some kind of criminal activity you've nothing to fear from me."

Ford started to say, "If you're alleging — "

Then the sneer left his face and he went on, "You're being facetious, of course."

"Of course," Quinn said.

"I'm glad to hear it."

96

"You may be even more glad to hear that I'm on holiday — or supposed to be — for the next couple of weeks. Apart from which, I don't write a gossip column . . . and so I'm not interested in tittle-tattle about your family or your friends."

Carole said, "Now that we've reached an understanding, that will be all." She glanced from one to the other and shook her head sadly. "If it wouldn't make you look even more like silly little schoolboys I'd insist on your shaking hands."

Quinn said he was sorry if he had behaved badly. Neil Ford mumbled something in the nature of an apology.

For the time being their instinctive antagonism was pushed into the background. But, as Quinn told himself, it was only for the time being.

Why Ford resented him was something that only Ford could explain. Perhaps it was true that he'd been badly treated by the local Press. Perhaps it was merely an excuse.

It made hardly any difference. The friction between them was there. Best thing they could do was keep out of each other's way.

For one brief moment he wished he'd never met Carole Stewart. If he had not gone to that party by mistake . . . What was the fellow's name? Ah, yes, Hinchcliffe.

. . . Damn' silly thing to do. He was old enough to have more sense. And getting himself plastered was absolutely stupid . . .

The door-bell chimed. Carole looked at Ford and said, "I wonder who that can be. Did you hear a car?"

"No. Certainly can't be Michael and Adele. It's too soon."

"They wouldn't ring the bell, anyway. Both of them have a key."

She went to the door and opened it and said, "Oh, hallo! Come in. I haven't seen you for ages. How are you?" Her voice was polite but it was the stilted politeness that women use to conceal dislike.

Quinn saw a stockily built woman with fluffy hair cut short and hazel eyes that flitted here and there like those of a bird. Her smile exposed a lot of teeth.

She wrapped it round Quinn when she was introduced to him. In a deep, masculine voice, she said, "How d'you do . . . "

Then she asked, "Have we met before?"

It was an unnecessary question. She expected him to say no, but the query established some kind of tenuous relationship.

He said, "I don't think so. This is my first visit here."

"Yes, I guessed as much. Never forget a face. Names go in one ear and out the other, but I've got a photographic memory for faces. One of those things, you know. Runs in the family . . . like noses."

At that she laughed as though she'd said something vastly amusing although a trifle vulgar. It was a high-pitched laugh in complete contrast to her normal voice.

She didn't need much encouragement to go on talking about herself. With her eyes flitting over Quinn's face as if looking for a place to settle, she said, "Mine was a crazy family. I've never forgiven my parents for calling me Ariadne. You can just imagine what I went through at school."

With her head tilted back and her eyes almost closed, she asked, "You know who Ariadne was . . . don't you?"

Again she wanted him to say no. Quinn said, "I learned very little Greek mythology, but if I remember correctly she was a goddess, daughter of Minos, the King of Crete."

"My, my!" Her eyes flicked open and fixed themselves on his with the hypnotic stare of a cat. "How about that? You are clever, aren't you?"

She looked at Carole and Ford as though displaying some new acquisition. Then she went on rapidly, "Don't confuse me with the lady of the same name. There's no royal blood in my family. Father was one George Wilkinson, tea importer of Mincing Lane. Quite a small way of business . . . "

With no change of tone, she went running on, "Hope I'm not being a nuisance. Merely walked across to borrow something that Adele promised me. Judging by all the signs and portents I'm going to get a soaking on my way home."

"If it rains I'll run you back," Carole said.

"Well, how about that? Aren't you sweet?" She glanced from Quinn to Ford and back to Quinn. "I do know the nicest people. Where are they, anyway? Michael and Adele, I mean."

Neil Ford had remained aloof from the one-sided conversation. Now he interposed, "She missed the bus from Salisbury. Michael's waiting for the one that gets in at ten to nine."

"Oh, really? I've never known that happen before. Where has she been?"

"Wood Lake."

"How strange . . . If she caught her usual train she'd be in plenty of time for the bus."

Carole said, "It's quite possible she missed the train. All we know is that she didn't arrive at the eight-ten."

"Then you'd think she'd have phoned, wouldn't you? Unless . . . " Miss Wilkinson's deep voice dwindled away to nothing.

Ford asked, "Unless what?"

With another high-pitched laugh, Ariadne said, "Don't be short with me, my dear man."

"I wasn't being short with you. But, if you know of any reason why Adele wasn't on her usual bus, for heaven's sake don't make a mystery out of it."

"Reason?" Miss Wilkinson tilted back her head and looked at him through half-shut eyes. "How would I know? I wasn't even aware that she'd gone to Wood Lake."

"Now you're being evasive."

"Don't be absurd! It could be any one of a dozen reasons. Perhaps she and Michael squabbled. Perhaps she thinks it might be a good idea to let him do without her for a change."

Neil Ford said testily, "That's ridiculous."

"Very probably. I wouldn't profess to know what a woman does when she quarrels with her husband. I've never been married."

"How do you know they quarrelled?"

"Who's being ridiculous now? Don't all married people quarrel? It's called the War of the Sexes. Making a man and a woman live together in the same house day after day is like putting a lion and a tiger in the same cage."

Quinn was watching Carole and he saw a shadow settle on her face. At the back of his mind he remembered a parcel of freshly-laundered shirts and underwear and pyjamas in the cottage near Basingstoke.

Carole said, "It's a good job we know you too well to take you seriously. Think I'd better switch the light on. It's getting quite dark. Wish the rain would come." She sounded restless and on edge.

Through the windows facing south, lightning glowed on the horizon. It lit up Ariadne's plump face and Quinn saw that she was smiling. There was a cruel look in her eyes as she watched Carole walk to the switch by the door.

Upstairs he could hear Irene Ford moving around, her heels tapping across a stretch of bare parquet floor. Then there came a muffled thump — thump — thump — thump as she walked over a carpet. She turned on a tap, turned it off again almost immediately. Water made a gurgling noise in a waste pipe.

Something clattered in the wash basin. The tap ran again briefly. All the little sounds were very distinct and he knew she must have left the bathroom door open.

Then Carole switched on the light. She said, "That's better. I always get a tingling feeling when there's electricity in the air. I can remember as a child having to get out of the bed during a thunderstorm because the mattress seemed to prickle."

In a deep mocking voice, Ariadne said, "Shows how different two people can be. I like it when there's lightning about. Makes me feel vital and alive all over. I get a thrill out of the noise of a storm, especially when it crashes right overhead. Do you think it's because" — she gave Quinn another sleepy look — "because I'm the seventh child of a seventh child?"

Quinn said, "Could be. Perhaps your parents knew what they were doing when they called you Ariadne."

She laughed her high-pitched laugh with both hands thrown up. Then she said, "How about that? I've often thought I was born three hundred years too late. I should've been a witch . . . "

She went on talking with a brittle air, glancing at each of them in turn to see their response to her forced wit. Quinn told himself she was determined to be funny if it killed them. After a while he shut his mind to her chatter and listened only just enough to know when to make the right noises.

Neil Ford said hardly anything. Carole spoke no more often than was absolutely necessary. Several times she looked at her watch and then glanced through the window at the elm trees towering against the overcast sky.

As time passed, Neil Ford became increasingly restless. He moved about, picked up an ornament and put it down again, and seemed unable to remain still.

Ariadne Wilkinson must have noticed it but she made no comment. She was too busy giving Quinn facetious pen-pictures of the people of Castle Lammering.

Eventually Ford went over to the bar and poured himself a drink. When he put it down again after barely tasting it, Carole asked, "Aren't you hungry?"

"No. We had afternoon tea rather

late and I'm not in the mood for eating right now. I'll have a bite when Irene comes down."

In a disgruntled tone, he added, "That'll probably be in time for breakfast. She takes longer to wash her face and comb her hair and put on a spot of make-up than any woman I know."

Miss Wilkinson said, "Oh, I'd forgotten about your wife. Of course, she's here, isn't she? I can't imagine what made me think you'd come on your own. Anyhow — "

She stopped and held up one finger, her mouth pursed, her eyes flitting bird-like from face to face. In a peculiarly hushed voice, she said, "Isn't that a car? Seems I was wrong, doesn't it? Adele must've been on the later bus, after all. That'll be Michael bringing his little wifie home to the bosom of her family."

Quinn saw the elms silhouetted by the lights of a car as it climbed the road from the village. He told himself it could hardly be Michael Parry returning from Blandford.

. . . Unless the bus got in early . . . and he drove like hell all the way back. His wife must be mad to travel with him at all. If he's ever stopped by the police and given a test for alcohol the breathalyser will change through all the colours in the rainbow and go off with a bang . . .

Ariadne Wilkinson said, "If that's Adele I hope she knows what I came for because I've completely forgotten . . . although I don't see how it can be her. The bus doesn't get to Blandford before eight-fifty and it's just turned five minutes to nine now. I know Michael drives like a maniac but this is ridiculous."

The car swung round in front of the house and pulled up smoothly outside the door. It wasn't Michael Parry's Rover 2000.

Through the tall window Quinn saw a man get out, look up at the sky, and then hurry into the porch. As the bell chimed, the first heavy drops of rain streaked the window. Before it rang again trees and car and pebbled drive were almost blotted out by a cloudburst that came down in solid sheets.

Ariadne Wilkinson said, "How about that? I knew Michael couldn't have got back so soon. That's Dr. Bossard's car. Is somebody ill . . . or is this a social call?"

Carole said crisply, "I'm glad there's something you don't know. I was beginning to think — "

"Better keep it till later. Poor Dr. Bossard will be half-drowned if you don't let him in."

She flicked a glance at Quinn and he caught the same look in her eyes that he'd seen once before when she was watching Carole. She said, "Isn't this rain delicious? Listen to it . . . just listen to it. If I were at home right now I'd be tempted to take off all my clothes and walk through the garden, quite naked, and let myself be washed clean and wholesome and innocent like a child — like we all were in the beginning. Don't you ever feel that way?"

He wanted to tell her if he did he'd have himself certified. While he was thinking of something more politic to say, Carole opened the door and let Dr. Bossard in.

" . . . Good evening, Doctor. You got here just in time. Shocking, isn't it?"

Bossard said, "Yes. But the farmers will be pleased . . . if they're ever pleased at anything. A good soaking will do their root crops all the good in the world . . . "

He was a slim-built man with good features and a well-shaped head. Quinn got the impression he was the ex-army type — clipped moustache, keen eyes, hair greying slightly at the temples.

He looked superior and yet approachable — the kind of man who would be part of the atmosphere of the bar in any four-star hotel. His eyes crinkled in a smile when he shook hands with Quinn and he gave Neil Ford a pleasant nod.

" . . . Nice to see you again. How's Mrs. Ford?"

Ariadne Wilkinson said, "Don't answer that or you'll get a bill at the end of the month."

Bossard gave Quinn a wry look and said, "One of the drawbacks of my job, Mr. Quinn, is that people make me the target of the same old jokes, year in and year out. What do you do for a living?"

"I'm with the *Morning Post*."

"Oh, that's quite a novelty. We've had all sorts and conditions of men visiting Castle Lammering from time to time but I think you're the first newspaper man I've met here. Wouldn't you" — he smiled at Carole — "wouldn't you agree?"

Before she could answer, Miss Wilkinson said, "Well, how about that? A real live journalist. You and Michael Parry should have quite a lot to talk about."

There was no mistaking the sting in her voice as she added, "He's a writer, too, you know. Can't tell you what sort of stuff he writes because I've never read any of it, but it certainly keeps him busy. I'm sure one of these days he'll startle all of us."

The downpour had slackened. Quinn could still hear the intermittent rumble of thunder but now it came from a long way off. The storm was moving north.

He said, "Mr. Parry's vocation and mine are poles apart. I've never deluded myself that I could write a book. Of course, I don't suppose he could do my job, either."

Ariadne Wilkinson gave another high-pitched laugh. She said, "The former may be put down to modesty, but I'm sure there's no doubt about the latter."

The she turned to Bossard and asked, "Is this a personal or professional visit, Doctor?"

"Oh, personal . . . at least, I hope so.

Mrs. Parry invited me to come round this evening."

"But she's not here. I popped in, too, because I wanted to see her but she's not back yet."

"I didn't know she'd been away," Bossard said.

"Oh, yes. She should've been on the eight-ten bus at Blandford but it seems — "

The phone bell rang. Like a man standing apart from the others in his own web of reality, Quinn looked from Carole to Ford to Miss Wilkinson to Dr. Bossard and asked himself how he came to be there.

It had been a mistake — a very big mistake. These were not his people, this was not the kind of place where he could be himself. He still thought Carole was cute but even Carole had a fence round her now . . .

The bell went on ringing. Neil Ford said, "I'll take it. Might be from Adele to say she's — "

He picked up the receiver. Dr. Bossard

walked quietly across to Carole Stewart and began talking to her in an undertone. Miss Wilkinson watched them, her hazel eyes bright and predatory. More than ever, Quinn felt he didn't belong. He was on the outside looking in.

Neil Ford said, "Hallo . . . no, not yet. We haven't heard anything since you rang before . . . yes, it is. Most peculiar. Have you spoken to the bus people? They might — "

He stood pulling at his ear while he listened, his womanish mouth drawn down in fretful lines. Then he said, "I don't know what to suggest . . . yes, naturally you're getting worried. Best thing you can do is to come back here. Won't serve any purpose to stick around in Blandford in the rain . . . m-m-m . . . m-m-m . . . quite possibly, but damned inconsiderate of her, all the same. If you like I'll phone Wood Lake and ask them — "

The look on his face changed. He said stiffly, "Oh, all right, if you prefer to do it yourself. I just thought it would save time . . . no, why should anything be wrong? We'll find there's a perfectly innocent explanation for the whole thing. Maybe she asked somebody to ring you and the person forgot . . . O.K. See you soon."

He hung up and looked at Carole and spread out his hands aimlessly. He said, "Adele wasn't on the eight-fifty bus, either. Michael's getting himself into quite a lather. He's imagining all sorts of things."

Ford turned to Bossard and asked, "Did you get the impression, Doctor, when Mrs. Parry invited you here this evening, that she expected to be home late?"

Dr. Bossard said, "No. As I was saying a minute ago I didn't know she intended to go away."

Carole said nothing. Her eyes followed Bossard as he walked over to a settee and sat down and clasped his hands behind his head.

Ariadne Wilkinson moved closer to

Quinn and murmured, "Perhaps there's a story here for you: Rich and Beautiful Woman Disappears. How about that?"

"You've got the wrong idea of the way newspapers work," Quinn said. "People aren't presumed to have disappeared just because they return home a little later than expected. Could even be that her husband got the time or the date wrong. Such things have been known."

"Especially with Michael Parry," Miss Wilkinson said.

In the same deep whisper, she added, "Was he the worse for wear when you got here?"

She made Quinn feel like a fellow-conspirator and he resented the feeling. He had no wish to become involved in the scandal-mongering of a woman with a poisonous tongue.

He said, "I saw nothing wrong with Mr. Parry. He was very pleasant, very hospitable. We spent only a few minutes together but in that time he made me thoroughly at home. I like him."

Carole said, "Good for you."

The look in her eyes reminded him of that moment when she'd stooped to kiss him. Now it didn't mean very much . . . if anything at all. He had no hope of competing with, for instance, someone like Dr. Bossard.

. . . Good-looking fellow. Grooming, education, the grand manner: he had everything . . .

Men like Bossard never failed to give Quinn a sense of inferiority. It had been like that all his life. Journalism gave him professional status but it was one of the fringe professions — not like Bossard.

. . . He was trying to make conversation with Carole while Ford was on the telephone but she didn't seem very responsive. Wonder how long they've known each other? Seems a nice fellow . . . the balanced type that doesn't suffer from inhibitions. Not like Parry or Neil Ford or this waspish wench Ariadne. When she told me she should've been a witch

117

I nearly asked her if she spelled it with a B . . .

Part of his mind heard Bossard say that maybe in the circumstances he should leave. When Mrs. Parry got back she wouldn't want to be bothered with stray visitors when she had week-end guests.

" . . . Perhaps somebody would give me a ring to-morrow and let me know if everything ended up O.K."

Although he didn't look at anyone in particular he was talking to Carole. Quinn knew that with certainty. She was Bossard's real reason for calling at Elm Lodge.

. . . Yet she doesn't seem to fancy him. Wonder why? I'd have thought he was more than eligible . . . unless he's married, of course. Not, when I come to think of it, that she'd let that stand in her way. She as good as admitted she'd been living with a man at her cottage . . .

It was a pity she'd told him. He never liked to know that sort of thing

118

about a woman. Somehow it spoiled the image he always created in his own mind.

. . . What image? She's a slim dark little girl with a cute smile and grave dark eyes that look at you innocently. Says she's a TV producer. Says the cottage near Basingstoke belongs to her. How d'you know what she is or what she owns? She might be a high-class tart or a low-class liar . . .

Carole could be playing the eligible Dr. Bossard on a long line. The hard-to-get technique often did the trick.

. . . He's sweet on her all right. Get a helluva shock if I told him everything I'm wearing except my shoes and the suit I've got on belongs to the man she was sleeping with until he walked out without bothering to take his laundry . . .

Bossard had hesitated as though waiting for someone to ask him to stay. But Neil Ford merely nodded and Carole stared down at her hands.

So the doctor stood up and smiled

at Miss Wilkinson and asked, "Can I give you a lift?"

With a look of surprise, she said, "Oh, that's very kind of you . . . but Miss Stewart has already offered to run me home and I wouldn't want — "

"Don't worry about that," Carole said. "So long as it won't be taking Dr. Bossard out of his way . . . "

Bossard said, "Not at all. Besides it wouldn't matter if it did on a night like this."

There was no concealing the disappointment in Miss Wilkinson's eyes. She said, "How about that?"

From under her stubby eyelashes she gave Quinn a sardonic look. "See what happens when you're past your youth and unwanted? Not that I don't appreciate dear Dr. Bossard's offer. I think it's uncommonly handsome of him to — "

Somewhere on the floor above a woman screamed — a wild and frantic scream that shocked Miss Wilkinson into silence. With her mouth pointed like a narrow funnel she stood motionless, her hands clasped tightly together.

For a long moment the others didn't move. Then Neil Ford said huskily, "What the devil's happened?"

Upstairs there were running footsteps that skittered on a bare stretch of floor. Quinn saw Irene Ford at the top of the staircase. Her eyes were wild and she was gasping for breath.

In a broken voice, she said, "My God . . . oh my God! It's Adele. She's in the nursery. Please do something . . . please . . . "

Dr. Bossard rushed towards the stairs. As he ran, he called out, "It's all right, Mrs. Ford, it's all right. Stay there."

She didn't seem to hear him. Before he reached the foot of the staircase she began to sway, her eyes as lifeless as the eyes of a wax dummy. Then her knees gave way and she collapsed on the floor close to the edge of the top step.

4

QUINN was close behind Bossard and Ford as they ran upstairs. When they stopped to attend to Mrs. Ford he squeezed past and carried on along the semi-circular corridor overlooking the floor below.

The two rooms nearest the head of the staircase were bedrooms. In one the light was on and he saw an open suitcase resting on a chair. It was the case that Neil Ford had brought in from his car.

The next room was larger and it had twin beds and slightly more ornate furniture. One of the beds looked as though it had been lain on. The other was badly disarranged, bedspread half pulled off and trailing down almost to the floor.

Next door there was a well-appointed bathroom . . . then another room with the door wide open. In there the light was on, too.

It was a white-walled room with scenes from fairy tales painted on the dado: Mother Goose . . . the Pied Piper . . . Jack and the Beanstalk . . . the Sleeping Beauty . . . and many more.

There was a playpen, a rocking horse, a large Teddy-bear, a table on which stood a lamp with a shade that had coloured pictures of the Seven Dwarfs. All the furniture was white-enamelled and three-quarter adult size — except the bed standing just behind the wide open door.

On the bed lay the most beautiful woman that Quinn had ever seen. She had red hair, dark eyelashes, and a smooth, flawless skin. She was fully dressed except for her shoes which stood neatly together, half under the foot of the bed.

She lay with her arms by her sides in a pose of complete relaxation — this woman who was perfection in face and body from her provocative breasts to her small-boned ankles and graceful feet. He didn't want to move or to make a sound in case he disturbed her. He had the feeling that if she were left alone she would remain like this forever . . . like the Sleeping Beauty on the wall just above where she lay.

Outside, near the top of the staircase, he could hear Neil Ford and Dr. Bossard talking . . . Ariadne Wilkinson asking questions down below . . . Carole saying " . . . No, we don't need any help. You stay where you are. There are enough of us up here to take care of everything."

Then she went on, "Better go and see what's happened, Geoffrey. I'll give Mr. Ford a hand with his wife."

Geoffrey . . . Geoffrey . . . The name registered distantly in Quinn's mind. It only brought confirmation of something he realised he'd already known.

. . . Does Bossard spell his name with a G or a J? Does it matter a damn how he spells it? They've been behaving as though they're comparative strangers

124

but in the stress of the moment Carole's now betrayed herself . . .

Not that it mattered very much. Nothing really mattered except the woman who lay asleep in a room that had been designed and created for a child.

Her eyes were veiled by sweetly curving eyelashes tinged with bronze, her lips were slightly parted. To Quinn she seemed neither alive nor dead. She was someone who existed in a realm outside Time where nothing changed, no one grew old — a realm where the beautiful were immune from the ravages of decay.

He went a half step closer and touched her hand. She felt cool but not cold.

Then as he bent over her the clock that had stopped began ticking again. The moment of illusion was over.

He saw her sunken cheeks, the sagging of her jaw, the discolouration around her nose and mouth. Death was engraved on her face. What had seemed for one endless moment to be so lovely now became disfigured by the ugliness that precedes corruption.

Yet she was unmarked. There were no injuries so far as he could see: nothing but the stamp of death. It could almost have been that she was, indeed, asleep.

As he drew back from the bed footsteps came steadily along the corridor. He listened to them with confusion that was almost chaos in his mind.

Then Dr. Bossard walked into the room. He looked at the dead woman, his pleasant face very sombre.

He said, "This is a damn' funny business. I don't understand any part of it."

Quinn said, "Well, I can tell you one thing. She's dead. Finding out how she died is your line of country. She doesn't show any sign of injury."

"We'll see." Bossard leaned over the bed, opened one of her eyes, and studied it by the light of a pen torch. "We'll see."

He sniffed at her mouth and mumbled something under his breath. Then he used the torch again.

Quinn turned away and stared at the bedside table. Perhaps the answer would be there. Perhaps Dr. Bossard wouldn't have far to seek.

There was a brandy glass on the table with what looked like half an inch of brandy in the bottom. Partly submerged in the spirit were two yellow capsules.

. . . Be no problem if that's what she took. They'll analyse it in no time. Wonder if Bossard's noticed the glass? It's half hidden by the stand of the lamp and it may have escaped his attention . . .

That wasn't very likely. Doctors were trained to notice details, taught to use every one of their five senses. The best doctors had a sixth sense, too.

. . . But right now his first job is to satisfy himself that she isn't still alive . . . although there's not much

doubt. You can always tell by the appearance of the face . . . not so much a change as the lack of a quality that's always present in living people, awake or asleep. When they're dead they have a look which says there's no one at home . . .

Dr. Bossard was still mumbling to himself. At the top of the stairs, Carole and Ford were talking together . . . and now Quinn could hear Irene's voice, too. She was plaintively asking something over and over again.

He listened to the jumble of talk until a door closed and cut off all the voices. Then his mind switched to thoughts of Michael Parry.

. . . Going to get a helluva shock when he hears the news. She must've been very lovely . . . He had a beautiful wife and pots of money, so what made him take to drink? Maybe he was an alcoholic before he met Adele . . . but I can't see her marrying him in that case. With her looks and her money she could've chosen any one of a hundred

men. Wonder how she came to choose him . . . ?

Bossard had turned away from the bed. Now he was studying the brandy glass on the bedside table. His face was no longer sombre and he seemed unconcerned by the presence of death.

. . . You'd think he'd show some sign of being upset by her death. After all, they must've been on friendly terms or she wouldn't have invited him here socially. Yet I suppose he's got to be impersonal about things like this. It's called the clinical approach. When a man takes up medicine he either starts out different from other men or he becomes different. They talk about not becoming emotionally involved . . .

His mind flitted from Bossard to Michael Parry again. Then he found himself listening to the sound of muffled wailing from the bedroom at the top of the stairs.

. . . She's certainly gone all emotional. Whether she was very attached to her sister-in-law or not it must've been no

joke to walk in and find Adele stretched out on the bed all nice and peaceful like the Sleeping Beauty . . .

The pattern of what had happened seemed clear enough. It should be quite a straightforward job for the police.

. . . Looks as if Adele came home when there was no one in the house and took a stiff brandy laced with something lethal. But why come in here to die? And was she upstairs when Michael got back from his favourite pub? Or was he at home when she got back and did she find him sleeping it off? . . .

High heels came clip-clopping across parquet floor . . . and carpet . . . and parquet floor . . . and carpet. As they approached the nursery, Dr. Bossard looked up and shook his head in warning. Quinn nodded but his mind was still a long way off.

. . . Something else puzzles me — something about those two beds in the other room. Michael would use only one bed for his siesta and

yet both of them have been disturbed. Why both . . . if she died in here? Could be she lay down in the other room and then changed her mind and decided she preferred the nursery . . . or there may have been a third person in the house? . . .

That thought came out of nowhere. If it had any substance it changed everything.

. . . Might even be that Michael didn't have a nap at all. Maybe Adele went from bed to bed until she found the most comfortable one . . . like Goldilocks. They seem to have forgotten the story of the Three Bears when they were decorating this room . . .

It was a bizarre idea. While he was still toying with it the high heels came to a halt on the carpet outside.

Carole poked her head in at the door. She looked rather pale and her eyes were even more solemn than usual.

In a small voice, she asked, "Is it true?"

131

Quinn said, "Yes."

"But how did it happen? What was she doing in here?"

"Those are just two of the many questions that people will be asking very soon," Quinn said.

"Can I see her?"

From behind the open door, Dr. Bossard said, "There's nothing to see and you'd only be in the way. Go back and look after Mrs. Ford. If she doesn't calm down soon let me know and I'll give her a sedative."

Carole didn't argue. She just made a face, waved her hand to Quinn, and went away.

When she'd gone, Bossard moved back from the bed, and asked, "Would you do something for me, Mr. Quinn?"

"Sure. What is it you want?"

"Go downstairs and ring the police without making too much fuss. Ask for Inspector Elvin and tell him what's happened. Say I'll stay up here until he arrives so as to make sure nothing's disturbed. Got that?"

"Not altogether," Quinn said. "I can hardly tell him what's happened when I don't know myself."

With a slight frown, Dr. Bossard said, "You know enough."

"Oh, no. In my philosophy, enough is never sufficient. Since this isn't the kind of thing that can remain hush-hush, how did she die and when?"

Bossard withdrew into himself, his handsome face puckered in thought. Then he said in a cautious voice, "Anything I told you would be largely assumption. We won't know the facts until we've had a post-mortem."

"That's all right. Whatever you're willing to assume will satisfy me for the time being."

"You won't quote me, I hope?"

"No, of course not. I'm not asking these questions in the line of duty. Officially, I'm on holiday but I happen to be of a curious nature and I always like to know what makes the wheel go round."

"Well, I can only tell you one thing,"

Bossard said. "There's no particular mystery about this affair."

"You could be wrong, Doctor. This affair's got square wheels. There are so many questions to be answered, the police won't know where to begin. I'll ask you one. How long has she been dead?"

The doctor's manner changed perceptibly. He said, "With all due respect, Mr. Quinn, I don't think I'm entitled to discuss the details with you. After all, Mrs. Parry was a patient of mine and I see no reason why I should satisfy your curiosity . . . apart from which this is now a police matter."

His shrug closed the subject. With a pleasant smile that left no room for offence, he added, "If they wish to pass on the preliminary information I give them . . . "

Quinn said, "You insist on treating me as a reporter but actually I'm a guest here."

"Then, if you'll forgive my saying so, you're not behaving like a guest. It's not very tactful to probe into the affairs of people who are suddenly involved in a tragedy."

It was like a rehearsed speech that Bossard had prepared in advance. Quinn knew that if he argued he would get nowhere.

He said, "You're right, of course, Doctor. I shouldn't be so persistent . . . but old habits die hard. Now, instead of asking any more questions, I'll go and phone the police."

As he was going out, he looked back and said, "Supposing Mrs. Ford gets hold of me and wants to know about her sister-in-law, what do I say?"

"As little as you can. She's already aware that Mrs. Parry's dead. The rest she'll learn" — Bossard glanced down at the woman on the bed — "sooner or later . . . like everybody else."

He was still standing there, his eyes on Adele Parry's dead face, when Quinn left him. There were quiet voices in the room near the top of the staircase, the distant sound of a car, the soft, all-pervading hiss of the rain.

As Quinn went downstairs he could hear Irene Ford saying " . . . It doesn't seem right. She had so much to live for. It just doesn't seem right . . . " Behind her puling voice he heard the nursery door close with no more than the faintest click of the latch.

★ ★ ★

He had only just finished talking to the police when a car pulled up outside and Michael Parry came in. He now appeared to be cold sober.

With a fretful look in his pale blue eyes, he asked, "Is that Dr. Bossard's car out there? When did he come?"

"A little while ago."

"Where's he gone? Where are the others, for that matter?"

Quinn said, "Carole and Mr. and Mrs. Ford are upstairs. Mrs. Ford isn't feeling very well."

"Oh, too bad. Hope it's nothing

serious. Is that why they sent for the doctor?"

"No, he just happened to be passing and he called in to say hallo. He'd have been gone by now — "

"While we're on the subject, I don't feel too good myself. Worry, you know. This business has got me properly rattled. My wife wasn't on the eight-fifty bus, either. She hasn't phoned, has she?"

"No . . . and there's something I've got to tell you. If you'll sit down — "

"Queer, damn' queer. She knows how to look after herself but all the same . . . "

A puzzled look came into Parry's weak face. Behind that look lay something that could have been fear.

He stroked his moustache with an uneasy hand and asked, "What do you mean there's something you've got to tell me? What's going on?"

Quinn said, "Your wife's here."

Parry's hand followed the shape of his moustache and carried on down to his chin. He said, "What're you talking about? How can she be here if she wasn't on the bus?"

"I don't know that any more than I know what time she came home but I can assure you she's upstairs. Dr. Bossard's with her."

"Is she — " Parry faltered and began again. "Is she ill?" He made the question sound as though he knew the answer.

Then his face became blank. In a string of little disjointed phrases, he went on, "She's here — but you don't know what time she came home — and Bossard's with her — "

His hand crept up until it covered his eyes and he shivered like a man gripped by sudden cold. When he looked at Quinn again, he said, "I don't understand any of this. I'm just not with you. She's been taken ill . . . that's what you're trying to say, isn't it?"

Quinn said, "I'm afraid it's worse than that. She's dead."

Parry's mouth opened and remained open. After a long time he swallowed and said, "I don't believe it. It can't be true. I've got a feeling I'm going to wake up in any minute. Adele's the healthiest person I've ever known. Never had a day's illness in her life. How can she be dead?"

Suspicion entered Quinn's mind like the touch of a small cold hand. He said, "I'm no doctor, so I can't say. All I can tell you is that she was dead when we found her."

In a pinched voice, Michael Parry asked, "Where? Where was she?"

"Lying on the bed in the nursery."

"What was she doing in there?"

It wasn't meant as a question. He was talking to himself, his face as numb as his voice.

Like an echo, he repeated, "What was she doing in there?"

"That's for the police to decide," Quinn said. "I phoned them just before you came in."

"The police? I don't see . . . "

The fretful look showed again momentarily in his eyes. Then he nodded and said, "Yes, of course. It was the right thing to do. Don't pay any attention to me. I can't think straight."

His hand felt for his moustache as he asked, "Who was it that — found my wife?"

"Mrs. Ford."

"How did she come to do that? No one ever goes in there. The nursery isn't used."

"I didn't get the chance to ask her. She threw a fit of hysterics and fainted at the top of the stairs."

Parry covered his eyes again as though they hurt. Then he took his hand away and asked, "What does Dr. Bossard think happened to my wife?"

Quinn said, "He wouldn't tell me . . . either because he didn't know or because he thought it was none of my business. But whatever it was that caused her death she didn't look as if she'd suffered at all. That may be some consolation to you when you've had time to get over the shock."

With the faintest spark of interest, Parry said, "You've seen her . . . have you?"

"Yes, I got there before anybody else. When Bossard arrived he turfed me out."

"Do you think" — Parry swallowed — "do you think he'd let me see her . . . just for a moment?"

It wasn't the kind of thing a husband should have needed to ask. Judging by his tone he didn't care whether the answer was yes or no.

Quinn said, "I don't see how he can stop you. If you want to go upstairs I'd advise you to do it now before the police get here."

Parry seemed unable to decide. When he turned and looked up to the top of the stairs his eyes were reluctant.

At last, he said, "I'd rather not, right now. Perhaps later. There's no hurry . . . is there?"

141

"It's entirely up to you," Quinn said. "Won't change things whether you see her now or later or not at all."

"That's true enough. She's dead" — he sat down and slumped forward with his hands dangling between his knees — "she's dead and there's nothing I can do about it."

After a long pause he looked up at Quinn and asked, "Does Dr. Bossard know what time she died?"

"If he does he wouldn't tell me. My opinion, for what it's worth, is that she was probably dead when Carole and I got here."

With no expression, Parry said, "I don't understand any of this at all. She wasn't in the house when I got back about half past three, so she must've come home after that. Why didn't she wake me up if she felt ill? Better still, why didn't she phone and ask me to pick her up at Blandford or even Salisbury? Doesn't make sense that she'd creep into the house and let me go on sleeping . . . "

142

His voice tailed off and he stared down at the floor. Quinn said, "I think you should prepare yourself for the possibility that your wife didn't die a natural death."

Parry closed one hand over the other. In a small tight voice, he said, "Go on. Don't wrap it up. Say what you have to say."

"There was a brandy glass on the table beside the bed with a little brandy in it and a couple of yellow capsules. I've no idea what they were — "

"Sleeping pills," Parry said. He sounded very sure. "Dr. Bossard prescribed them and she's been taking one occasionally. Now I begin to see . . . "

He took a long breath and let it out again. Then he shook his head as though there was nothing more to say.

Quinn asked, "What do you see?"

"Why she was in the nursery. It's never used. She's kept it exactly as it was when the baby died."

As though recalling details that now had a new significance, he added, "The kid was only a few months old. She never really got over it."

"How long ago did it happen?"

"Five or six years . . . may be more. Lost her first husband not long afterwards."

Once again he seemed to be searching his memory. Then he said, "I met her about eighteen months later. We got engaged and married in a matter of weeks . . ."

While he listened Quinn had a picture in his mind of two beds that had been disturbed and the face of a beautiful woman disfigured in death. Perhaps she had gone into the nursery because she wanted to die surrounded by memories of a time that had been all too brief.

. . . Yet that doesn't explain who used the second bed in the other room. Unless she went from bed to bed until she found the most comfortable one for her last sleep . . . like Goldilocks. But

Adele Parry didn't have golden hair — she was a red-head . . .

A phrase came back to him from his childhood: " . . . *Then Goldilocks woke up and saw the three bears and she was very frightened. So she jumped out of bed and climbed through the window and ran all the way home to her mummy.*"

But Adele had nothing to be afraid of — except life itself. She might have been one of those people who were born under an unlucky star. Whatever happiness she had known with her first husband came to an end when she lost her baby and then he died. After that she'd had nothing.

So she'd tried to begin again. And this time it hadn't worked out, either. This time she'd had to stand and watch Michael become a dipsomaniac.

It might have been too much. Years of frustration and disappointment might well have reached culmination point on this last afternoon.

. . . *She found her husband in a*

drunken sleep. It wouldn't have been the first time but this was once too often. The police should have a pretty straight-forward case . . .

Except for two things . . . They would want to know why she had returned home hours before she was expected: why she had lain down on that second bed in the twin-bedded room — the room that she obviously shared with Michael — and then changed her mind and gone into the nursery.

Michael Parry was still looking down at the floor. As though following the trend of Quinn's thoughts, he said, "She never let me know she was coming back early. That's what I can't understand."

He hadn't yet shown any signs of grief. When he heard that his wife was dead he'd been shocked but not distressed, confused and bewildered but not sad. Now the look in his eyes was that of a man with a problem in which grief played no part.

Quinn asked, "Could she have returned before you got back this afternoon?"

Michael seemed to be enmeshed in his own inner problem. When he managed to rouse himself, he said, "Mrs. Gregg — that's the daily woman — doesn't leave until after one . . . and I came home about a quarter past three."

"Well, that means the house was empty for at least two hours . . . doesn't it?"

"Yes. But I can assure you my wife wasn't anywhere about when I got in."

"She might've been — if you went straight upstairs for your afternoon nap. You wouldn't have known whether anyone was in the house or not . . . providing they didn't make any noise."

After he'd swallowed a couple of times, Michael said, "You think she was in the nursery?"

"It's quite possible. After all, you

147

didn't go in there. Why should you?"

"Yes, but" — he had to get rid of something in his throat again — "but she must've kept very quiet and I don't see . . . "

"She didn't want you to find her before it was too late," Quinn said.

Michael Parry stared down at the floor, his hands dangling loosely, his face empty of all feeling. He seemed to be limp and yet alert — as though awaiting something he knew was bound to happen.

Upstairs a door opened and closed . . . careful foosteps walked along the semi-circular corridor . . . another door opened. Voices murmured at a level that was just audible.

Dr. Bossard said, " . . . No, Miss Wilkinson, I'm afraid you can't come in here. The police are due any moment and, besides, there's nothing to see. So I suggest you go home. It may sound rude but you'd only be in the way."

Ariadne Wilkinson's deep voice gave him barely enough time to finish. Quinn heard her complain " . . . be reasonable, doctor. How do you expect me to get home? You were going to take me, if you remember. I don't mind waiting until you're free."

In a sharper tone, Bossard said, "Now you're being awkward, Miss Wilkinson, and you know it. I'll probably have to stay here for quite some time. In any case, it isn't raining now."

"But, doctor — "

"A quarter of an hour's brisk walk will do you good. Help to keep your weight down. Aren't you always saying that's what you want?"

Miss Wilkinson said, "You're a beast, Dr. Bossard, nothing but a beast. What harm is there in letting me take a peep at an old friend before they take her away?"

"The answer's still no. You can pay your respects when you attend the funeral." There he raised his voice. "Good night, Miss Wilkinson."

Quinn heard the door close firmly.

Then Ariadne Wilkinson came down the stairs.

She scowled at Quinn and said, "How about that? Who'd have thought a man would make me walk home at my time of life?"

Her little hazel eyes flitted to Parry and she went on, "Hallo, Michael. Sad affair, very sad. You have my sympathy."

Without looking up, Michael said, "Thanks."

"If there's anything I can do just let me know." She opened the door and poked her head out and then she looked back at Quinn.

She said, "I hate that man. He's so right. It has stopped raining. But I'll guarantee it'll come down in buckets before I'm half-way home. Serve him right if I get pneumonia and he has to visit me three times a day."

When she was going out she looked back again and added, "Don't forget, Michael, if there's anything I can do . . . Nighty-night."

Parry raised his head just long enough to say, "I won't forget." Then at last she had gone.

Part of the overcast had lifted and the banked-up clouds in the western sky burned red in the light of the setting sun. As Ariadne Wilkinson crossed the drive she walked into a broad swaithe of that fiery light, her shadow bobbing behind her like a monstrous companion.

She seemed to lose substance the farther she went. Quinn watched her until she was hidden by the clump of elm trees glistening wet and green after the rain. He told himself he would scarcely have been surprised if she had come sailing over the topmost branches on a broomstick.

Inside his head he could hear her saying " . . . *Do you think it's because I'm the seventh child of a seventh child? . . . I've often thought I was born three hundred years too late. I should've been a witch.*"

Perhaps she was merely being

facetious. Perhaps, on the other hand, he had been meant to take it seriously. She was a strange woman — a strange and somewhat unpleasant woman.

. . . Funny how I didn't notice she wasn't downstairs when I went down to use the phone. Wonder where she was all the time Dr. Bossard and I were talking together in the nursery? Probably hidden in the bathroom next door with both ears flapping. She's not the kind to miss very much . . .

He pushed her out of his mind and thought instead about Irene Ford and her reason for going into the nursery. According to Parry, no one ever went in there.

Could be that Michael Parry wasn't very reliable. His wife had evidently not had much faith in him . . . or he'd have known she was coming home sooner than arranged . . . assuming that was true and she hadn't really told him. With someone like Parry a lot of things had to be assumed.

5

INSPECTOR ELVIN was a spare, wiry man with protruding cheek-bones and a head of silver hair brushed smoothly back without any parting. His tie matched his dark blue suit, his collar was crisply white, his shoes had been meticulously polished.

The plainclothes officer who came in with him was big and burly and heavy featured. Elvin introduced him almost as an after-thought.

" . . . Oh, and this is Sergeant Taylor. He knows the district very well or we'd have taken a lot longer to find the house."

The sergeant bobbed his head and grunted something unintelligible. Then he hid both hands inside his hat and looked up at one of the light fittings as though he had never seen anything like it before.

153

When the introductions were over, Elvin shared a roving glance between Quinn and Parry and murmured, "Very unfortunate business . . . very unfortunate. I won't trouble you any more than I can help, Mr. Parry, but I have to make certain inquiries . . . certain necessary inquiries. You understand, I'm sure."

In a faraway voice, Michael Parry said, "Yes, of course. But there's so little I can tell you. This has come as a great shock to me."

"That's only natural, sir, very natural. We'll talk the whole thing over later when I've had a word with Dr. Bossard. For the moment I suggest that you try to relax — just relax."

His face and his tone changed as he turned to Quinn and said, "You're the gentleman who phoned me, aren't you? Was it you who found Mrs. Parry?"

"No, it was Mrs. Ford, her sister-in-law."

"And where is Mrs. Ford now?"

"Upstairs. Her husband's with her

and so is Miss Stewart, a friend of the family. They're keeping Mrs. Ford company because she's been very distressed."

"Then I won't disturb the lady just for the moment. There's no hurry, no hurry at all. Dr. Bossard's still in the room where Mrs. Parry was found?"

"Yes."

"Oh, I'm glad of that . . . very glad. Now would you take me to him, please?"

Sergeant Taylor remained downstairs, his eyes shifting from one light fitting to another, his flabby face quite impassive. Michael Parry never even looked up when they left. He was still sitting in the same position, his head bent, his hands clasping and unclasping between his knees.

At the top of the stairs, Quinn said, "The Fords and Miss Stewart are in that room there. The one next to it is Mr. and Mrs. Parry's room."

Without taking his eyes off Quinn's face, Elvin said, "I see."

"There's something I'd like to show you, Inspector, if you've got time."

A pale smile passed over Elvin's face. He said, "For the necessary things I make time, Mr. Quinn. It's the only way, in my experience, the only way. There's always to-morrow."

Quinn led him into the empty bedroom. When the door was shut, he said, "Mr. Parry told me he returned home about half past three, went straight upstairs, and took a nap It would seem he was still asleep when Miss Stewart and I arrived at seven-thirty."

Once again, Inspector Elvin said, "I see."

"You don't — not yet. But I think you will. Parry says there was no one in the house when he got back. His wife had been to a place called Wood Lake and she wasn't due back until this evening . . . "

Elvin listened to the story, his face remote. Then he said, "M-m-m . . . Strange affair, very strange. Didn't anybody see her return home?"

"Not that we know of. But it must've been quite a while before Miss Stewart and I got here. I'd say she'd been dead some time when we found her just before nine o'clock."

With a leisurely glance at his watch, Inspector Elvin asked, "Have you much experience of these things, Mr. Quinn?"

"A fair amount."

"In what way?"

"I'm crime correspondent for the *Morning Post*. Over the years I've had a lot of dealings with the police and this sort of business."

Elvin raised his silver eyebrows. He said, "Interesting . . . yes, indeed, very interesting. Have you some idea at the back of your mind that Mrs. Parry's death is not entirely what it would seem to be?"

"Hardly an idea, Inspector. Just a teeny-weeny thought that worries me."

"Based on what?"

"Those two beds. They've obviously been lain on . . . both of them."

With slow deliberation, the inspector stared at one bed and then at the other. He said, "Yes, so it would appear. But there's nothing unusual about that . . . nothing unusual at all. What're you trying to say?"

"Just this. Unless Parry slept in more than one bed, someone else must've taken a lie-down in this room. And the odds are it was Mrs. Parry. But she was found dead next door in the nursery. So I've been asking myself why she flitted from one room to the other. What difference did it make which bed she died in?"

Inspector Elvin gave Quinn a sidelong look and nodded thoughtfully. He said, "That's a good question . . . a very good question. You may be quite a useful man to have around, Mr. Quinn."

"It's been known," Quinn said.

"I'm sure it has . . . quite sure. When I've spoken to Dr. Bossard I'd like to hear if you have any other ideas."

Elvin looked down at the twin beds

again. In the same remote voice, he asked, "Are you an old friend of the Parrys'?"

"Never met them before to-day."

"Then how do you come to be here?"

"Miss Stewart invited me to spend the week-end at Elm Lodge. We'd hardly been in the house five minutes when Michael Parry dashed off to meet the bus his wife was supposed to be on . . . so I haven't had much chance of getting really acquainted with him. And the first time I set eyes on her she was dead."

"Not a very auspicious start to your week-end . . . not very auspicious, at all. On the other hand" — there was a questioning light at the back of Elvin's eyes — "they say all is grist that comes to the mill. There may be a story in this for you."

Quinn said, "I don't want a story. I'm on holiday. The paper will have to get on without my works of genius for the next couple of weeks."

"Ah, yes, but there's such a thing as a busman's holiday."

"Neither busman's nor boatman's. My interest in this affair is purely academic. I'm puzzled by Mrs. Parry's strange behaviour, that's all."

"Oh, I can see that. It is peculiar . . . very peculiar."

"Of course, people who are about to commit suicide often do peculiar things."

"That sounds like a question," Elvin said.

He sucked in his cheeks while he gave Quinn another sidelong look. Then he added, "You have a suspicious mind, Mr. Quinn. I always thought that was the special privilege of the man in my job."

Quinn said, "Newspaper men share it as well. They learn the facts of life at an early age."

"I've no doubt they do . . . no doubt at all. And talking about facts" — he gave the twin beds a final scrutiny and then he opened the door — "I think it's

160

about time I heard what Dr. Bossard has to say."

"Let's hope he tells you more than he told me," Quinn said.

"Wasn't he very communicative?"

"I'm not sure he even admitted that Mrs. Parry was dead."

"Does he know you're a newspaper reporter?"

"Oh, yes. Everybody in the house has learned my ghastly secret by this time."

"Well, there's your answer. Dr. Bossard is police surgeon for this area and as such he doesn't make statements to the Press. But there's nothing personal in his attitude, nothing personal at all."

Inspector Elvin gave Quinn a nod and added, "Would you mind waiting here until I come back?"

"No, I don't mind . . . but is there any special reason why I shouldn't go downstairs? I could do with a drink."

"I'm sure you could and I won't delay you a minute longer than is necessary — absolutely necessary. Soon as I've got a little information from Dr. Bossard I'll be back."

"That still doesn't explain why I have to wait here."

"It should . . . if you think about it."

"Thinking tires me," Quinn said. "Life's a whole lot easier when I get things spelled out for me in simple language."

"More often than not, it's the use of language that makes life complicated — very complicated."

"Now you're trying to blind me with semantics. Why not just answer my question?"

"All right. Until I get back I don't want anybody to disturb this room before I've had a chance to search it."

Quinn said, "Now who's got a suspicious mind? If you feel that way, what makes you think you can trust me?"

"One thing — and one thing only." A little frown put lines in Inspector

Elvin's smooth face. "You're a stranger in this household, Mr. Quinn. That's why I think I can trust you."

As he was closing the door, he added, "I hope you don't do anything to spoil that trust . . . anything at all."

* * *

For a quarter of an hour, Quinn paced the room backwards and forwards, passing and re-passing the long landscape window which looked out on fields and woods fresh from the rain. Slanting russet shadows now lay everywhere as the sun went down.

He had a new problem. No policeman he had ever known went out of his way to confide in a stranger. Yet Elvin had talked as though they were close confidants.

. . . He says he trusts me but his reason is a load of codswallop. For one thing, he talks too much. And any copper who agrees with me all the

163

time and chucks compliments around is suspect from the word go. Trouble is I can't see what he's after . . .

Voices murmured in the room where Neil Ford and Carole were taking care of Mrs. Ford. The set-up there was peculiar, as well.

. . . Why is Ford keeping out of the way? You'd think he'd be somewhat curious to know what had happened to Adele. After all, his wife could've been wrong. How does he know Adele Parry's dead? She might've had a heart attack . . . or nothing more serious than a fainting fit. Yet he's been stuck in there ever since his wife passed out with hysterics. And not because he's a devoted husband. That I won't believe . . .

Michael Parry's behaviour was also rather odd. He acted like a man crushed by the weight of events . . . but it was a piece of acting and not very good acting, at that.

He didn't really care. His wife was dead but the fact of her death hardly

164

seemed to have impinged on him. If anything, his chief reaction could almost have been one of relief.

. . . You'd think he was glad. Well, maybe not exactly pleased but near enough . . .

There was no sound from the nursery. Whatever was taking place between Elvin and Dr. Bossard they were keeping their voices down.

. . . Of course, if Parry and his wife didn't get on very well, I wouldn't expect him to be crying his eyes out. Unless she's pulled a fast one on him he'll probably inherit all her money . . . and that must be a tidy sum. She may have been heavily insured, as well . . .

It was the lonely who committed suicide. Few people took their own lives unless they had no one they could turn to.

. . . Seems such a waste. Rich and beautiful and, as Irene Ford said, so much to live for. Yet Mrs. Adele Parry must've considered that what

165

she possessed didn't compensate for the things she lacked . . . if she committed suicide. If not . . .

The door opened and Michael Parry came in. He looked much less dispirited now.

When he caught sight of Quinn he gave a little start and said, "I didn't expect to find anyone in here. I thought you and the inspector would be with Dr. Bossard."

"No, Elvin wanted to talk to him on his own. He left me" — Quinn couldn't resist the temptation — "to play watchdog, as it were."

Michael wiped a hand over his face. It seemed to replace the harassed look he'd worn downstairs as though he were putting on a mask.

Then he asked doubtfully, "What do you mean by watchdog?"

"Just a figure of speech. Elvin merely wants me to see nothing's interfered with in this room while he's having a chat with Dr. Bossard."

"Interfered with? What on earth are

you talking about?"

"Ask the inspector. I'm only quoting what he told me. I gather he's going to make a search in here when he gets back."

Michael Parry's mouth opened and shut again. He said, "This is absolutely fantastic. What does Elvin expect to find?"

"Your guess is as good as mine," Quinn said.

"But there can't possibly be anything in this room that — " Like a man who had been on the verge of saying too much, Parry stopped and moistened his lips.

Then he went on weakly, "It's bad enough that my wife committed suicide without all this on top of it. Still, I suppose the police have their own way of doing things and they won't change their system out of consideration for my feelings."

Quinn said, "You can be sure of that . . . if nothing else. They never go by appearances. Although it does look as if your wife committed suicide."

Something showed momentarily in Parry's eyes. He said, "Of course she did. What else could it have been?"

"Are you asking me or yourself?"

"No, I just wondered if Inspector Elvin thought it might've been an accident."

"Possibly. For the sake of you and the other members of the family I hope that's what it turns out to be. Save a lot of embarrassment all round."

Parry said, "Thanks." He looked grateful. "That's very decent of you. I suppose all we can do is keep our fingers crossed."

"That's all. But if it's an encouragement to you the average Coroner's jury leans over backwards to avoid bringing in a suicide verdict."

Through Quinn's mind ran the thoughts he'd had before. Now they were more positive.

. . . This bloke doesn't care a damn that his wife's dead. His only concern is for himself. Wonder if he realises he's

bound to be asked a lot of questions at the inquest. Won't sound good if they prove she must've swallowed the stuff — whatever it was — after he got back home . . .

Nobody would believe Parry was so drunk he hadn't heard anything. Whatever pub he'd been in the landlord would know if he'd had a lot to drink.

. . . You can bet all your wife's money — every sausage of it — that the landlord will be asked what sort of state you were in when you left . . . and where you were . . . and why . . . and how . . . and what time you went rolling home . . .

Parry said, "If you're right it'll make me feel a lot better. Not that anything can ever — "

A door closed not far away and he broke off to listen. As footsteps came near and halted outside he rubbed his hands together as though he felt cold.

Then Inspector Elvin walked in. He looked at Parry and said, "Ah, I'm glad

169

you're here, sir, very glad. I think we can have our little talk now and clear up various matters."

His eyes switched to Quinn and he went on, "Perhaps you wouldn't mind leaving us. When you go downstairs I'd be grateful if you'd tell Sergeant Taylor to phone for the ambulance . . . very grateful."

Quinn had reached the door when Parry said, "I'd like you to stay. Pass on the inspector's message and then come back, there's a good fellow." He made it sound more like an order than a request.

Inspector Elvin coughed and said, "I see no necessity for a third party to be present — no necessity at all."

A look of aggression came into Parry's pallid blue eyes. He said flatly, "What you see or don't see is quite immaterial. This is my home and I look on Mr. Quinn as a friend. So I want him to stick around while you question me. Any law against it?"

"No. I never suggested that there

was. It's just that — "

"Have you got some personal objection?"

"None at all." The inspector bent his silver head and looked down as though admiring the shine on his highly-polished shoes. "I merely think it's rather ill-advised. That's all — ill-advised."

"Why?"

"Well, I suppose you're aware that he's a newspaper reporter?"

There was nothing offensive in either the words or the tone but Quinn felt resentment at being involved. He said, "You make it sound as if I were a prostitute."

Elvin looked up without raising his head. He said, "The comparison is rather unfortunate, if I may say so — rather unfortunate."

"You've already said so. I get the point."

"I'm afraid you choose to misunderstand me. However, if Mr. Parry wishes you to stay there's no reason why you

171

shouldn't . . . no reason at all. But please oblige me by remaining quiet. We'll get on much quicker that way."

For a moment longer than was necessary he kept his eyes on Quinn's face. Then he turned to Michael Parry and asked, "Would you excuse me while I give instructions to my sergeant?"

He left the door open when he went out. Quinn heard the clip-clop of his shoes on the stairs . . . subdued talk that lasted only a few seconds . . . the tinkle of a phone bell. He wondered if Sergeant Taylor had gone on studying the light fittings all the time he'd been alone.

. . . Typical plain-clothes dick. Looks the kind who'd shop his own grand-mother. Wouldn't like to trust this fellow Elvin, for that matter. One minute he pretends we're the best of pals, and the next thing you know he acts as if he wouldn't trust me with the church collection . . .

Inspector Elvin was coming upstairs

again. As he reached the top, someone came out of the adjoining bedroom.

Quinn heard Carole's husky voice. She asked something that he couldn't make out.

Elvin said, "Yes, I'm from the police. May I ask who you are?"

"I'm Carole Stewart. Is Dr. Bossard still here?"

"He is. Do you want him for any special reason?"

"Well, I think he might take a look at Mrs. Ford. It was she who found Mrs. Parry and you can understand — "

"Yes, of course. Have a word with the doctor yourself. You'll find him in the nursery."

. . . Funny how Carole and Bossard behaved as if they hardly knew each other. They wouldn't act that way unless they had something to hide. Maybe they were pretty close at one time and then she took up with somebody else . . . that man who stayed at the cottage, perhaps . . . or it was Bossard himself who shared

the love-nest. Don't suppose he'd be amused if he knew I was wearing his shirt. Bound to get altogether the wrong idea of how I came to be there . . .

Carole said, "Thank you. Do you know where Mr. Parry is?"

"In the next room. But he's not free for the moment. You'll be able to see him later."

Michael Parry was listening although he pretended to be indifferent. His eyes looked strained.

. . . In every sense I'm odd man out here. They've all got their little secrets but I don't feature anywhere. I feel as if I'm looking through a peephole . . . like that thing they used to have on the pier at Yarmouth: What the Butler Saw . . .

Elvin was coming back. He walked with the unhurried, confident tread of a man who was very sure of himself — a man who had everything under control.

. . . If that old boy old boy character, Reg, hadn't gone off to get another

drink I wouldn't have got myself mixed up in all this . . . Carole had no need to come looking for me. What I did, or didn't do, was no concern of hers. I'd either have slept it off in that wench's bedroom . . . what was her name? Caroline? Gwendoline? No, Jacqueline, that was it . . . or they'd have tossed me out on my ear . . . Some day I must look up Charlie Hinchcliffe and see what he's like . . .

At the back of Quinn's mind, Reg was talking in a superior voice that sounded as though he had something hot in his mouth. *"Charlie isn't short of the old folding money, you know. His wife left him pretty well fixed . . . very considerate woman. Went and snuffed it while Charlie was in the prime of life. Ever since then he's been having a whale of a time . . . got rid of his handicap and came into a packet . . . some fellows have all the luck, don't they?"*

Fellows like Michael Parry. It was a

grim thought and it stuck in Quinn's mind.

Yet Parry didn't want people to think his wife had committed suicide. He would prefer a verdict of Accidental Death. If he could be believed . . . if anybody could be believed in this damned house.

6

THEN Inspector Elvin returned. He shut the door, leaned back against it, and slid his hands into his jacket pockets with his thumbs left outside.

He said, "Now, where were we? Ah, yes . . . I suppose you know the circumstances of your wife's death, Mr. Parry?"

After a hesitant start, Michael said, "I only know she died from — from something she took. At least, that's what I've been told."

"You haven't been to see your wife?"

"No, I — I couldn't face it. The thought of her being dead . . . " He looked down at his restless hands.

"Have you any idea why this should have happened?"

"Not a clue. If I'd had even the

faintest idea . . . but how could I know?"

"That is a point." Elvin bobbed his silver head in agreement. "How could you know?"

For a few moments he waited as though expecting an answer. Then he went on in a confidential tone, "Well, I feel I ought to tell you what we think caused your wife's death, Mr. Parry. She would appear to have died from an overdose of some hypnotic drug, probably a barbiturate called Pembrium. Was she in the habit of taking sleeping pills?"

"I wouldn't exactly call it a habit . . . but she did take one now and again."

"Were they Pembrium?"

"That's something I couldn't say. All I know is that Dr. Bossard prescribed them for her."

"Do you know of any reason why she should've suffered from sleeplessness?"

With a touch of his old hearty manner, Parry said, "Well, now, that's making too much out of it. Just because she took an odd pill once in a while . . . "

He seemed to lose the thread of what he had been going to say. His eyes shifted from Elvin to Quinn and then dropped to his hands again.

In a clipped voice, Inspector Elvin said, "It was not an odd pill that your wife took this afternoon, Mr. Parry. It was a massive and fatal overdose. What I am trying to establish is her reason for doing such a thing. And I know you want to help me . . . don't you?"

"Of course. But I'm as much in the dark as you are."

"Had she been worried recently about anything — I mean anything that could've made her depressed, not quite herself?"

Michael Parry rubbed his eyes while he thought. Then he said, "Worried is hardly how I'd put it, but she did seem a bit off-colour. Inclined to get irritable over trifles, I noticed. That's why I thought it a good idea when she suggested going to Wood Lake for a few days."

"What sort of place is Wood Lake?"

"Oh, it's one of those slimming resorts that women go to. Fancy diets and massage and sauna baths and beauty treatment and all that kind of thing."

"Did she go there often?"

"Yes, every two or three months."

"And came back each time feeling better in health?"

Parry looked as though he'd been asked a trick question. Eventually, he said, "That wasn't really why she went to Wood Lake. Her health never troubled her. She was always a very fit person."

"But she took sleeping pills," Elvin said.

In a bluff voice, Michael said, "So do most people nowadays. I've read that half the population take drugs of one kind or another."

"But half the population don't commit suicide. And that's what your wife has done ... or appears to have done. Isn't it?"

Michael looked at Quinn as though for support. He asked, "Couldn't it have been — an accident?"

Inspector Elvin said, "That's for a Coroner's jury to decide, Mr. Parry. However, I would doubt it very much. I can't see anyone accidentally taking a large dose of barbiturate in the middle of the afternoon ... can you?"

"No, I suppose not."

"And then there are all the other factors that have to be taken into account. You've had plenty of time to think about them by now — plenty of time."

The inspector paused. When Michael Parry had waited until he could wait no longer, he asked, "What factors?"

"From what I understand you thought she wouldn't be coming home until some time this evening. That is what you did think, isn't it?"

"Yes. I'd arranged to meet the eight-ten bus at Blandford. In fact I went there and hung around until the eight-fifty had come and gone."

"You received no word from your wife to say she'd changed her mind?"

"No, she never got in touch with me at all from the time she went away."

"When was that?"

"Last Monday."

"Where is this place Wood Lake?"

"Just outside Chobham."

"That's near Woking, isn't it?"

"Yes, three or four miles from there."

"How did your wife usually get to Wood Lake?"

"A taxi would call here and take her to Blandford. From there she'd get the bus to Salisbury where she caught a train. At Woking she'd be met by a car from Wood Lake."

"I see."

Inspector Elvin moved his feet farther apart and repeated, "I see."

Then he asked, "Did she always return the same way?"

"Yes. I usually picked her up at

Blandford instead of letting her get a taxi home."

"Didn't you ever take her there in your own car when she was going off to Wood Lake?"

"Yes, sometimes."

"But not on this last occasion?"

An uncomfortable look came into Michael's puffy face. He said, "No, she didn't want me to."

"Any special reason?"

"Not really. She preferred to take a taxi, that's all."

Elvin made no attempt to hide the disbelief in his eyes. He said, "I do wish you'd be frank with me, Mr. Parry. It would make my job so much easier and save you inevitable distress."

"I'm being absolutely frank. I've no reason to be otherwise."

"Then please answer my question. Why didn't your wife want you to run her to Blandford last Monday?"

Parry glanced at Quinn again. Then he said, "What difference does it make? Will any of this alter what's happened?"

"No, of course not. Nothing can do that. But the Coroner's going to ask me a lot of questions, Mr. Parry — a lot of questions — and he'll expect answers to them. With your help we may be able to satisfy him."

"But I still don't see — "

"Above all else we must try to fathom your wife's state of mind on the day she left here to visit Wood Lake. I'd have thought that was obvious — very obvious."

"Why? What good will that do? It's days ago."

"She may have brooded over it while she was away. That's quite possible if" — the inspector stared at him with guileless eyes — "if, for example, you had a quarrel on the day she left."

Michael Parry said in a flat voice, "My wife and I never quarrelled."

"Never?"

"Once in a while we might've had a difference of opinion but that was as far as it ever went."

"Did you have a difference of opinion

last Monday before she went away?"

Quinn saw anger flare in Michael's eyes. Then defeat took its place.

He said, "It was quite trivial . . . not worth mentioning. But women get these damn' silly ideas. There was no reason why I couldn't have taken her to Blandford."

"But she preferred to go by taxi. Why?"

"Because I'd had a couple of drinks at lunch time and she was afraid I might be stopped and given a breathalyser test."

Quinn told himself Michael Parry was lying. " . . . *Michael, me boy, you're a first-class, one-hundred-per-cent liar. She wasn't afraid merely because you'd had a couple. You must've been stinko — so damn' plastered you weren't fit to drive. She wasn't going to trust herself in a car with you driving.*"

Inspector Elvin nodded amiably. He said, "Good. That's one thing out of the way."

185

As though tabulating his thoughts, he went on, "She left in a taxi, you stayed here . . . and there was no quarrel of any kind before she left. Have I got it right?"

"Yes. That's exactly how it was."

"And you didn't hear from your wife at any time while she was at Wood Lake?"

"No."

"Was that usual?"

"Yes. She seldom, if ever, got in touch with me when she went away for just a few days. Anyway, I'd arranged to pick her up at the bus stop this evening, so there was nothing for us to talk about."

"But she didn't keep to the arrangement, Mr. Parry. She must've returned some time this afternoon. Can you suggest any reason for that — any reason at all?"

"No, I can't . . . but evidently she changed her mind."

"Without telling you?"

A harassed look came into Parry's

washed-out blue eyes. He said, "Maybe she tried to phone me and I was out."

"If you were, would there be no one here to answer the telephone?"

"Not after one o'clock. That's when Mrs. Gregg leaves."

"And who is Mrs. Gregg?"

"Our daily woman. She comes at nine and goes about one."

"Every day?"

"Except Sunday."

"If, by any chance, your wife did phone, surely Mrs. Gregg would have told you?"

"She'd gone by the time I got back."

The slightly puzzled look on Elvin's face cleared. He said, "Ah, now I see. But wouldn't Mrs. Gregg make a note of the call and leave it beside the phone?"

"Yes, I suppose so."

"You don't sound very sure, Mr. Parry — not very sure at all. Hasn't she had instructions to write down any phone calls received while you and your wife are out?"

"Oh, yes . . . and she always does."

"So we can take it" — Elvin's voice dropped half a tone — "that no call was received. In other words, your wife didn't phone."

Michael Parry played with his hands while he thought. At last, he said, "She might've done between the time Mrs. Gregg left and the time I returned."

"When did you return?"

"About half-past three . . . I think."

"So for roughly two and a half hours there would be no one in the house?"

"Yes. And that's when" — Michael's face brightened — "that's when my wife probably tried to ring me."

Inspector Elvin shook his head. In a tone of reproof, he said, "No, Mr. Parry. I doubt it — I doubt it very much. She must've set out from Wood Lake before one o'clock to get here during the afternoon. She had to get to Woking . . . take a train to Salisbury . . . a bus from Salisbury to Blandford . . . and then some form of transport from there to Castle Lammering."

"But she might — "

"There's no might about it, Mr. Parry. That sort of journey takes time. If she intended to return home earlier than arranged she'd have had to make her decision long before one o'clock . . . and your Mrs. Gregg would still have been here."

Something new showed behind Elvin's smooth courtesy as he asked, "Do you follow my line of reasoning?"

Parry agreed a little too hastily. He said, "Oh, yes . . . yes, I do. But I've already told you I just can't explain it — any of it."

With artificial sympathy, Inspector Elvin said, "It is a problem — quite a big problem. However, I'm sure we'll find the answer if we go about it the right way. So let's start from the beginning. What time did you leave home this morning?"

189

"About eleven o'clock. I had some shopping to do . . . " Parry left the rest in mid-air.

"Where did you go — Blandford? There aren't any decent shops much nearer than that, are there?"

"Well, actually I went to Poole. Needed a haircut and I like to use the same barber . . . "

He looked across at the bed where the eiderdown trailed almost to the floor. His face stiffened as he went on, "I thought I'd spruce myself up a bit because Adele" — he faltered — "because my wife was coming home and I wanted to look my best."

"How long did you stay in Poole?"

"A couple of hours or so. After I'd had a haircut I bought some odds and ends and then I had a bite of lunch."

As though he wanted to change the subject, he added, "Good shopping centre is Poole. Not many places round here where you can get bow ties — I mean the kind you tie yourself, not those ready-made-up horrors that are

190

all right for the peasants."

Downstairs the phone rang and Quinn heard Sergeant Taylor talking briefly. Elvin waited, his eyes fixed on Parry's face, until the bell tinkled again.

Then he asked, "Did you come straight home, Mr. Parry, after you'd done your shopping and had lunch?"

"No, I called in at some pub or other, met a bunch of sociable fellows, and got chatting. You know how it is."

"Yes, of course. Time does tend to pass quickly when you're having a drink with friends. Always a lot to talk about — even when you've met only the other day."

The implied question left Parry with no choice. He said, "Oh, they weren't friends. I'd never seen them before. But when you pop into a strange pub you have to be sociable, haven't you?"

Once again, Elvin said, "Yes, of course. What time did you leave this pub?"

"Two-ish, I'd say."

"And yet" — the inspector looked no more than politely surprised — "you didn't get back here until half past three? Surely that must be wrong?"

"I don't see — "

"Come now, Mr. Parry! It's only fifteen or sixteen miles from Poole. That couldn't have taken you an hour and a half, could it?"

Michael Parry's manner underwent a sudden change. In an angry voice, he said, "Look, we seem to be getting off the point. I don't have to account to you for every minute of my time. Where I went and what I did and how long I took to do it is my business. I'm not going — "

"Just be patient," Elvin said. "Bear with me a little longer. I'm merely trying to ascertain if it's possible that your wife did phone. Before we eliminate the possibility we must have an accurate time-table. You see that, don't you?"

Quinn wondered if Parry would

192

believe anything so obviously false. But maybe it wasn't obvious to him. Elvin had the right approach.

. . . Yet you can see which way the wind blows. He's going to get Michael into a corner where there's no way out and then use the chopper on him . . .

Michael Parry said, "A time-table of my movements can't have any bearing on what my wife may, or may not, have done. But if you must know I stopped at the Bird-in-Hand in Castle Lammering on my way back. Got there about — " He gave the inspector a sour look. "You want me to be exact, I suppose?"

"As exact as you can be," Elvin said.

"Then I'd say it was something between two-fifteen and two-twenty."

"And you left when . . . ?"

"Close on half past three. I know it was nearly twenty to four when I got home."

Inspector Elvin bobbed his head and looked pleased. He said, "Thank you, Mr. Parry. We're getting along famously. Now take your time and think — think very carefully. What did you do when you entered the house?"

"I came straight upstairs to this room."

"Any indication that your wife had returned home?"

"None at all."

"Was that" — Elvin pointed — "her bed?"

The numb look settled again on Parry's puffy face. He said, "Yes."

"Do you remember if it was in that disarranged condition then?"

"No, I wasn't paying any attention."

"Surely you'd have noticed — "

"There's no surely about it," Parry said. His voice was too loud. "You asked me and I've told you. I don't know what state the bed was in. It was a hot day and I'd had a couple of drinks and I wanted to put my feet up for an hour or two. Anything wrong with that?"

"No, of course not. You mustn't — "

"It never struck me that my wife might be home . . . if she was. How was I supposed to know she'd changed her mind without telling me?"

Inspector Elvin said gently, "How indeed? So you lay down on the bed and fell asleep. Is that right?"

"Yes. I dropped off almost at once."

"Anything disturb you — anything at all?"

"Not a thing. I slept like a log until" — he looked at Quinn — "until Miss Stewart and my friend here arrived. It was the ringing of the door-bell that wakened me."

"What time was that?"

"Half past seven."

"So you'd slept for nearly four hours?"

In an unpleasant voice, Parry said, "Is it a crime for a man to sleep as many hours as he likes in his own home?"

Elvin looked apologetic. He said, "I didn't suggest that anyone had committed a crime. All I want is to clear up the mystery of your wife's return home. Did she take any luggage with her when she left last Monday?"

"Yes, one case."

"Have you seen anything of it?"

"No, it wasn't downstairs. And" — Parry's eyes made a tired survey of the room — "it doesn't appear to be here."

"Is this where you'd expect it to be if she'd been going to unpack?"

"Yes."

"Where would the empty case go?"

"In the spare room where we keep trunks and cases and things like that."

"We'll go along there shortly and have a look," Elvin said. "Meantime would you mind if I searched this room?"

"No, of course not." Parry's resentment came to the surface and then as quickly subsided. "Why should I mind?"

He watched the inspector glance under the twin beds, look behind the dressing-table, slide back a door in the fitted wardrobe. Quinn didn't think

Michael Parry was very interested.

There were shoes on a floor rack, eight or nine suits on a rail. Elvin didn't bother to open a set of drawers running from floor to head height.

In the centre compartment he found nothing of interest, either. It was when he pushed back the right-hand door that he stopped and looked over his shoulder at Parry and asked, "Did you say something?"

Parry said, "That's the case I was talking about — my wife's travelling case. What's it doing in the wardrobe?"

Inspector Elvin brought it out, laid it on the floor, and unfastened the catches. When he raised the lid, he said, "What indeed? Doesn't look as if she even started to unpack."

The case was full of neatly folded items of clothing held in place by two elastic straps. Nothing appeared to have been disturbed.

Elvin said, "This affair becomes more and more peculiar the further we go. Your wife would seem to have returned home, carried her bag upstairs, and put it in the wardrobe. After that she lay down on her own bed — for how long, we don't know."

He stared up at Parry and added, "If you were going to say we know singularly little about anything you'd be quite right."

Parry said, "It's not my place to comment. Won't help you if I keep on saying I'm completely baffled." He seemed unable to take his eyes off the suitcase.

"That's hardly surprising," Elvin said. "Her behaviour was certainly very odd . . . to put it mildly. Some time later she appears to have got up, taken a glass of brandy — heavily doped with some kind of barbiturate — and carried it into the nursery. There she swallowed enough of the drug to kill herself. If anyone" — his eyes travelled from Parry to Quinn — "can put forward an explanation, I'll be glad to hear it."

Quinn said nothing. After a couple

of false starts, Parry said, "Don't ask me. I haven't a clue. It just doesn't make sense."

"You're quite right. It doesn't make sense — none of it. Above all, why did she come home secretly to commit suicide? Why didn't she do it at this place, Wood Lake? Eh, Mr. Parry?"

"Maybe she forgot to take the sleeping pills with her when she went away," Parry said. He didn't sound very confident.

"And so she came all the way back determined to take her own life?" The inspector shook his head. "I've dealt with one or two suicides — and I've also read quite a bit on the subject — and I can tell you that the circumstances here don't follow the established pattern."

He bent over the suitcase as though looking for something. When he straightened himself again, he went on, "People nearly always commit suicide on impulse. In the majority of cases it's done on the spur of the moment. If it fails — or if anything intervenes to stop the attempt — most of them don't try again . . . at least, not for the time being."

"What you're saying — "

"I'm saying nothing," Elvin said. "I'm merely thinking aloud. And these are my thoughts. In your wife's case she had time to change her mind. Furthermore, I can't believe that anyone who needed even an occasional sleeping pill would go away for several days without taking them with her."

Michael Parry might have tried to hide the look of mingled fear and bewilderment that came into his eyes but he failed. As though all the strength had gone out of his legs he sat down on the edge of the nearer bed and slumped forward, his hands dangling between his knees.

In a wooden voice, he said, "Now I'm lost, utterly and completely lost."

Then he looked up at Quinn and asked, "Why do you just stand there like part of the furniture? Why don't you say something? Are you afraid to open your mouth?"

Quinn said, "This isn't my party. I never poke my nose into a police investigation. Anyway, I was ordered not to interfere."

Inspector Elvin made a little apologetic noise in his throat. He said, "Not ordered, Mr. Quinn, merely requested. A man of your experience knows" — Quinn saw him staring at the table between the twin beds — "knows that a three-handed discussion often confuses the issue in an affair of this kind. Confining it to two people avoids the risk of being side-tracked, of losing sight of important points."

He was talking for the sake of talking as he walked across to the table and bent down and reached under it. When he stood up again he was holding a transparent plastic bag with printing on it.

Michael Parry had turned his head to watch him. The inspector asked, "Is this yours?"

201

"Yes. It's what my shirts are wrapped in when they come back from the laundry."

"So I thought. The name of a laundry in Blandford is printed on it. Any idea how it came to be behind that table?"

"No. Probably fell on the floor when I took out a clean shirt."

In sudden irritation Parry got up and said, "What difference does it make? Honestly, Inspector, you baffle me with some of the questions you ask. It's just a polythene bag — the kind that's used by a thousand laundries every day of the week. Why should you be interested in the way my shirts are wrapped?"

"Because I have an inquiring mind," Elvin said. "May I keep this bag?"

"Of course. I'll give you a dozen more if you're collecting them."

Parry laughed without any trace of humour. Then he asked, "Is there anything else you want to know?"

"Just one thing. Had your wife recently been receiving psychiatric treatment?"

202

Once again a look of withdrawal came into Michael Parry's faded blue eyes. In a cautious voice, he said, "Not to my knowledge."

"That isn't a very satisfactory answer, Mr. Parry. Wouldn't she have told you if she had consulted a psychiatrist?"

Michael Parry made a little sound of disdain. He said, "If my answer wasn't very satisfactory, your question is positively daft. Did my wife tell me she was going to commit suicide? Did she confide in me that she was in the mood to do something terrible like this? Did she ever, in fact, have the slightest respect for me? Now go ahead and pick the bones out of that lot."

Inspector Elvin said, "I will, Mr. Parry, I certainly will. My first thought, naturally, is that you and your wife weren't very happy together. Would you agree?"

"This is becoming farcical," Parry said. "If she'd been happy would she have killed herself? Now, if you've no objection, I'm going downstairs to get something to eat. My last meal was at lunch time and I'm damned hungry."

He went out and pulled the door shut with more force than was necessary. As his footsteps marched aggressively towards the top of the stairs, Quinn said, "And that's that — the gesture of the little man in the face of authority. Mind if I go now?"

Elvin looked at him absentmindedly and then asked, "Where are you off to?"

"I still want that drink I was going to have when you talked me into staying up here."

"You could have had it long ago if you hadn't let Parry talk you into keeping him company. Why did you?"

"Mainly for your sake."

"Indeed?"

"Yes. I thought you'd like me to be present in case he made a liar of himself."

"And why should he do that?"

"He'd have a good reason if he

were responsible for his wife's death," Quinn said.

Inspector Elvin nodded and went on nodding while he turned to look at the disarranged bed again. Then he said, "You are a man of ideas, Mr. Quinn. How would you force or persuade or fool someone into taking a lethal dose of barbiturate?"

"Might not be all that difficult. If the stuff hasn't got an unpleasant taste, or if whatever taste it has could be masked by the liquor, then I'd slip it into the lady's brandy."

"Do you happen to know if Pembrium tastes nasty?"

"Never tasted the stuff, so I can't say. Why don't you ask Dr. Bossard?"

"I intend to," Elvin said. "Rest assured I intend to."

He folded the plastic bag twice, turned it over to study it back and front, and then asked, "Do you ever watch television, Mr. Quinn?"

"Occasionally. Why?"

"Oh, I just wondered if you'd seen

that Ministry of Health thing about keeping polythene bags out of the reach of children and domestic pets. Know the one I mean?"

Quinn said, "Yes. And I also know what you've got in mind."

With a smile in his eyes, Elvin said, "That's very clever of you."

"Not really. In the world where I earn my living, two and two always make four."

"All right. Tell me."

"You think that polythene bag might've come in handy if Adele Parry had taken too long to die," Quinn said.

Inspector Elvin retired behind his smile. In a tentative voice, he asked, "And what do you think?"

"I'm not sure you're right. It all depends."

"On what?"

"On whether Mrs. Parry was worth more dead than alive. She controlled the purse-strings . . . and she was a very wealthy woman. Her will would make interesting reading."

"Hasn't he got any money of his own?"

"Not according to my information."

"From a reliable source?"

It was an awkward question. For the first time Quinn realised that he might have been taking far too much for granted.

He said, "On our way here, Miss Stewart gave me the background to the Parry family. From what she says, Michael Parry's financial dependence on his wife has been common knowledge."

"Does that mean he hasn't got a job of any kind?"

"Ostensibly he's a writer, but I imagine that's merely a front to hide the fact that he's — "

" — been living on his wife's money," Elvin said.

"Well, yes, that's the impression I got."

"M-m-m . . . Interesting situation . . . full of possibilities."

"As I see it there's one that sticks out

a mile," Quinn said. "Some time this morning before the daily help arrived, Mrs. Parry phoned her husband and told him she was returning home earlier than arranged. My guess is that she also made it clear they'd reached the parting of the ways. Maybe she'd found someone else: or maybe she'd decided that there was no future in their marriage and she didn't want to go on living with him. The effect of all this on Michael Parry was — "

" — to make him decide that if she wouldn't go on living with him he'd see she wouldn't go on living without him," Elvin said.

Quinn remembered the look on Parry's face when he'd opened the door — a befuddled look compounded of drink and sleep. He'd hardly seemed like a man who had just murdered his wife. And yet he must've been in the house around the time when she'd died. And that posed a different problem.

"It might not have been quite as it looks," Quinn said. "Supposing she came home and found him in a drunken stupor? If she'd reached the stage where she couldn't take that sort of thing any more she might — I say she just might — have yielded to a sudden impulse and committed suicide. If so, where does that put Michael Parry?"

Inspector Elvin looked dubious. He said, "I'm not sure I follow you."

"Then let's take it step by step. Michael wakes up with a head like a bucket and the first thing he sees with his little bleary eyes is his wife. She's lying on the other bed and he discovers soon enough that she's not just sleeping. This gives him quite a shock . . . not because he'll go into mourning for a year if she dies but chiefly because it might be suspected that he had something to do with her death."

"As has indeed happened," Elvin said.

"Exactly. Now let's take it from there. While Michael's racking his inebriated wits for a way out, the door-bell rings. In case it's just a chance caller he lies low and does nothing. But it rings again . . . and again . . . and he hears voices outside. One of them is the familiar voice of somebody he knows very well — Miss Carole Stewart. By this time he's scared stiff . . . and I don't blame him. What would you have done if you'd been in his shoes?"

"The situation isn't likely to arise," Elvin said. He seemed faintly amused.

Quinn asked, "Why not? Aren't his shoes big enough?"

Inspector Elvin shook his head disapprovingly. He said, "Dear me . . . the old joke about the size of a policeman's feet. I'd hoped for better things from you. What I meant was that I could never land in Parry's situation because my wife isn't a wealthy woman. But please go on."

"There's not much more. Either Michael Parry hadn't expected week-end guests or we'd arrived earlier than anticipated. The way he was placed it didn't make any odds. He needed time to think and he wouldn't get it if visitors walked in and found Adele dying from an overdose of sleeping pills. He had to put her some place where she wouldn't be found before he'd thought of a way to dispose of her."

"What you're saying is that he let her die," Elvin said. "That makes him out to be a ghoul."

"Well, he's either a ghoul or a loving husband. You can take your pick. I know which I'd choose. He didn't need her — just her money. But everybody knew that so he had to play it clever . . . or he might take the blame for something he hadn't done."

"Letting his wife die when there was a chance of saving her life is tantamount to murder," Elvin said.

"We don't know that there was a chance. She might've been too far gone. But supposing she could have been saved? What would he be charged with? How could you ever prove that either she wasn't already dead when he found her or that she wouldn't inevitably have died no matter what he had done?"

Inspector Elvin said, "The answer to the last question encompasses all the others — I couldn't."

With a morbid look on his face he went back to the table between the twin beds and studied the glass top from various angles. As though talking to himself, he repeated, "I couldn't . . . "

He bent over the top and examined it more closely. Then he said, "A wet glass has been standing here. There's a ring" — he stooped lower and touched it with the top of his finger — "a ring that's still damp. It feels sticky — so it can hardly have been made by water."

Quinn said, "There's your confirmation. She drank her doped brandy, put the glass on the table, and then lay down to sleep. By the time Michael woke up she was either dead or in a state of advanced coma. So he carts her into the nursery where no one ever goes, gets rid of the brandy glass, ditto her travelling case, and hopes she won't be found until he's thought of a way out of his quandary. It all fits, doesn't it?"

Inspector Elvin went on looking at the wet ring on the bedside table. At last, he said, "You could be right . . . but I'm not happy with your explanation. Parry couldn't keep his wife's body hidden indefinitely. Concealing her death was only going to make things worse for him in the long run."

"Not if he were able to dispose of her body outside the house," Quinn said. "She'd gone off to Wood Lake and she hadn't come back. That would be his story. You couldn't prove he was lying unless you found the person who brought her home."

Elvin nodded. He said, "That might be well-nigh impossible . . . if it had been Parry himself who met the train or bus or whatever it was. Which brings us back to square one."

"Suicide or murder," Quinn said.

"And the circumstances fit both equally well. Only two things remain that I don't really understand. One is Mrs. Parry's shoes."

"What about them?"

"Well, she probably took them off before she lay down on the bed in this room . . . if she committed suicide. If she didn't, then her husband removed them before he dragged her into the nursery to avoid leaving scratches from her heels on the parquet floor of the landing."

"So?"

"Just this: either way, he put her shoes in the nursery. But why should he have bothered to be so tidy? Did you notice how carefully they'd been placed under the foot of the bed?"

Quinn said, "Yes, I did notice. But I didn't think it was all that important."

"Maybe it isn't . . . and yet maybe it is. The other point has to do with Mrs. Ford. How did she come to find her sister-in-law's body? I understood that no one ever went into the nursery."

"Could be that she saw the door was open and took a look inside out of curiosity."

"Why should the door be open if the room's never used?"

"That's something you'll have to ask her."

"I will," Elvin said.

He stood listening to the sound of a vehicle droning its way up the slope from the village before he went on, "Rest assured I will . . . That must be the ambulance. Go and get your drink, Mr. Quinn. I'll have another word with you soon's I'm free. You'll be stopping here overnight, I presume?"

"That's up to my host," Quinn said. "After what's happened he'll hardly be in the mood to entertain company."

Elvin said, "If I'm any judge, he'll

be even less inclined to stay alone in the house. So don't suggest that you'd like to leave."

"Why not? This isn't the kind of place I'd choose for a riotous week-end."

"Neither would I. But you could be of considerable help to me if you stayed."

"How?"

"By keeping your eyes and ears open."

"In other words you want me to act as an informer."

"If you wish to put it that way, yes. I need hardly remind a man like you that it's your duty to assist the police."

"It isn't my duty to abuse the laws of hospitality," Quinn said.

Inspector Elvin stroked his silver hair in an affected gesture. He said, "You're jumping to conclusions, Mr. Quinn. There's nothing definite to connect Parry with the death of his wife . . . or even with concealment of her death. By staying on at Elm Lodge you may be doing him a very great service. And, of course, at the same time . . . "

"Yes?"

"You'd enjoy my confidence," Elvin said.

He seemed to think there was nothing more to say. As he went out he didn't even look back.

From the bedroom window Quinn watched a white-painted ambulance roll to a halt outside the front door. Then there were voices down below . . . footsteps on the stairs . . . the irregular tramp of feet going past . . . more voices from the direction of the nursery.

He stayed at the window and listened and thought about Adele Parry. He didn't want to see what they were doing.

It wasn't long before the same footsteps passed the bedroom door again and went slowly and carefully down the stairs. He heard someone saying " . . . easy . . . hold your end up . . . O.K. I've got it . . . "

Two men came out of the porch bearing a stretcher covered from head to foot by a blanket tucked in all round. With the ease of long practice they loaded the stretcher on rails and slid it into the ambulance like delivery men returning a tray of bread to a baker's van.

In the failing light, Quinn saw them slam the doors . . . and walk briskly round to the front of the ambulance . . . and climb in. He turned away as they drove off.

Down below the phone bell tinkled. Then Inspector Elvin came back into the bedroom.

With a quizzical look, he asked, "Haven't you had your drink yet?"

"I don't need one. I've changed my mind," Quinn said.

"You may change it again when you've heard the latest news. I've just been on the phone to Wood Lake."

"And?"

"Mrs. Parry hasn't been there this week. They haven't seen anything of her since" — Inspector Elvin raised his eyebrows in mock surprise — "since the last time she visited the place . . . which was about two months ago. Be interesting to know where she has been — very interesting."

7

WHEN Quinn went downstairs he found Parry and Neil Ford talking quietly together near the central hearth. Carole was in the kitchen making sandwiches.

He stayed in the doorway and stood watching her. She seemed older — older and more serious and very different from the girl with the cheeky smile whom he'd met at Charlie Hinchcliffe's party.

It felt like a lifetime since he'd yielded to a crazy impulse and kissed her. That had been a stupid thing to do. If he'd known about the man who'd lived with her at the cottage he'd never have done it. For all he knew there might have been more than one man.

. . . Don't believe she's like that. Whatever else, she isn't a tart. As

220

I see it she invited me here for the week-end because she didn't want to be available for Bossard while she was at Elm Lodge. I was her excuse for keeping him at arm's length. So he must mean a lot to her and she doesn't want to show it . . .

Out of nowhere came a thought that took shape, piece by piece, like an irregular structure built with a child's set of bricks. It wasn't very solid but it stood up long enough to give Quinn a new awareness of many things that had perplexed him since he'd arrived at Castle Lammering.

. . . Adele didn't really mean anything to anybody. Bossard's behaviour when he saw her lying there seemed peculiar at the time . . . the look on his face wasn't right . . . but now I understand. That look was one of relief — as though her death had taken a load off his mind . . .

Ariadne Wilkinson hadn't shown any grief, either. Neil Ford didn't even pretend to be sorry. Carole was thoughtful and withdrawn, but not sad. Her friend — a kind, hospitable friend — had died suddenly and tragically, but Carole shed no tears.

And Michael Parry . . . He didn't act like a man who had lost his wife. The only emotion he betrayed was fear — an underlying fear that could have been caused by any one of a dozen reasons. Neither in his voice nor his eyes was there any hint of sorrow.

That left Irene Ford. She'd been shocked into a state of hysterics, but with a woman like Irene that could have been expected.

. . . She's a twitching neurotic. It needn't have been affection for her sister-in-law that made her hysterical. She'd probably have reacted the same way if she'd discovered the body of a complete stranger. Not that I blame her for being upset. Finding a corpse in the next room is enough to make any woman jump out of her roll-on. But not every woman would scream

the house down . . .

Carole looked up and gave him a little forced smile. She said, "Hallo . . . You've been upstairs a long time. Has that inspector finished asking questions?"

"I'd say he's only just started," Quinn said. "We've a long way to go before we see the end of this business. How's Mrs. Ford?"

"Dr. Bossard's with her now. He's given her a sedative and he says she should be all right after a good night's rest . . . but it'll take a little time for her to get over the shock."

"That's only to be expected. How do you feel?"

"Oh, I'm all right." She brushed some crumbs together with the edge of her palm and gathered them into a mound. Without looking at Quinn, she added, "A lot better than I'd have felt if I'd been the one who found Adele."

Quinn said, "That's something I've wanted to ask you. Did Mrs. Ford tell you what made her go into the nursery? I understood that no one ever went in there."

"The light was on. She noticed it when she was leaving her own room to come downstairs. From what she says the nursery door wasn't quite shut. Naturally, that made her curious . . . "

"If it hadn't got suddenly dark she wouldn't have seen the light in the nursery," Quinn said.

"No, I don't suppose she would. What I don't understand is why Adele should have needed to use the light on a day like to-day."

"Me, neither. And I've no doubt Inspector Elvin will make three."

Carole went on toying with the mound of crumbs. Then she said, "Maybe Michael could suggest a reason. He might know if Adele had recently been in the nursery after dark."

"If he doesn't, no one else will," Quinn said. "I'll ask him."

Parry didn't know. He didn't seem very interested, either.

It was Neil Ford who made an issue of the question. He said, "I heard my wife saying something about the light being on in the nursery . . . but I don't see why that should concern you." Once again he had an offensive look in his eyes.

Quinn said, "I thought the war was over. So you don't get the wrong idea let me tell you I'm merely quoting Inspector Elvin. It's he who wants — "

"Then let Inspector Elvin ask for himself. In the circumstances, don't you think your presence here is rather unnecessary?"

Carole came out of the kitchen with a tray of sandwiches and crockery and a pot of coffee. She said, "I'll tell you something, Neil. That old adage isn't true: it doesn't take two to make a quarrel. You do very well all by yourself."

Ford said, "I didn't mean anything more than that this was hardly the time to have strangers around."

"That's merely your opinion. Besides,

Mr. Quinn isn't a stranger. He's a guest of the house. I invited him to spend the week-end at Elm Lodge and it isn't his fault that this has happened."

In a restless voice, Michael Parry said, "I don't want to take sides . . . but it's for me to say who stays here and who doesn't."

"If that means what I think it means" — Ford's womanish mouth tightened and his face lost some of its colour — "you won't need to say it twice. If Irene's all right we'll leave in the morning."

Michael threw up his hands. He said, "Oh, don't be a bloody fool! I don't want you or anyone to leave. Now can't we drop this whole silly business and behave like civilised people?"

Quinn said, "If nobody minds me butting in I'd like to mention that Inspector Elvin wants me to stay on . . . either here or somewhere nearby. I think he's got an idea I might be needed at the inquest."

It was a weak excuse but they seemed to accept it. Michael said, "Then that's that. You'll all stay . . . at least until after the inquest. Since the week-end is bound to delay arrangements, I don't suppose it'll take place before Monday at the earliest."

"I have to get back to Ringwood first thing Monday morning," Ford said. "I've got my business to look after. In any case they won't need me. Irene's the one who found" — he gave Parry a long look — "who found Adele. Strange affair altogether when you come to think of it."

Michael asked, "What's strange? Why shouldn't it have been Irene?"

"No reason at all. She just happened to be the first to go upstairs. If it had been any one of us we'd have wondered why the light was on in the nursery . . . same as she did. That's not what I meant when I said it was a strange affair."

"Then what did you mean?"

Carole said, "I wish you'd leave all

227

this talk until later. The coffee's getting cold."

"No." Michael turned his back on her and folded his arms and stared at Ford belligerently. "If you've got something on your mind, let's hear it. Let's bring it out into the open. What did you mean?"

Neil Ford shrugged. He said, "Nothing that everybody else hasn't already thought of . . . including Dr. Bossard and that police inspector. Adele must've been in the house all the time . . . and yet you didn't know."

With a slight narrowing of his faded blue eyes, Parry asked, "Are you suggesting that I did know?"

Ford said, "Now who's being foolish? Of course I'm not! I just mentioned that it was rather strange. If you'd only thought of looking in the nursery — "

"Well, I didn't. I went straight up to my room for a lie down and I was asleep when Carole and Mr. Quinn arrived. Adele wasn't supposed to be coming home until this evening, anyway, so why should I have gone and looked in the nursery . . . of all places? You're as bad as that damn' policeman with some of the things — "

"O.K. O.K. Don't get excited. I was only trying to help."

In a voice that matched the sour look in his eyes, Parry said, "You'd do a lot better if you went and looked after your wife."

Neil Ford drew in a quick breath. As though the words were fighting to get out, he said, "And you'd have done a lot better if you'd looked after yours . . . "

There he faltered, his plump face pale and scared. Then he mumbled, "I'm sorry. I had no right to say a thing like that. Don't pay any attention to me. It's been a trying time for all of us and . . . "

His voice tailed off again. Then he said, "Maybe I should go and see how Irene's getting on."

Carole said, "Ask her if she'd like

229

something to eat. I'll make her whatever she wants. And tell Dr. Bossard there's some coffee waiting for him."

Ford hurried upstairs as though afraid that Parry would stop him. When he had gone, Carole looked at Michael and said, "You deserve a medal for restraint. How you controlled yourself I'll never know."

He brushed up the ends of his moustache and gave her a weak smile. He said, "I was tempted to punch him in the nose but it wouldn't have done any good. This is neither the time nor the place for that sort of thing. Let's have a friendly cup of coffee and a sandwich and forget Adele's" — he stumbled over the next word and took a moment to recover himself — "Adele's relations."

To Quinn it was all unreal. Michael Parry might as well have said that they should forget Adele herself. She had died . . . her body had been removed . . . and now the gap had closed. It was as though she had never been.

Through his thoughts he heard Parry saying " . . . haven't eaten since lunch time and that was before one o'clock. You've no idea how appetising those sandwiches look."

Then he turned to Quinn and asked, "How about you?"

Quinn said, "I'd like a cup of coffee but that's all. I had a pretty good meal when we got here."

Perhaps Michael Parry guessed what he was thinking. In an uncomfortable voice, Parry said, "There's something I want you to know. Maybe it's not really any of your business — "

"Then don't tell me," Quinn said.

"I must . . . for my own sake I must. You see, whatever my faults and failings, I've never been a hypocrite. And I'm not going to start now. Do you understand what I'm trying to say?"

Quinn nodded. At the back of his mind he was asking himself why a man who had lived on his wife's money, who had been little better than a parasite, should object to being thought a hypocrite.

. . . Now he's going to tell me the old story. Why does a husband always use the excuse that his wife doesn't understand him? He might be a lot worse off if she did . . .

Michael Parry said, "I can't pretend I'm overwhelmed with grief. It's a terrible thing to have happened . . . of course it is . . . and I'm sorry . . . but that's all. In my position I should be heartbroken but I'm not. I just don't feel anything. All I want is to get the whole business over and done with so that I can get away — as far away as possible from this damned house. Whatever I've been, she made me. Nobody realises — "

"Don't say that," Carole said. "If you hadn't been drinking you'd know how dreadful it sounds. Anyone hearing you would imagine all sorts of things."

Quinn said, "He isn't drunk. Let him talk. Nothing he says can make the situation any worse."

Parry looked at Carole and said, "I told you, didn't I? They think I killed Adele. Just because I didn't know she'd come home they think I got rid of her."

Carole said, "That's a load of nonsense."

Then she turned and stared at Quinn and asked, "Isn't it?"

He wondered why Michael was so anxious to talk about his relationship with Adele . . . why he seemed to have forgotten that he was hungry . . . and why Carole wanted to protect him. Nobody at Elm Lodge behaved true to type.

Quinn said, "All I can tell you is that Inspector Elvin isn't satisfied with Mr. Parry's account of what happened this afternoon. There's not much doubt that Mrs. Parry lay down on the bed in her own room when she came home. The fact that she was found in the nursery makes Elvin think she was put there by someone who didn't want her to be discovered before she was dead."

Michael Parry picked up a sandwich, looked at it, and tossed it back on the tray. Then he rubbed a hand across his eyes.

He said, "See how they've got it all worked out? I was the only one in the house from half-past three until the time you and Quinn arrived . . . so it must've been me. Either I deliberately killed Adele or I let her die. Take your choice."

Carole shivered. With no emotion in her face, she said, "It's horrible . . . just too horrible."

She doesn't believe it, Quinn told himself. But somehow I think she wants to. And there can be only one reason for that.

. . . *Wish I could find a reason for Michael's behaviour. Publicising all this isn't in his own interests. Why should he invite the lightning? Or did he know he'd be suspected and is this his method of making people think that a guilty man wouldn't go out of his way to attract suspicion?* . . .

It was tempting to lay the blame on Parry. If he were responsible for his wife's death — directly or indirectly — then there would be no questions left unanswered.

. . . Maybe he's using me now as a contact between himself and Inspector Elvin and that's why he asked me to stay in the room while Elvin was questioning him . . . and also why he put out the red carpet for me soon's I got here . . .

It seemed far-fetched. And yet . . .

Carole was looking at him, her wide, dark eyes like the eyes of a stranger. She asked, "Is all this true?"

Quinn said, "In substance — yes. The police are thinking along those lines."

"Did the inspector say he thought Michael was responsible for Adele's death?"

"Not in so many words. It was just mentioned — along with several other things — as a possibility. Elvin has a lot of inquiries to make before he'll be able to say exactly what happened here this afternoon."

"Never mind Inspector Elvin. You know pretty well as much about the affair as he does. What do you think?"

It was an awkward question. And Carole wasn't the type to be fobbed off with half an answer.

. . . From Basingstoke to Castle Lammering must be approximately sixty-five miles . . . and from her cottage it'll be a little less since it's this side of Basingstoke. If she averaged forty miles an hour she could've done the return journey in roughly three hours . . .

That didn't allow for what had to be done at Elm Lodge. But there would still have been plenty of time.

. . . I slept like a pig from the early hours until about a quarter past five in the afternoon. If she'd known that Adele would be arriving home some time after the daily woman left at one o'clock . . . if she got to Elm Lodge, had a drink with Adele, and doped

236

*her brandy . . . if she escaped from
the house before Michael returned at
three-thirty or thereabouts she'd have
had ample time to get back to the
cottage by five-fifteen and waken me
with a cup of coffee . . .*

Quinn said, "I'd say it was too early
to draw conclusions. I'm willing to
believe that Mr. Parry didn't know
his wife was in the nursery when he
returned home."

Some of the bitterness left Michael
Parry's face. He said, "That might not
be much but it's better than the way
Inspector Elvin talked to me. If it
were left to him I'd be locked up
right now."

Carole said, "I'm sure you're wrong.
You just feel depressed because you've
had a very trying day."

As she began pouring out a cup of
coffee, she added, "Drink this and have
a bite to eat and then go to bed. Things
will look better to-morrow."

Michael said, "Thanks. I'm glad you
two are here . . . and I hope you'll

stick around until everything's cleared up . . . "

The opening of a door on the floor above stopped him. There was the sound of subdued voices . . . someone saying " . . . I'll look in again in the morning." Then Quinn saw Dr. Bossard coming downstairs.

With a peculiar look on his face Michael Parry turned his back, piled three or four sandwiches on a plate, and carried them along with his cup of coffee to a bench seat near the central hearth. When he sat down he kept his back towards Bossard.

All Quinn's attention was on Carole. He hated himself for what he was thinking but he couldn't get it out of his mind.

. . . She used you as her alibi. When she went to Charlie Hinchcliffe's party she must've been on the lookout for some mug who'd fancy going home with her. If necessary she'd have been prepared to sleep with him . . . after he'd drunk a nightcap fortified with a

few Pembrium capsules which would've kept him safely in dreamland all next day . . .

Dr. Bossard was smiling at Carole and asking, "Do you think I might have a cup of coffee before I go?"

Carole said, "Of course. It's not very hot, I'm afraid. If you like I'll make some more."

"Oh, no. This'll do nicely. I've got to get back, anyway, in case there are some late calls for me."

They went on talking small talk while Bossard drank his coffee . . . and Michael Parry sat alone beside the hearth . . . and Quinn thought bitter thoughts about the cute little girl with dark eyes and dark hair and the kind of smile that melted his cynicism. The pity was that it always left him wide open to be fooled.

. . . She was lucky in picking you up. Since you were stinking drunk she didn't have to undergo a fate worse than death . . .

Bossard was saying good night. Carole

239

said she would see him to the door . . . Michael Parry mumbled something . . . Quinn answered mechanically.

. . . All that smooth explanation about going out to buy a razor for you was just a load of malarkey. She wanted a cover-up in case you'd roused and found she wasn't there. Not that there was much chance of you waking up too soon when you had a bellyfull of sleeping pills . . .

By then Carole and Bossard were walking to the door. Quinn told himself this was his opportunity to catch her unawares.

He said, "Before you go, Doctor, do you mind if I ask you something?"

Dr. Bossard turned without haste and looked at him with raised eyebrows. In his usual mellow, courteous voice, Bossard said, "Not at all . . . providing it won't keep me too long. I really must be off."

Quinn said, "This'll only take a moment. Are you now able to say what time, approximately, Mrs. Parry died?"

Carole looked startled. Dr. Bossard was obviously taken aback. Only Michael Parry remained unmoved.

In a slightly pompous tone, Bossard said, "I don't think that's the sort of thing we should discuss — at this juncture."

"Why not? Inspector Elvin didn't put an embargo on the information, did he?"

"No. I just think this is hardly the place to go into details of a nature that might cause — distress."

"Distress to whom, Doctor? I never knew the lady: Miss Stewart" — Quinn glanced at her briefly — "won't require smelling salts . . . whatever you choose to disclose: and Mr. Parry, I'm quite sure, actually wants the answer to my question."

Bossaid said, "Perhaps so. But there will be plenty of opportunity later for him to be told."

Michael Parry put down his half-eaten sandwich and swung round. He said, "Later won't do. I want to be told

241

now. I'm entitled to be told. What you and Inspector Elvin and a few other people seem to have forgotten is that Adele was my wife."

Quinn liked that. It was much more than he had expected.

. . . Fine stirring speech. Wonder what made him change his tune all of a sudden? Could be he thinks I'm pally with the law and he wants to have a friend at court . . . if that's not an unfortunate way of putting it. I'd say that either he already knows the time his wife died or he doesn't care a damn. If the latter, then he must feel pretty safe . . .

Dr. Bossard put his hands behind his back and rocked to and fro while he thought. It didn't take him very long to make up his mind.

Eventually, he said, "Very well. I didn't imagine it would be all that important, but if you really wish to know . . . In my opinion, when I examined Mrs. Parry she had been dead approximately five hours. That is to say, death took place around four o'clock. Of course, it might have been as late as four-thirty. These things can't be calculated to within half an hour."

He stopped bobbing up and down and shared a well-groomed smile between Parry and Quinn. He said, "That's about all I can tell you."

His smile meant nothing. It was merely a cover behind which he tried to conceal his dislike of being questioned.

Quinn said, "There's one thing more. How long does it take for an overdose of barbiturate to cause death?"

Dr. Bossard moved impatiently. He said, "That's something I can't really answer. It would depend on a number of factors, the most important one being which of the barbiturates — "

"Assuming it was this stuff Pembrium, and also assuming the minimum fatal dose, how long do you think it would have taken?"

"Until we have the results of a post-mortem" — Bossard looked at his watch — "I've got just no idea.

It's far too early to make positive statements."

Michael Parry stood up. He said, "It wasn't too early for Inspector Elvin to question me in detail about where I went this morning and what I did and when I returned home and why I didn't know my wife was in the house when I got back. He seemed pretty sure that she must've been here at half past three . . . which can only mean you told him she couldn't have taken the Pembrium after that time."

Bossard waved a hand in mild protest. He said, "Don't blame me because the inspector arrives at his own conclusions. All I did was to express the opinion that fatal results of an overdose would not ensue in less than an hour . . . might've been as much as two hours but unlikely to be less than one."

"That's the same thing expressed in a different way," Parry said. "If my wife died at about four-thirty and those sleeping pills needed at least an hour to take effect — "

He faltered. Then he went on, "I mean she wouldn't have died for at least an hour after taking them . . . and so she must've been in the house before half-past three . . . and yet I didn't know."

"By that time she would be in a state of narcosis," Bossard said.

With neither regret nor sympathy in his face, he added, "Now I must go. Good night."

At the door he murmured a few words to Carole and Quinn heard her say " . . . It won't do any good . . . but I'll think about it."

Parry turned away and sat down. Quinn stood listening to the quiet voices talking in the doorway.

. . . Something damn' funny about the life and death of Adele Parry. She isn't yet cold but her husband doesn't care two hoots and neither does her doctor. You'd think she'd done them a favour by dying. Michael's attitude I can understand — he probably inherits her money. But what does

*the handsome Dr. Bossard get out
of it? Maybe Carole knows. If she
does, I'll lay any odds she won't tell
me . . .*

Then Bossard got into his car and
drove off. Carole came back inside and
closed the door and said, "It's raining
again. I think we'll have a wet day
to-morrow."

Michael Parry said, "Wet or fine, the
morning can't come too soon. This has
been the longest day of my life."

He stretched and yawned and then
got stiffly to his feet. He said, "If
nobody objects I think I will go to bed.
Show Mr. Quinn his room, Carole,
there's a good girl . . . "

At the foot of the stairs he glanced
over his shoulder at Quinn and added,
"Sorry about all this carry-on. You
picked the wrong week-end."

Quinn said, "I didn't pick it. Until
this afternoon I'd never even heard of
Castle Lammering. It was all Carole's
idea."

"Doesn't matter. Good to have you."

He climbed a couple of steps and looked back again. "I don't expect you to be on my side . . . but I'm glad you're here, all the same . . . "

Carole waited until his bedroom door closed and then she said, "I'll never understand that man. One time I feel sorry for him and the next I think he needs kicking."

"Lends a touch of variety," Quinn said. "What are your feelings about him right now?"

With her lower lip held between her teeth she looked at Quinn thoughtfully, her eyes troubled. At last, she said, "I don't know. Honestly, I don't know. But I'm afraid."

"Because you think he poisoned his wife? Or are your fears for somebody else?"

A spot of colour came into her cheeks. She said, "That's not a very nice thing to say. I don't believe anyone would've wanted to harm Adele. If she died from an overdose of sleeping pills, then she must've taken them herself."

"Try telling that to Inspector Elvin. He's got a notion that this is a case of murder . . . and he'll take a lot of convincing that it isn't. From what I've seen and heard since I entered this house I'm inclined to agree with him."

"What have you heard?"

"Enough to tell me that no one loved Adele Parry. Like the song, she was a poor little rich girl. Everybody's going to be better off now she's dead — or so they like to think."

"You mean financially?"

"Sure. She'll have left some nice bequests to her family and friends, won't she?"

"No, that's where you're wrong. She never made a will."

"How do you know?"

"She told me. A few weeks ago, apropos of something else, she mentioned that she'd always hated the idea of making a will but one of these days she'd have to do so. Apparently her lawyers had been urging her not to be superstitious. For the sake of all concerned it was her duty to make a will."

"And now all concerned are devoutly hoping that she wasted no time in following her lawyers' advice," Quinn said.

Carole gave him a barbed look. She said, "You've changed since last night. You're a completely different person. I don't like you in this mood."

"It's the only one I've got. I'm like a chameleon: my disposition changes according to my surroundings. And this environment is hostile . . . or haven't you noticed?"

She smiled at him without showing her teeth. It wasn't the kind of smile that had attracted him to her in the beginning.

She said, "You're good with words . . . so I'm not going to get involved in an argument. Let's leave it like that. Now I'll take you up to your room."

He followed her upstairs . . . past the first two bedrooms . . . and the bathroom . . . and the nursery. A couple of doors farther on, she said, "You'll be quite comfortable in here. Sleep well."

"And the same to you," Quinn said. "Say good night for me to Neil Ford . . . if you should happen to see him."

Carole stopped. She said, "For some reason best known to yourself you're trying to make me lose my temper. You know perfectly well there's nothing between Neil and me."

"How about Michael Parry?"

"That's even more ridiculous. Why do you want to annoy me? Didn't you say you hoped we'd be friends?"

"Friends are honest with each other," Quinn said. "That lets you out."

With her dark eyes narrowed in a frown she studied him carefully. Then she asked, "Just what do you mean?"

"Well, to start with, you might've told me I was only invited to spend the week-end at Castle Lammering because it served your purpose."

Her mouth opened in swift denial

but she left it unspoken. He saw the conflict in her eyes before at last she said, "What difference would it have made if I had? You were on holiday and had nowhere to go. It served your purpose, too, or you wouldn't have accepted the invitation."

"That's not the same thing. I didn't pretend."

"Neither did I."

"You led me to believe you wanted my company. And that wasn't true, was it?"

"Oh, yes, it was. I thought someone like you would be — " She broke off with a shrug.

"Useful is the word you're looking for," Quinn said.

She tightened her lips and he thought she was going to walk off and leave him. After a little struggle, she said, "I see you're determined to pick a quarrel . . . although I still don't know why you should want to row with me."

"There's only one thing I want right now," Quinn said. "I'm sick and tired

251

of being led by the nose. Why not tell me the truth for a change?"

"About what?"

"The part you play in all the funny business that's been going on here. You invited me to spend the week-end at Elm Lodge because you thought I'd act as a fence between you and somebody else. If the man isn't Neil Ford or Michael then it must be Dr. Bossard. Am I right?"

She opened the door of Quinn's room, switched on the light, and glanced here and there. When she looked at Quinn again, she asked, "Supposing you are right? What's it got to do with you?"

"Quite a lot . . . if he's the man who went off without his laundry."

"I can assure you" — her eyes were hard and bright — "he isn't bothered about a few odds and ends like that."

"No, but I am," Quinn said. "I don't fancy walking around in your former lover's shirt."

Carole smiled the wrong kind of

smile. She said, "He wasn't my lover . . . but it's true that I hoped you'd keep him away from me. Unless I'm very much mistaken, Adele didn't really ask him to come here this evening. He invited himself because he wanted to see me again. That's all."

Quinn said, "If he wasn't your lover how did he come to be staying at the cottage? Don't tell me he merely used it as a dressing-room."

She shook her head. In a tone of mock pity, she said, "You're not very clever, are you? A man and a woman are entitled to live together if they're legally married."

"Do you mean he's your husband?"

"Not any more. We're separated."

Conflicting thoughts tumbled over each other in Quinn's mind. He asked, "Do the others know about this?"

"No, they were never told. My marriage broke up before Geoffrey took over his practice in Blandford. Adele knew that he and I were friendly — but nothing more than that. I think

253

recently she must've guessed there was something between us because she kept trying to bring us together . . . or so I imagined. Of course, Geoffrey might've had a lot to do with that. He wants me to go back to him."

"And will you?"

"I don't know if I dare take the chance. He swears it'll never happen again . . . but I'm afraid to take the risk that I'll be hurt like I was hurt the last time."

Her voice tailed off and there was a glint of tears in her eyes. Quinn told himself she hardly looked the type to trick anyone into providing an alibi so that she could commit murder.

. . . She'd need to have a motive — and I don't know of any. The prospect of being left a fair sum of money wouldn't be a strong enough urge to kill somebody who was her friend. It takes more than that . . . money isn't Carole's problem . . . she has bigger troubles . . . easy to see she's still in love with Bossard . . . he must

earn a comfortable income . . . and she's got a good job . . . if she went back to him they wouldn't go short of anything . . .

Lack of motive was the stumbling block. Inspector Elvin thought he had found one — the only one worth pursuing. But Elvin might well be wrong.

Quinn said, "Forget all the nasty cracks I've made. If you're looking for a shoulder to cry on, try mine. Sometimes it helps to talk this sort of thing out of your system. So come on in and tell me all about it."

Her eyes searched his face and he gave her an encouraging smile. When she still hesitated, he asked, "Are you afraid you'll be compromised?"

She went on looking at him as though his question merited a serious answer. Then she shook her head.

In a solemn little voice, she said, "No, that's not what I was thinking of."

She walked past him into the

bedroom. With both arms hugging herself she waited until he had shut the door before she said, "There isn't much to tell. Maybe you'll say I did the wrong thing. I sometimes feel that way myself. Maybe I should've tried to understand, to see it from a man's point of view, but at the time I couldn't. Now it's probably too late."

"While you're alive, nothing's ever too late," Quinn said. "When I've heard the story I'll give you this man's point of view — if you want it."

"Oh, yes, I do." She sat down on the edge of the bed and looked up at him. "That's exactly what I do want . . . "

It was a disjointed account of a marriage between two people who met and fell in love and married without knowing very much about each other. As Quinn listened, the impression grew on him that Carole had needed Geoffrey Bossard more than he had needed her.

" . . . He was a ship's doctor. That's how I first met him . . . on a trip to the

United States. I went over there to do a programme on race relations in New York. Instead of flying I went by sea because I'd been working hard and I thought a few days' rest would do me good . . . "

Bossard came to see her the next time he was on leave. In the following months they saw each other frequently, but always in snatches. She learned very little about him except that he was tired of life aboard ship and wanted to settle down somewhere permanently.

" . . . A country practice was what he kept talking about . . . Dorset or Somerset or even farther west in Devon. I happened to mention it to Adele one week-end when Geoffrey was away and she said her own doctor in Blandford had been looking for a partner because his health wasn't good and he couldn't run the practice on his own much longer. Of course, Adele didn't know that Geoffrey and I were more than just friends . . . "

So Bossard had gone to see the

man in Blandford . . . and they had agreed on a three-month trial period, to commence when Bossard completed his contract with the shipping company . . . and then he had asked Carole to marry him.

" . . . We decided to live at my cottage until Geoffrey was free to take up the partnership offer. He had only a few days' leave . . . we got married . . . and on the Monday he went away. Some people from the studios attended the wedding . . . but I didn't get the opportunity to tell anyone at Castle Lammering because I never saw Adele for some weeks . . . "

They had been married about two months — during which time Bossard was at home every couple of weeks — when Carole was given another assignment in the United States. She went away on first October and didn't return until the middle of November.

" . . . Perhaps I shouldn't have left him so long . . . but we'd agreed that I should carry on working until such time as he settled down in practice at Blandford. Anyway, I hadn't been home more than a couple of hours when I discovered that he'd had another woman at the cottage. Whether he'd got himself a mistress or she was just some bird he'd picked up, I never bothered to find out. I didn't know which was worse and I didn't care . . . "

That was the end of their marriage. Bossard didn't deny he'd been unfaithful: he merely asked her to believe it had only happened once. He was sorry — he'd always be sorry. For the rest of his life he'd regret having yielded to a crazy impulse. If she would try to forgive him he would do his best to make up for what he'd done.

But Carole couldn't forgive. So they'd separated.

With her hands resting limply on her lap, Carole said, "That's the whole story. He finished his contract with the shipping line and went into practice in Blandford. I heard that not long afterwards his partner had died . . . so as things turned out, Geoffrey did quite well for himself."

"Except that he's neither married nor single," Quinn said. "It's not a very comfortable situation for either party. Have you ever discussed the subject of divorce?"

"No."

"Why not? I can understand that he's not keen on the idea because he still hopes you'll go back to him, but don't you want your freedom?"

She shrugged and said, "I've never given it much thought."

"What's kept you from thinking about it?"

"I don't know." She turned her hands over and studied them as though admiring her long slim fingers.

Quinn said, "You do know . . . and so do I. You're still in love with him. All that stands between you and your lawful husband is wounded pride."

She looked up slowly and sat nibbling her lower lip. Then in a dry voice, she said, "That's not true. I could never live with him again."

"You really mean that?"

"Yes . . . yes, I do."

"And you've no intention of remarrying?"

"Not at present. If and when the right man comes along . . . " She shrugged again.

"Until that time you're content to go on living the life of a celibate spinster?"

"Yes . . . of course." She seemed vaguely surprised.

Quinn said, "I see. How long is it since you and your husband separated?"

"About — twelve months."

"And all this time you've been keeping yourself pure and unsullied for some good man whom fate may bring your way before you're too old to get any fun out of it?"

Her air of surprise changed to annoyance. She said, "I don't know what you think I am — "

"Then I'll tell you," Quinn said. "I

think you're as human as any other girl who's once had a husband. Sleeping with a man is an acquired taste. Once you've acquired it, you don't readily break the habit. Now, in your case — "

"That's enough," Carole said.

" — you can do as you like. You don't owe your ex-husband either loyalty or anything else. So there's no reason why you shouldn't satisfy a perfectly natural desire . . . is there?"

"I'm not" — she stood up — "I'm not going to listen to any more."

"You don't have to. That's the lot . . . except for the man's opinion that I promised to give you."

"Don't bother. I can do without it."

"How do you know until you've heard what it is? I think there's only one way you can get Geoffrey Bossard out of your system . . . and that's by sleeping with another man. So" — Quinn pointed to the bed — "why not hop in and give both of us a treat?"

As he came towards her she backed away, a look of open disbelief on her face. She said, "Don't you dare. If you touch me — "

"You'll scream," Quinn said. "How quaintly Victorian . . . You invited me here for the week-end hoping, or anticipating, that I'd try to make love to you — not because of my good looks or charm or sex-appeal but merely because I was a man. You wanted to compare somebody else with dear Geoffrey."

"That's nonsense!"

"Oh, no, it isn't. So let's make a proper comparison. Let's do the job completely. I'll have a bit of fun . . . and you'll resolve the problem of your relationship with Geoffrey Bossard. Yes?"

She drew in a long breath and then she let it out again very slowly. She said, "You can't really be serious. This is your idea of a joke."

"Why should I be joking? I'd like to sleep with you . . . and you can't find me altogether repulsive or you wouldn't have taken me home to your cottage and then asked me to spend the week-end with you at Castle Lammering."

"I — " She shook her head and began again. "I explained all that and I thought you understood."

Quinn said, "What you explained was only what you wanted me to believe. It wasn't necessarily the truth. But now I've discovered the truth for myself."

She watched him half-fearfully as he went to the door and opened it. He said, "You're a one-man woman, Carole. When you became Mrs. Bossard it was for keeps. Whatever your husband did made no difference. He's still your husband . . . and he always will be. Now get out before you ruin my reputation."

Her eyes were still afraid as she passed him. She said, "To you this is still some kind of game. If I'd known I wouldn't have confided in you."

"It wouldn't have made any difference whether you had or not. The fact that you and Dr. Bossard were married was bound to come out pretty soon. By this time to-morrow, Inspector Elvin will have a complete history of everyone in this house."

"You make it sound as if" — with both arms wrapped round herself again she looked back at him — "as if I had something to hide."

Quinn told himself she was asking a question. She wanted to know how much he knew.

He said, "Maybe you have. But you won't be able to keep it hidden for very long. And when the time comes . . . "

"Yes?" She was still standing at the half-open door looking back at him.

"Don't rely on me," Quinn said. "I owe you nothing — neither you nor anyone else connected with Adele Parry. Whatever I learn while I'm here I'll tell the police."

8

HE slept well and awoke just after seven. By the time he had washed, shaved and dressed it wasn't yet eight o'clock.

The house was quiet. So far as he could tell the others were still asleep. There was no sound from any of the bedrooms as he went downstairs.

It had stopped raining and the sun was high. Among the elm trees that crowned the road to Castle Lammering the birds were singing. Except for a sprinkling of petals around some bedraggled rose bushes and a few broken twigs on the drive there was little trace of the storm.

If everything hadn't gone wrong within an hour and a half of his arrival, to-day would've been the start of an enjoyable week-end. He had looked forward to it so much: a luxury

266

house in the country, hospitable people, lovely June weather. A man could ask for nothing more.

But Adele had spoiled it all. Adele had gone and died.

. . . Why couldn't she have picked next week-end? Might not have happened like this if she'd gone away a week later. Wonder where she went when she was supposed to be going to Wood Lake? If Michael knew, then he lied to everybody. If he didn't, then Adele lied to him. Must've had a reason. Wish I knew what it was . . .

He hadn't wanted to become involved but now he was part of a nasty tangled affair. Elvin would think it funny if he packed his bag and left.

. . . Suppose he'd think it even funnier if he knew it wasn't your bag and the things in it weren't yours, either. Could've blackmailed Carole into sleeping with me if I'd threatened to tell Bossard I was wearing his shirt and how I came to

get it . . . with a few embellishments that she'd never convince him were all in my imagination. She'd hate him to think she was as bad as he'd been. To keep that sort of thing from him she'd share my bed any time I liked . . .

The thought fanned into life a dark flame of desire. He'd only be taking what she'd been willing to give on the night she took him home to her cottage.

. . . You could be wrong about her — wrong from beginning to end. And, even if you're not, since when did you crawl into the gutter for your pleasures? No matter what she may, or may not, have done, she's another man's woman. If you made her sleep with you, you wouldn't sleep too well with yourself for as long as you lived. So forget it. If you can't, go and take a cold bath . . .

The flame shrank low and then snuffed out. He told himself that a cup of hot coffee would make sure it didn't flare up again. Nobody would mind if he fixed some breakfast. They were all in bed. When he'd had something to eat he'd go for a walk.

As he crossed the sitting-room there were little sounds of movement in the kitchen . . . a cup tinkling in a saucer . . . a chair creaking . . . the rustle of a newspaper.

It was Irene Ford. She was sitting at the table with a teacup in one hand and a folded newspaper in the other.

When he drummed on the door with the tips of his fingers she looked up, her eyes startled. Then she giggled nervously while she fanned herself with the paper.

She said, "Oh, dear, you gave me such a fright. I didn't know anyone was there."

Quinn said, "I'm sorry. If I'd thought — "

"No, it wasn't your fault . . . not really. My mind was miles and miles away."

In the same colourless voice, she added, "It's only to be expected . . . isn't it? After what's happened . . . I mean."

"Of course. You must've been badly shaken. How are you feeling now?"

"Oh, a lot better. But it'll take time for me to get over it. Only natural . . . when you get a shock like that . . . don't you think?"

There she hunched up her narrow shoulders as though the sunlight was cold. All her movements were nervous and jerky like those of a bird prepared for instant flight.

Quinn wondered how a man of Ford's type could ever have married her. She didn't seem to have a drop of warm blood in her veins.

. . . *Couldn't imagine anybody making love to her unless he was desperate. Soon's hubby starts getting excited, I'll bet she giggles. And if there's anything can put a man off at the critical moment, that's it . . .*

He said, "Yes, quite natural. I'm

surprised to see you up and about so early. I understood that Dr. Bossard had given you something to make you sleep."

With a little self-conscious wriggle, Irene Ford said, "Oh, that sort of thing doesn't have much effect on me. I could take fifty of those pills and — "

Her mouth stayed open but no sound came out. She had a shrivelled look on her thin, pallid face as she stared up at Quinn miserably.

At last, she said, "Poor Adele . . . Terrible when someone young dies like that . . . unexpectedly, I mean . . . isn't it?"

"Very terrible," Quinn said.

She looked here and there, played with her cup, and eventually asked him, "Would you like some coffee . . . or do you prefer tea? I'm sure you want a hot drink. I always need one in the morning . . . to wake me up . . . if you know what I mean."

"I'll have coffee, please, if it's no trouble."

"Oh, no . . . no trouble at all. There's some in the pot on the stove."

Without making the slightest move, she went on, "You sit down, Mr. Quinn. After all, you're a guest. Let me get it for you."

"No need for that," Quinn said. "I can help myself . . . if it's all right with you."

"Yes, of course. Why should I mind?" A look of tired helplessness came into her eyes. "This isn't my house. I'm not even sure I'll be welcome here from now on."

Quinn poured out a cup of coffee and brought it back to the table. As he sat down, she said, "Maybe I shouldn't say a thing like that. It sounds awful . . . but I know you won't tell Michael . . . although it's true . . . unfortunately."

"What makes you think he doesn't like you?"

Her face brightened. She said, "Oh, it's not me. I get on well enough with him. It's Neil. They seem to rub

272

each other the wrong way. Of course, Michael's inclined to be — difficult. Doesn't mean any harm, really, but you've got to understand him. And that was Adele's trouble . . . although it doesn't seem right to find fault now that she's . . ."

The rest trailed off into uneasy silence. Quinn asked, "What was Mrs. Parry's trouble?"

Irene gave herself a little shake. With her fingers travelling over the surface of the newspaper as though she were reading braille, she said, "I always told her she should have more patience. But she was never very patient with anyone . . . not even my brother . . . and he was the easiest man to get on with that you could hope to meet. Anyone who knew him would tell you that."

"Weren't they happy together?"

With a nervous wriggle, Irene said hurriedly, "Oh, yes, very happy. I don't think they ever had a wrong word. Of course, I'd say that was mainly because he was so easy-going . . . and we can't all be the same, can we?"

"So they say," Quinn said. "You think that if Adele had been more patient with Michael she might be alive now?"

"Well, no one" — Irene wriggled again — "no one can be sure of that . . . can they? I'm only going by what she told me on the phone . . . nothing to make me think she meant to poison herself, of course, and I can't believe it even now . . ."

There was another awkward silence until Quinn asked, "What did she tell you on the phone?"

Very deliberately, Irene linked her thin hands together and hunched forward. In a worried voice, she said, "Well, maybe I shouldn't say anything . . . I don't want to cause trouble . . . but that's what upset me most of all last night when I had time to think about it . . . and it can't do her any harm now she's, well, dead . . . if you know what I mean."

Quinn said, "I'm afraid I don't know

what you mean, Mrs. Ford. The one thing you can be sure of, however, is that nothing you might say will do Mrs. Parry any harm and it could relieve your mind of needless worry. So why keep it to yourself?"

She drew back a little and looked guilty. She said, "It's probably not worth repeating. You'll think I'm just silly for making a fuss over nothing. My husband always says I exaggerate and if he heard — "

"He won't," Quinn said. "Not from me, he won't. So now — what did Adele say to you on the phone?"

"It was about her and Michael . . . and she sounded as if she'd really made up her mind."

"What about her and Michael?"

"She was going to divorce him . . . or ask him to divorce her. I'm not sure which. But it doesn't make any difference really . . . does it?"

"Depends on the circumstances," Quinn said. "In this case it might make all the difference in the world.

Can't you remember what she said?"

"No, I didn't pay much attention. To me it was the same thing either way. Of course, if I'd known what was going to happen . . . but you can't see into the future . . . even a few hours . . . can you?"

She separated her hands and gave another wriggle as though her clothes felt tight. Quinn wondered how any man could put up with her interminable questions, her lack of ordinary common sense.

He said, "You weren't to know, Mrs. Ford. So don't blame yourself. When did you get this phone call from Adele?"

Her face sharpened in a look of surprise. She said, "I've told you. It was only a few hours before — before I got here. She rang me yesterday morning when I was at home."

"Just to say that she and Michael were going to be divorced? Why couldn't she have kept the news until you arrived?"

276

"I asked her that and she told me she hadn't known whether we were coming or not. We hadn't said definitely when we were here the last time . . . and, anyway, we might not want to come when we knew she might be going off as soon as she'd talked to Michael."

"But it didn't stop you?"

Irene hunched up her shoulders. She said, "Oh, no, of course not. You surely don't think I was going to stay away and let her break up her whole life . . . just like that . . . do you?"

"But if she'd made up her mind — "

"It was still my duty to give her a good talking to . . . wasn't it? I had to make her realise what she was doing. After all, Michael wouldn't have grounds for divorce unless she did something . . . something wrong . . . if you know what I mean."

"I can guess," Quinn said. "But Mrs. Parry wasn't a child. You couldn't be responsible for what she did."

"No, but people talk. And it isn't nice . . . not really. Is it?"

There was no answer to that, no means of communication. Quinn told himself there was nothing so impenetrable as the barrier of stupidity.

But one question had to be asked. He said, "Did Mrs. Parry tell you where she was speaking from?"

Irene looked momentarily lost as though he had interrupted her train of thought. Then she said vaguely, "Oh, yes . . ."

As her eyes strayed down to the newspaper again, Quinn said, "This is important, Mrs. Ford. Where was your sister-in-law yesterday morning?"

"In London. She'd been there all week. She wanted to get away from everybody and everything so she could decide what to do . . . about Michael. It was only when she'd finally made up her mind that she phoned me from the hotel."

Once again, Irene retired within herself. Quinn asked, "Do you know the name of the hotel?"

"It's the one where she always stayed

when she went up to town — the Cavendish . . . at least, I think so."

"But she didn't say so?"

"Well, no. But she never went anywhere else. It was very convenient when she wanted to see her lawyers because their office is just round the corner."

"Was that one of the reasons why she was in London — to see her lawyers?"

With her shoulders hunched up, Irene Ford sat and thought. Then she said, "I don't know. Adele never mentioned anything about them. She just said she'd gone away for a few days because she wanted time to think . . . and she felt that I ought to know what she'd decided . . . since I was the only relation she had, as it were . . . apart from Michael, of course, and she'd made arrangements about him. So you see — "

"What had she arranged for Michael?"

"I don't know. It wasn't my place to ask . . . although I did wonder what she meant."

There was no future for Quinn in the realm of things that aroused Irene Ford's wonder. He asked, "Did Mrs. Parry say when she would be returning home?"

"Yes, I understood she'd be back before we arrived. That's why I thought it strange when she wasn't here. I never dreamed . . . it was the last thing in the world . . . "

Her lips trembled and she made a thin wailing sound in her throat. Then she stood up clumsily, her hands feeling for the corner of the table as though she were blind.

Without looking at Quinn, she said in a muffled voice, "You'll have to excuse me . . . oh dear . . . oh dear . . . oh dear . . . "

He watched her cross the wide expanse of living-room and go upstairs, her shoulders stooped, her arms wrapped round her middle as though she was in pain. In his mind lingered an impression that he had heard her whimper " . . . It was wrong. He shouldn't have done it. I don't care what she was . . . "

Long after she had left him her plaintive voice went on repeating the words again and again inside his head. He could still see the look of desolation on her face as she got up from the table — a look that left him feeling some of the cold she felt when she thought of Adele lying dead in the nursery.

She was afraid . . . like Carole was afraid . . . and Michael, too. When Adele Parry died, fear took her place at Elm Lodge.

* * *

Inspector Elvin was interested. He said, "Thanks for ringing me, Mr. Quinn. What you've learned from Mrs. Ford should save us quite a lot of trouble. When I asked you to stay on at the house I knew you'd be a useful chap to have around — most useful. Keep up the good work."

281

"Only if our association isn't intended to be a one-way affair," Quinn said.

"Meaning . . . ?"

"You know perfectly well what I mean. Anything I may be able to do will be done strictly on a *quid pro quo* basis. If I help you I want to be kept informed of progress."

The phone hummed distantly while Elvin took time to think. Then he said cautiously, "If it's to be strictly a *quid* for a *quo*, it'll also have to be strictly unofficial. I'm not supposed to divulge — "

"And I'm not supposed to be a copper's nark," Quinn said. "In case you don't know it, this isn't my idea of a holiday."

"No? I'd have thought you were doing all right. I wouldn't mind being a guest at a country house in perfect June weather, all found, and with something to keep my mind gently occupied."

"Then your tastes differ from mine. Ever heard the saying: '*Where every prospect pleases and only man is vile?*'

There's nothing gentle about life at Elm Lodge."

Elvin said, "Your misquotation is from a hymn by Bishop Heber and the correct line starts '*Though ever prospect pleases* . . . ' My mother used to sing it."

"I never knew that policemen had mothers," Quinn said. "And let's not get off the point. Is it a deal?"

"Providing that your idea of reciprocation doesn't conflict with my idea of duty — yes, it's a deal. What do you want to know?"

There were sounds from upstairs . . . a door opened and closed . . . slippers flapped their way along the corridor . . . another door thumped shut.

Quinn said, "Nothing — right now. The house is beginning to wake up. You'll be paying us a visit some time to-day, I suppose?"

"I'd intended to come out this morning . . . but in the light of your information I'll make a quick trip to London, instead, and have a chat with the people at the Cavendish. You don't happen to know the name of the late Mrs. Parry's lawyers, do you?"

"No, but I could find out from her husband. Want me to ask him?"

The phone went quiet again except for that empty humming sound in the distance. Then Inspector Elvin said, "No, better not. I'll get hold of it some other way."

With a smile in his voice, he added, "We have our methods . . . as that pompous and overbearing character, Mr. Holmes, was fond of saying."

"This seems to be a day for mis-quotations," Quinn said. "The phrase he used was: '*You know my methods . . .*'"

Elvin said, "*Touché*. How do you propose to spend your time until I get back from London?"

"Enjoying the delights of the countryside. When I've arranged some breakfast I'm going for a walk."

"Don't go too far. I may want to give you a ring."

"Not to worry," Quinn said. "I won't get lost."

★ ★ ★

He made some toast and washed it down with the last of the coffee. Then he lit a cigarette. By that time he could hear people talking on the floor above. One of them sounded like Carole.

What he had said to her the night before had been a mistake. He hadn't any right to be jealous of Bossard. After all, Dr. Bossard was still her husband — even if they were separated.

. . . And that's your trouble: you are jealous. Why don't you go and get your own woman instead of casting covetous eyes at another man's wife? Anybody'd think she was a raving beauty . . .

Asking himself questions to which there were no answers wouldn't help. He'd tried to frighten her with a threat as though nailing his colours to the mast. And that had been mean.

"Don't rely on me. I owe you

nothing — neither you nor anyone else connected with Adele Parry. Whatever I learn while I'm here I'll tell the police."

Now he realised they'd been foolish words — just an empty threat. In the event he hadn't told Inspector Elvin that Carole was Dr. Bossard's wife. It did no good to excuse himself by saying that the information wasn't relevant, that it had no bearing on the death of Adele Parry. That hadn't been his real reason.

. . . You were just trying to atone for the nasty thoughts you had about her, trying to be a gallant gentleman. Trouble is you don't know how to be gallant and you'll never be a gentleman . . . If I'm any judge there's not much wrong with that girl. She's been hurt once and I don't want to see her hurt again . . .

Yet he knew all the time he was blinding himself to reality. He believed in her because he wanted to believe in her.

Threatening her on the one hand and keeping things from Inspector Elvin on the other was what the Yanks called playing both ends against the middle. And the Yanks always contended there was no future in that.

Now he'd manœuvred himself into the middle position and the quicker he got out of it the better. Carole was married. Carole had volunteered the information quite readily. If she hadn't wanted anyone to know she shouldn't have told him.

He stubbed out his cigarette and crossed the living-room and unlocked the front door. One half of his mind was listening to someone on the floor above complaining about the lack of hot water. This time it sounded like Irene Ford's voice.

As he went out he was turning to look back and he nearly bumped into Miss Wilkinson. She was dressed in white sandals, tight, pale-blue jeans, and a yellow sweater that emphasised her shapeless bust. Around her hair she wore a chiffon scarf tied in a bow under her chin.

In exaggerated self-defence she held up both hands and said, "Well, how about that? Almost got knocked over by the sleuth of Fleet Street himself . . . and I'll bet you couldn't say that if you were tiddly. Where are you dashing off to so bright and early — if it's any of my business?"

Quinn said, "I was just going for a walk. The others aren't up yet . . . or I should say they're up — "

"But not down . . . good."

She came closer to look up at him and he could see little yellow flecks in her hazel eyes. She said, "It's you I want to talk to this beautiful morning — not the others. So would you mind postponing your walk for a few minutes?"

"Why not come with me? I won't go far."

"That's the trouble" — she gave him a coy look — "with all the men I meet. They never go far enough . . . and if

288

you don't smile at that you'll embarrass me because I'll think you don't think I'm joking."

"Then consider that I'm smiling," Quinn said.

"If you are, it doesn't show. But never mind. It's not the first time my poor attempts at wit have fallen flat."

She lowered her voice as she went on, "I don't want them to see me going off with you. They'll think I'm telling you something they're not supposed to hear."

"Such as what?"

"Such as the motive behind Adele's death."

"Telling me won't do any good. It's the Coroner's job to decide why she would want to commit suicide."

Miss Wilkinson fluttered her eyelashes and asked, "But supposing it wasn't suicide? Supposing somebody might've had a reason for wanting to get rid of her?"

"Anyone might've had a reason for doing anything," Quinn said. "Why not be a little more specific?"

"Oh, I can be a lot more specific. But if I am" — she looked past him at the open door and dropped her voice lower still — "I don't want my name to be mentioned."

"Why? What are you afraid of?"

"My neighbours. I've got to go on living round here. And if they thought I kept an eye on their comings and goings, that would be the end of my social life. So anything I say must be between ourselves. Otherwise . . . " She put a finger to her lips and then waved it in Quinn's face.

He said, "O.K. If anything results from what you tell me, I promise not to disclose the source. Now let's hear it. Whose comings and goings have you been keeping an eye on?"

Miss Wilkinson stood on tip-toe to look past him again. Then she said, "Dr. Bossard's. About a year ago he started calling here pretty often. During the day, at that, when Michael wasn't at home. He never gets back from the

Bird-in-Hand until nearly four . . . and Mrs. Gregg leaves at one o'clock . . . so the doctor and Adele had the house all to themselves."

"Don't see anything wrong in that," Quinn said. "She was one of his patients — almost certainly a private patient. He was entitled to visit her whenever she asked him to call."

Cynical lines etched themselves around the corners of Miss Wilkinson's nose and mouth. She said, "Two or three times a week? They can hardly have been professional visits."

"I don't see why not."

"Because if she needed medical attention all that often she must've been suffering from some chronic ailment . . . and I can assure you she wasn't."

At the back of Quinn's mind he could hear Michael Parry saying " . . . *It can't be true . . . Adele's the healthiest person I've ever known. Never had a day's illness in her life . . .* "

Quinn asked, "Did Dr. Bossard only

call here in the afternoons?"

With her eyes half-shut and her head titled back, Ariadne Wilkinson stood quite still while she thought. Then her eyelids flicked open like those of a doll.

She said, "It was the afternoons when I saw him . . . the time of day when Adele would be alone in the house. That's why it's obvious — "

"Only if you jump to conclusions," Quinn said. "I don't know about you, but I'd prefer to tread cautiously. To begin with, what evidence have you got that the doctor came to the house two or three times a week?"

"The evidence of my own eyes. I can see Elm Lodge from the bedroom window of my cottage. It's" — she pointed vaguely in the direction of the high ground to the west — "it's over there. The drive here in front of the house is clearly visible . . . and I can't mistake the doctor's car."

"So for the past year you've been keeping watch every day," Quinn said.

Her mouth drew down again. She said, "How about that? I try to be of help . . . and for my pains I'm charged with snooping. You're not very nice to know, are you?"

He said, "That's not what I want. You say Dr. Bossard started calling on Mrs. Parry about a year ago. I just wondered if these visits of his had gone on up to the time she went away last Monday."

"If I could answer that" — Ariadne Wilkinson was faintly triumphant — "it would mean I'd been snooping seven days a week for the past year . . . and I can assure you I haven't. I lost interest months ago. It was none of my business if our local doctor chose to make a fool of himself with an over-sexed married woman."

"That's a dangerous thing to say about a professional man," Quinn said. "You've no proof they were having an *affaire*."

She looked at him with a wide-eyed pretence of astonishment. In a

293

tone that was even deeper than her normal voice, she said, "How about that? Who'd have believed you were never told the facts of life?"

Quinn said, "Let's cut out the quips. What has all this to do with Mrs. Parry's death?"

"Just about everything. Can you imagine how Michael would've felt if he'd discovered what was going on behind his back?"

"Yes. I can imagine how any husband would feel in those circumstances. Are you suggesting he had found out?"

"No, but he was bound to do so very soon. And then what do you think he'd have done?"

"The same thing as most other husbands . . . if she'd been like most other wives. He'd have divorced her. But she was different from other wives. She was a rich woman. Because of that he might've been prepared to turn a blind eye to — "

"You're no judge of human nature," Miss Wilkinson said roughly. "There are very few men who'd put up with that sort of thing. Besides, if he wanted money, he could get it by suing for divorce and charging the doctor with enticement . . . or whatever it's called. That way he'd get a tidy sum, wouldn't he?"

Quinn said, "This isn't getting us very far. What you say may be true but it doesn't provide a motive for her death . . . assuming that she didn't commit suicide."

"Of course she didn't! Why should a young, rich and attractive woman poison herself? Not because she'd been crossed in love — that's for sure. A man-eater who's been married twice doesn't voluntarily give up the delights of the flesh."

The question echoed in Quinn's mind and roused a memory of Irene Ford's voice. He could hear her whining complaint again as clearly as he had heard it when he was going downstairs to phone the police.

" . . . *It doesn't seem right. She had*

so much to live for. It just doesn't seem right . . . "

He said, "I can give you one reason. Maybe she poisoned herself because she couldn't face a divorce action and all the notoriety that goes with it."

With a knowing smile, Ariadne Wilkinson said, "No, not Adele. She wouldn't be scared of notoriety. But I can tell you somebody who would — somebody who'd have been ruined if he were cited in a divorce suit . . . "

They were Quinn's own thoughts clothed in another person's words. Now he could understand what lay behind the fear in Carole's eyes. It had to be one of two things: either she had poisoned Adele Parry . . . or she guessed that Dr. Bossard had done it.

Miss Wilkinson's deep masculine voice ran on as though she were savouring each phrase with relish. This was her big moment.

" . . . Adele was his patient. Once she had her claws in Bossard I doubt if he could ever have made her let go.

And hanging over him all the time was the threat of what Michael would do when he found out . . . as he was bound to find out in the long run. Maybe not so long, at that."

Quinn said, "You're making a very serious allegation."

"Oh, yes, I know just how serious. But, of course, it's strictly *entre nous*."

"Now you're being silly. That sort of thing can't be kept secret."

"Who says it's a secret? Who says I'm the only one who's aware of the intimate relationship between Adele and her — for lack of a better term shall we call him her medical adviser?"

"I can't see how that has any bearing on — "

"Perhaps it hasn't . . . but you never can tell. The main thing is that a doctor gets struck off for what's described as unprofessional conduct. And adultery with a female patient isn't considered to be ethical treatment — even if that's the medicine the patient prescribes for herself."

For a moment longer Ariadne Wilkinson stared up at Quinn with wide hypnotic eyes. Then she said, "He was hooked, Mr. Quinn. Nothing could save him. Whether he realised it or not, the risk that Michael Parry would find out was becoming greater every day."

Quinn heard footsteps coming down the stairs. She must've heard them, too, because she drew back.

With a farewell wiggle of her fingers, she added, "Strange are the workings of Providence. Just in time his mistress let him off the hook. She went and died. How about that, Mr. Quinn of Fleet Street? How about that?"

9

WHEN she reached the spreading shade of the elms her brisk pace slackened and Quinn thought she was going to turn back. But it was only a momentary pause. Seconds later he lost sight of her beyond the trees.

Then Carole came out and joined him in the porch. She said, "Good morning. Who was that?"

"Your friend Miss Wilkinson."

A look of distaste spoiled the shape of Carole's mouth. She said, "No friend of mine . . . but that's by the by. What did she want?"

"Nothing particular. Just a social call."

"Which means she was on the prowl for gossip. Whose reputation did she try to blacken?"

"Nobody's," Quinn said. "She wasn't

here more than two or three minutes."

"That's long enough for Ariadne to bring down the government. Have you had any breakfast?"

"Yes, thank you. I helped myself. Hope that was all right?"

"Certainly. Adele always liked people — "

Carole shivered and looked away. In a small voice, she said, "I keep forgetting . . . What I meant was that nobody stands on ceremony in this house. You don't need to ask for permission."

"I'll remember that," Quinn said.

She left him and went into the kitchen. A little while later, Neil Ford came downstairs, followed not long afterwards by Michael Parry.

Ford gave Quinn a nod but no other greeting. He looked as churlish as he had been the night before. Quinn heard him talking in an undertone to Carole until one of them shut the kitchen door and blotted out everything except the intermittent murmur of their voices.

Parry seemed to have benefited from a night's sleep. His faded blue eyes were brighter and he was less subdued.

With the same air of *bonhomie* that he had worn when he welcomed Quinn to the house, he said, "Good morning, old man. Carole's not much good as a weather prophet, is she? Forecast rain . . . and it's as fine a day as you could wish for. Had breakfast?"

"Yes, thank you. I've been down quite some time."

"So I gathered from Irene. Says you two had a very interesting chat. Seems to have taken a liking to you, old man."

"I'm glad to hear it," Quinn said.

. . . She did most of the talking and all I had to do was listen. That's why she likes me. Don't suppose anyone ever listens to her — least of all her husband. Wonder if she was born inadequate or if parents and family and environment crushed her spirit? Marrying a man like Neil Ford would be the last straw . . .

301

Michael brushed up his moustache with the back of his hands. He said, "O.K. then. Think I'll go and see what's cooking."

He used both hands to point the ends of his moustache. Then he asked, "What do you intend to do with yourself to-day?"

It sounded like nothing more than an idle question. He was just being sociable.

Quinn said, "I think I'll enjoy some fresh air and sunshine. Don't often get much of either."

"Good idea. You do that. And if you want to do it the lazy way, borrow my car. The keys are in the ignition."

"Thanks . . . but won't you need it yourself?"

"I shouldn't think so. The odds are that Inspector Elvin will be calling on me again some time to-day."

"Did he say so?"

"No. But I've got a feeling in my kidneys that he's still got some questions up his sleeve."

Parry turned away. Then he glanced back and asked, "Have you heard from him since last night?"

It sounded like another artless question. But this time Quinn was not so sure.

He said, "No."

★ ★ ★

Mrs. Gregg arrived soon after nine o'clock. She was a sturdy woman with thick legs and a bovine face and black, skimpy hair. Her eyes were the type that missed nothing.

Quinn saw her studying him as she went round to the rear of the house. A minute or two later she came out of the kitchen and walked with a solid tread to where he stood just outside the front door.

She said, "They told me you were Mr. Quinn."

Her voice conveyed a mixture of protest and accusation. Then her mouth closed firmly and she stared at him with unmoving eyes.

Quinn said, "Whoever they are, they were right. I can't deny it."

Nothing changed in her stolid face. She said, "I'm Mrs. Gregg."

"Glad to know you."

Her mouth relaxed momentarily in a pretence of a smile. She said, "They're all in the kitchen except Mrs. Ford so I can't get started in there . . . and she's taking a bath . . . and there's a lot to do . . . so I hope you won't mind."

"Whatever it is, I won't mind at all," Quinn said. "But just out of sheer curiosity, what is it?"

In a patient voice, she said, "I'd like to make the bed and tidy up in your room. If I don't start somewhere I'll never get done."

Quinn said, "That's a very good thought. So far as I'm concerned, go right ahead."

"I won't be in your way?"

"No, you needn't worry about that.

The room's all yours. Take as long as you like."

As though she hadn't heard him, Mrs. Gregg said, "I don't want to cause no trouble. Sometimes it's not very convenient . . . and I like to make myself a convenience for people. But not everybody's like that, are they?"

"Offhand, I can't think of many," Quinn said.

"Yes, that's what's wrong with the world — no consideration. We shouldn't be surprised when terrible things happen."

"I'm never surprised at anything," Quinn said.

He knew what was coming. This was another one who wanted to talk.

. . . Must be something about me . . . yet it doesn't have the same effect on Bossard or Neil Ford. Maybe that's significant. Maybe it's because they've got something to hide and the others haven't. All the rest unburden themselves freely — even that smooth character, Elvin . . .

Mrs. Gregg spread her feet farther apart and folded her arms. With no trace of sentiment in her voice, she said, "Very sad about Mrs. Parry, isn't it? I always say life's short enough without dying."

Quinn said, "How right you are."

"Oh, yes, always look on the bright side, that's what I say. But it makes you think, doesn't it?"

"Sure does. Did you see Mrs. Parry before you left here yesterday?"

"No, she hadn't come back yet. And down in the village they're saying — "

"I wouldn't pay too much attention to what they're saying down in the village," Quinn said. "Anything you know you'd better keep to yourself. There's a police inspector making inquiries and he'll want to talk to you later on. If he hasn't arrived before you go I'll take your address so that he can call on you at home."

Mrs. Gregg's eyes became more intent. She said, "If the police are in it they must think there's something funny going on."

"Not necessarily. They always ask questions in a case of this kind. That's the way they do things."

"Oh, I know that well enough. I've seen it lots of times on the telly."

"Good. I'm sure you'll be very helpful. When Mrs. Parry went away last Monday did she tell you she'd be home Friday evening?"

"No, never said a word to me about going away. It was Mr. Parry what told me when I came on Tuesday."

"So you didn't know until then that she'd gone to London?"

With a slightly puzzled look on her dull face, Mrs. Gregg said, "It wasn't London she went to. It was that place they call Wood Lake . . . or something."

"How did you know that?"

"Mr. Parry told me. I asked him where she was and that and he said she'd gone off for a few days to — "

"Yes, I see. And I suppose he

mentioned she'd be coming back on Friday?"

"Oh, no, he didn't mention when she'd be back." Mrs. Gregg raised her folded arms a little higher and gave Quinn a shrewd look. "I'd have been surprised if he had the way things have been in this house . . . not that it's my place to talk about them but when the poor lady's dead and I'm the one what knows better than anybody why she done it . . . well, it'd be wrong of me to keep quiet, wouldn't it?"

"Very wrong," Quinn said. "How have things been recently?"

"Nasty. That's the only word for it — nasty. Of course, they weren't suited to each other from the start. I could see that. He wasn't" — she glanced over her shoulder to the kitchen door — "he wasn't anything like Mrs. Parry's first husband. Now there was a fine man for you. Never any arguing or quarrelling with him."

"You mean that Mr. and Mrs. Parry

quarrelled a lot?"

Mrs. Gregg unfolded her arms and rested one hand on the jamb of the door. She said, "Well, I wouldn't put it like that. You couldn't rightly say they quarrelled. No time for each other, I'd say. At least, she hadn't no time for him. Found out too late, you see. And after that there was nothing she could do about it. Trouble never does run smooth, does it?"

"Something like that," Quinn said. "What was it she found out too late?"

"Well, he wasn't" — Mrs. Gregg held Quinn's eyes with a long, unwinking look — "he wasn't exactly the man she'd expected . . . if you get my meaning."

"I don't. Many a woman has found that her husband didn't come up to expectations: it's more the rule than the exception. But most marriages don't end like this one."

"Too bad if they did. I believe in what it says: For richer, for poorer, in sickness and in health . . . and all that. We can't all be like Mrs. Parry, can we?"

"Now I'm not with you," Quinn said.

"Ah, that's because you don't see what I mean. We're not all the same, are we?"

"No . . . but I'm afraid you're getting away from — "

"Well, there's the whole point. Mrs. Parry was rich. Not like me. And it makes a difference, doesn't it? We wouldn't look at things the same way, would we?"

Quinn gave up the struggle. He said, "No, I don't suppose you would."

"Of course not. I've got to work for my living. Always have and always will. But don't get me wrong. That's the way I like it to be. Wouldn't have it any other way — even if I do know I can't. I don't believe in all this fratriciding by people who can't afford it."

She ended on a note of triumph. When she looked at Quinn as though daring him to contradict her, he said,

310

"How right you are! I couldn't agree more . . . to coin a phrase. Now we've got that settled let's get back to Mr. Parry and his failings. What do you think was wrong with him?"

In an artificially prim voice, Mrs. Gregg said, "Well, it's not exactly what I like to talk about . . . in the manner of speaking. But if you really want to know . . . "

"I do. And the police will want to know as well. So I'll help you to put your thoughts in order ready for the inspector's arrival this afternoon."

Once again she glanced over her shoulder to the kitchen door. Then she said, "I've always thought it needn't be the man's fault. A lot depends on the kind of wife he marries. With some women that sort of thing isn't all that important. Others can't get enough of it . . . if you follow me."

Quinn said, "Now I know what you're talking about. But how do you know that's what was wrong between them?"

"Because I've heard her complaining many a time. Not that I deliberately listened . . . "

"No, of course not. She just talked loud enough for you to hear her."

"That's right. Many a time. Told him he wasn't a man . . . had no right to marry her . . . if she'd known he never would've done. And then there was one day . . . "

Mrs. Gregg hesitated. The look on her heavy face invited Quinn to ask her to go on.

He said, "Yes? You may as well give me the whole story now."

"I don't know whether I should . . . you being a friend of his, and that."

"I'm far from being a friend. I met Mr. Parry for the first time yesterday evening. So don't worry. I won't repeat anything you tell me."

"Oh, I hope not. He'd say it was only because I don't like him. She was nice to me . . . but he's always had too big an opinion of himself. I once heard him call me Pathé's Gazette. I've never found out what he meant but I know it's rude and I don't think he's entitled to say nasty things about people when he's no better than they are. It is rude, isn't it?"

Quinn had a picture in his mind of a darkened cinema and the twin lenses of a movie camera on the screen as the newsreel came to an end. Then fade-out music coinciding with a legend: *Pathé's Gazette — The Eyes and the Ears of the World.*

He said, "Whatever Mr. Parry meant I wouldn't let it worry me if I were you. Instead tell me what happened that day you were talking about."

Mrs. Gregg came out on to the porch and pulled the door almost shut behind her. With her eyes fixed immovably on Quinn's face, she said hurriedly, "They must've thought I'd gone but I'd come back because I'd forgotten something and they didn't bother to keep their voices down so I couldn't help — " She stopped for lack of air.

" — overhearing them," Quinn said. "Quite natural. What did you hear?"

"It was about him drinking. She said it might be because he got drunk so often that he wasn't much use. And he said all she ever thought about was getting into bed. She might've killed her first husband but she wasn't going to kill him. That wasn't very nice, was it?"

Quinn said, "Depends on the circumstances. What did he say?"

"I didn't get it all. Just something about him taking too much for granted. All he cared about was himself. It wouldn't matter to him if she dropped dead. He'd have no financiery worries and that was all he was concerned about."

With an air of sadness Mrs. Gregg shook her head and went on, "Now the poor thing's dead and so he's got what he wants. Not that he had anything to do with it, of course, except it was through him she did it . . . but it makes you think, doesn't it?"

"You're so right," Quinn said. "And I'm going for a walk while I think some more. Anyone wants me, I'll be back about two. And tell Mrs. Ford or Miss Stewart I'm lunching out."

10

FOR more than two hours he wandered at random along quiet country roads under a sun that burned in the cloudless blue of the sky. Now and again he rested at the roadside, sprawled out on a bank where an overgrown brier cast its shade. And all the time he thought about a man called Michael Parry.

Carole had been right. Parry's life might have been different if he'd married someone for whom he would've had to work, some ordinary woman who'd have needed him to support her.

But circumstances had betrayed him. Adele was no ordinary woman. Her money and the physical demands she made on him destroyed all incentive, all ambition to create something out of his own life. Too much money left him with only a pretence of living. When the pressure became too great and he was forced to recognise what he had become he could always blot out the picture by means of drink — each time more and more drink.

. . . And he knows that everybody knows. Whatever he does is merely an act to protect his ego . . . and it doesn't even do that. I'd feel sorry for him except for the fact that nothing stopped him getting out. He was healthy and intelligent enough to earn his own living. His failing was that he didn't have the moral strength to break out of his cocoon . . .

Adele had made a slave of him — a kept man helplessly dependent on her. And the irony was that what she had bought with her money had failed its sole purpose. Michael had never satisfied her need.

. . . The situation was one that couldn't go on indefinitely. She was bound to take a lover . . . and Parry was bound to know it . . .

If she had phoned him to say she was coming home that afternoon instead of in the evening . . . and he had gone to Salisbury to meet her . . . and she'd told him their marriage was finished . . . she'd instructed her lawyers to make out a will leaving him nothing or next to nothing.

Yet it could have been Dr. Bossard who had met her at the station and driven her home. Same circumstances, different motive. All that needed to be known about Adele Parry had been provided by Mrs. Ford, Miss Wilkinson and now Mrs. Gregg.

. . . There's that business about the boot of the car being open. I saw that when Carole and I went round to the garage a minute or so after we got to Elm Lodge. Could be that Michael made the car ready in anticipation of bringing his wife's body down from the bedroom . . . but she took longer to die than he'd expected . . . and Carole and I arrived sooner than he'd expected . . . and so he had to drag Adele into

318

the nursery where she wouldn't be found . . .

Quinn told himself he'd been over the same ground already. If he were wise he'd get out and forget the whole thing. It was none of his business. He was supposed to be on holiday.

It seemed a long time since Thursday night and that stupid party. He'd already wasted two days. His best bet would be to leave the people at Elm Lodge to stew in their own juice.

Maybe no one would ever know how and why Adele Parry had died. There was no reason why he should care. He didn't even have to go back to the house. None of the things he'd left there belonged to him.

A bus from Castle Lammering would take him to Blandford . . . he could catch another bus to Salisbury . . . and from there a train to London. To-morrow he'd begin his holiday again — this time alone.

. . . That's the route Adele took last Monday. We know she went to

London. The police will verify that a taxi picked her up at the house and dropped her at Blandford. They'll also find out if she called on her lawyers and what she talked about. Be interesting to see whether it was her husband or Bossard . . . or if she actually did it herself . . .

He turned back and headed for Castle Lammering. There he caught the quarter to twelve bus to Blandford.

It was a pleasant town on a pleasant day but his journey served no other purpose than to show him there was a telephone box within a few yards of the bus stop. When he had wandered around for a while he took the next bus back.

By then it was twenty minutes past one and he had begun to feel hungry. If he looked in at the Bird-in-Hand he should be able to kill two birds with one stone. It seemed the kind of place where the beer would be cold and he could get an edible sandwich.

The bar was fairly busy. All the

customers were men and they looked and behaved like regulars. When he first walked in they stared at him, one or two of them gave him a friendly nod, and then they went back to their own affairs.

He ordered a sandwich. " . . . Anything'll do so long as it keeps the wolf from the door. I won't even say no to a piece of wolf between two slices of bread."

The landlord said, "We've had no wolves in these parts since the bad winter of 1721 . . . but I'll see what I can dig up for you. Before I get out my spade, would you risk ordering something to drink?"

Quinn said, "I'll have a pint of bitter. It doesn't seem to have harmed your other customers."

"That's merely because they've developed a natural immunity. You just passing through here?"

"No, I'm staying up at Elm Lodge. I believe Mr. Parry comes in quite a lot?"

The landlord finished drawing Quinn's beer, placed a cardboard mat in front of him, and stood the pint glass on it. Then he said, "Yes, he does. But from what I hear we won't be seeing much of him to-day."

"I shouldn't think you will," Quinn said.

"A very distressing business . . . by all accounts."

"It's always worse for those that are left . . . as they say," Quinn said.

"Yes, that's true enough. How's he taking it?"

"As well as can be expected," Quinn said.

"Give him my sympathies and tell him we were all very sorry to hear the news . . . will you?"

"Soon's I get back to the house," Quinn said.

The landlord nodded and said, "Sad life . . . but there it is. Now I'll go and see about that sandwich of yours."

Quinn drank beer and listened to the sporadic conversation around him. The cool half light of the bar was more than welcome after his long and dusty walk in the sun.

Then the landlord came back. "Here we are. Beef on fresh bread with home-made pickles. How's that?"

"Sounds all right and looks all right," Quinn said. He took a bite. "Tastes all right, too. Present my compliments to the chef."

"She'd rather have half a crown. Always has been one of the mercenary kind. Do anything for money — well, almost anything."

Quinn paid, bought the landlord a drink, and then asked, "How did you get to hear about Mrs. Parry?"

"Oh, the usual way we hear about everything that goes on. The milkman called at one of his customers — in this case it happened to be a friend of the Parrys — and she told him. Then the milkman told the postman and the postman told Mary Kemp who runs the village store and Mary Kemp told me . . . all inside about fifteen minutes."

"They do say news travels fast," Quinn said.

"And nowhere faster than in these parts. If Marconi had lived in Castle Lammering he wouldn't have bothered to invent radio."

The landlord raised his glass. "Cheers . . . Does anyone know when Mrs. Parry came home?"

"Not yet. I'd have thought your bush telegraphy system could provide all the answers."

"Oh, no. It only transmits things that are seen or heard . . . and apparently no one saw her. I knew she'd been away all week, of course. Mr. Parry always stays longer than usual at midday when he's on his own and since last Monday he's stood chatting to me until long past closing time."

"But he wasn't in yesterday, was he? From what he told me he went shopping in Poole and had lunch there and knocked back a few drinks and drove straight home to sleep it off."

The landlord shook his head. "You've

only got it half right. He was in Poole, true enough. And he also had a few in some pub there. But that didn't stop him dropping in and having a few more before he went home."

Quinn said, "Funny why he doesn't remember it."

"Wouldn't strike you as funny if you'd been in here. When he came in about half past two I could see he'd already had a pretty good session . . . not that he can't carry his drink, mark you."

"Oh, I know that," Quinn said.

"Still, there's a limit even for someone like Mr. Parry. I was the one who advised him to go home and sleep it off after he'd had one or two doubles. Even tried to persuade him to leave his car and walk but he wouldn't have it."

"All the same you succeeded in getting him to leave earlier than usual," Quinn said.

"Only because I put him in a bad temper. The moment I suggested that

325

he might be wise to leave his car he flared up and told me to mind my own bloody business. He's never been the sort of man to use bad language but he called me a few choice names before he dashed off as if he was going to a fire. When he'd gone I found he'd left his whisky. It's not like him, at all."

"Probably he was so tight he didn't know what he was saying. Doesn't even remember anything about it . . . so I wouldn't be offended if I were you."

The landlord said, "Takes more than that to offend me. In view of what's happened since then you can take it that the whole thing's forgotten."

He grinned, swallowed a mouthful of beer, and grinned again. "For your information, I've been insulted by professionals. If Mr. Parry had been himself he wouldn't have gone off the way he did. I've never known him leave before we bolt the outside doors."

"What time do you shut up shop in this part of the world?"

"Same time as in most other places.

We stop serving at three o'clock and then there's ten minutes drinking-up time before we turn the key in the lock."

"And so my friend Parry was out of here before ten past three," Quinn said. "Must've been real squiffy if he never finished his drink."

The landlord said, "I can assure you he didn't need it. He'd had more than enough . . . and that's an understatement. But for heaven's sake don't tell him you heard it from me. I'd hate to lose a good customer."

"I won't tell him," Quinn said.

★ ★ ★

He got back to Elm Lodge just before two. Irene Ford and Carole were sunbathing in the garden at the rear of the house, Michael Parry had gone to his room to write some letters. Neil Ford was in Ringwood.

" . . . That's where they live and his business is there," Carole said. "Made

327

an excuse that he had a couple of things to attend to but I think he was just bored. Says he'll be back for dinner and — "

"You can spare me the details," Quinn said. "I'll survive until our twin hearts are reunited. Any phone calls for me?"

"No. Where have you been since I saw you this morning?"

"Here and there . . . taking the sun at my leisure."

"Have you had any lunch?"

"Yes, thank you. Got a sandwich at the Bird-in-Hand and also sampled the local brew. Both were well up to standard. How about you? Been having a good time?"

She frowned and said, "Don't be facetious. If Michael hadn't asked me to stay I'd have left here this morning. I wouldn't ever come back again, either. This place is like a — " Her husky voice broke off.

" — morgue," Quinn said. "You've lost a dear friend and the whole

328

atmosphere's getting you down. What you need is a change of surroundings."

"I know that. But I've got to stay."

"Nevertheless, there's one way you could get all these unpleasant things off your mind."

"I'd like to know how."

"It's simple. Why don't you tell your erring husband that he can come home, all is forgiven?"

With a frosty look in her dark eyes, Carole said, "I've got an even better idea. Why don't you stop meddling in other people's affairs?"

★ ★ ★

There was a county cricket match on television starting at two-thirty. Quinn watched it without very much interest, smoked two or three cigarettes, and dozed in the big arm-chair, only one half of his mind awake. It would have been all very peaceful . . . if he could've forgotten Adele Parry, if he could've wiped from his memory the look of death on her calm and beautiful face.

Inspector Elvin arrived at twenty minutes to four. Quinn let him in, told him the gist of Miss Wilkinson's gossip about Dr. Bossard, and then asked, "What did you find out in the Big Smoke?"

"Oh, quite a lot . . . quite a lot. Mrs. Parry stayed at the Cavendish, all right. She got there last Monday afternoon and checked out yesterday morning. Received no visitors and no phone calls. Breakfasted in her room, didn't go out very much, and dined at the hotel each night. Behaved with propriety and decorum — as one would expect of a wealthy, respectable married woman."

"Who had a lover," Quinn said.

Elvin pursed his lips. "That has yet to be proved."

"I'm willing to believe it right now. We know from Mrs. Ford that her sister-in-law wanted a divorce."

"Doesn't mean to say she had a lover. She might just have got sick of a husband who spent all his time drinking. That's as logical as — "

"Not when you hear what Mrs. Gregg, the daily woman has to say . . . "

The inspector listened, his head bent, his hands in his pockets with the thumbs hanging out. When he had heard it all, he said, "Yes, it does point in that direction, I admit . . . it certainly does. But this London visit hardly seems to have been for the purpose of keeping an assignation. Nobody came to see her at the hotel."

"So far as they know. But even a high-class place like the Cavendish isn't able to keep watch on all their guests . . . which isn't the function of an exclusive hotel, anyway. What type of room did she have?"

"One of their best suites."

"Yes, that I'd expect. But was it single bed, twin bed, or double bed?"

"On the day she arrived the only accommodation they were able to give her was one with a double bed. She hadn't made reservation in advance and they were almost completely booked up."

"Did she ask them to let her know if another suite became available?"

"Not so far as I'm aware. There was no mention of it when I spoke to them . . . no mention at all."

"Then a man could have spent the night very comfortably with her as often as he or she wished, couldn't he? All he had to do was go straight upstairs at a pre-arranged time and he'd find the door unlocked. Next morning he could leave any time before the chambermaids started work — which is seldom very early — and nobody would've been any the wiser. Right?"

Inspector Elvin took a hand from his pocket, studied it as though he were reading his own palm, and then put it back again. He said, "Quite right. But without going into intimate details, I would suggest that two people who are so minded can make do with a single bed. The fact that she had a double bed at the hotel doesn't prove anything . . . doesn't prove anything at all."

"I'd still like to know if Dr. Bossard spent one or two nights away from home this week," Quinn said.

"Why need it have been Dr. Bossard? If Mrs. Parry was the over-sexed type of woman she might've had several men friends. Just because an inveterate scandal-monger likes to stir up dirt is no proof that the doctor's visits to Elm Lodge weren't perfectly proper."

"Then that leaves us with Michael Parry, back where we started."

"Not quite. We know a lot more than we did when we started. The hotel had a record of two phone calls made by Mrs. Parry. One was to a number in Ringwood, her sister-in-law's number — "

"Was that the one Mrs. Ford told me she received yesterday morning?"

"Yes, it must've been. The other was to a London firm of solicitors in the Haymarket: Cockburn, Watling and Company. I rang them from the

Cavendish and caught their senior partner, Watling, just as he was leaving the office. Another half minute and he'd have gone off for the week-end and I'd have had to wait until Monday to learn about a conversation Mrs. Parry had with him last Thursday afternoon."

"About making a will?"

"Yes. She phoned at midday to fix an appointment and called on him late in the afternoon. As a result of that meeting he drew up a will which she arranged to sign on her return to London early next week."

"If that's true it pretty well rules out suicide," Quinn said.

"Oh, it's perfectly true. These people are old-established solicitors and — "

"I wasn't questioning their integrity. I just wondered if she actually intended to go back to London."

Inspector Elvin stroked his sleek silver hair while he thought. Then he put his hand back in his pocket.

He said, "I considered that possibility,

too. But to make an appointment with no intention of keeping it seems rather pointless. In view of what you learned from Mrs. Ford I'd say Adele Parry would be very anxious to sign that will without delay."

"Which means it concerned her husband more than a little," Quinn said.

"He had everything to gain, or lose, depending on which way you look at it. She told Watling she meant to discuss her will with Michael during the week-end."

"What was in it for him?"

"If he agreed to institute divorce proceedings on grounds that she would provide he'd be named as a beneficiary in the sum of £20,000. Furthermore, she would sign an immediate financial undertaking in return for his cooperation: £5000 when divorce proceedings commenced, £5000 on the granting of a decree absolute."

"And if he refused to play?"

"He'd get nothing. She intended to

sell this house and go abroad and leave him without a penny."

"Had he any chance of redress if she'd gone ahead and done just that?"

"Not to my knowledge."

"So she had him by the short hairs. Any other beneficiaries?"

"Only one which might interest us. Apart from that one and the £20,000 that Parry would get if he was a good boy, all the rest of her estate — estimated at £180,000 — was to go to various children's charities after payment of death duties."

"What was this other bequest?"

"She left her jewellery to Miss Carole Stewart."

"Valued at what?"

"Well, it was insured for £8,000."

"Very nice, too," Quinn said.

Now he no longer doubted the truth of Miss Wilkinson's story. Adele must have been Bossard's mistress. If she hadn't known when their *affaire* began that he was married, she'd found out later that he was Carole's husband. And this had been her idea of conscience money.

Inspector Elvin asked, "What does that mean?"

"Just what it says. I'd like someone to leave me £8,000 worth of jewellery."

"Not if the someone was as young as Mrs. Parry. In ordinary circumstances she'd out-live you."

"In ordinary circumstances she might well have out-lived her husband," Quinn said.

Elvin bobbed his head in quick agreement. "At their best, the prospects for Michael were long term: he'd inherit £20,000 in thirty or forty years if he were still alive and — "

" — and if she hadn't changed her will in the meantime," Quinn said. "While she lived there was always that chance. So all he could be really sure of was the ten thousand pounds she'd give him for a divorce."

"Not much when you consider that she was worth a hundred and eighty thousand — not much at all."

"To him she was only worth ten thousand," Quinn said. "Unless she died before she signed the will."

Inspector Elvin used both hands to stroke his silver hair. Then he said, "Means, motive and opportunity . . . Let's go upstairs and see if Mr. Michael Pary will now tell me the truth."

11

PARRY was seated at a small table under the bedroom window with a writing pad and an open box of stationery. There were several sealed and addressed envelopes propped against the box. On the pad lay a part-written letter that he turned face down when they walked in.

He said, "I didn't hear you knock." His pale blue eyes were more afraid than angry.

"Perhaps your mind was far away," Elvin said.

"Or perhaps you didn't bother to announce yourself. Whatever you want it'll have to keep until later. I'm busy right now."

"What I want isn't the kind of thing that improves by keeping. Either we talk here or I'll have to ask you to accompany me to police headquarters

339

in Blandford. Which would you prefer?"

Without taking his eyes off Elvin's face, Parry folded the sheet of notepaper twice and pressed down the creases. Then he said, "Neither . . . but my preferences don't enter into the scheme of things, do they? I suppose you have authority for this intrusion."

He glanced at Quinn and asked, "Whose side are you on?"

Quinn said, "Your wife's. Wouldn't you say it's about time one of us started thinking of her?"

Parry folded the sheet of paper again, screwed it into a twisted roll, and then looked at it in surprise as though he had suddenly realised what he was doing. His hands were unsteady.

He said, "That's hitting below the belt."

His eyes turned to Inspector Elvin. "O.K. Now it's your turn. What's the bad news?"

Elvin said, "I have reason to believe you lied to me, Mr. Parry, when I questioned you last night. If that is so — "

"It isn't so . . . it damn' well isn't so. I can't explain what's happened but I've told you everything I know. Whether you believe it or not is up to you."

"Being aggressive won't help your cause, Mr. Parry, won't help it at all. I'd advise you — "

"Never mind the advice. How did I lie?"

"You told me your wife had gone to a place called Wood Lake when she left here last Monday afternoon."

"Well, what's wrong with that?"

"Everything, Mr. Parry. I've spoken to the people there and they assure me she hasn't been near the place this week."

Parry shut his eyes and held them tight shut as though in sudden pain. Then he looked down at the writing pad.

With the barest movement of his lips, he said, "That's not my fault. I only told you what she told me. When she left here I was under the impression she was going there and since then I've had no reason to think otherwise. If I had, why would I have gone to Blandford to meet the bus?"

Elvin nodded. In a tone that was no longer agreeable, he said, "You may think that's a rhetorical question, Mr. Parry, but I assure you it isn't. We'll come back to it later. Right now I want to know if you have any idea where she went last Monday afternoon?"

"No. She phoned for a car to take her to Blandford . . . and I carried her bag out to the taxi. If you like you can ask the car hire people — "

"I've already asked them. They confirm what you say. But of course they don't know where she went after she got out of the taxi."

"Well, neither do I."

"Then I can tell you," Elvin said. "She went to London, booked in at a West End hotel, and stayed there until

Friday morning. Can you explain why she should do that when she'd given you to understand she was going to Wood Lake?"

Michael Parry brushed up the ends of his moustache and stared at the screwed-up sheet of notepaper while he thought. At last, he said, "I can only suggest that she changed her mind . . . for some reason."

"Can you also suggest the reason?"

"No."

"Did she say she would be returning on the bus that arrived at eight-ten Friday evening?"

"Yes, she did."

"And she asked you to meet the bus?"

"Yes."

"After she left that day you didn't see her or have any communication from her?"

"No."

Inspector Elvin said, "Very well. Let us move on. We know where she was all week and that she didn't leave the hotel in London until yesterday morning. Between then and last night when she was found dead in this house, her movements haven't been traced. She wasn't on any bus from Blandford to Castle Lammering nor did she use the car hire firm: I've checked both. So we're faced with our original question. How did she return home?"

"If I knew I'd tell you," Parry said. "I've nothing to hide."

"All right. Was she the type of woman who would accept a lift from a stranger in Salisbury — assuming she went there by train from London?"

"I don't really know . . . but I doubt it." He sounded like a man who was afraid that whatever he said would be the wrong thing.

"So do I," Elvin said.

He took his hands out of his pockets and slapped them together several times very deliberately. Then he went on, "Wouldn't it simplify matters for all of us if you were to tell me the truth?"

"I've already told you the truth. I

had nothing — nothing at all — to do with my wife's death."

"Yet you are obviously being evasive. You admitted that you had a quarrel with your wife before she went away . . . did you not?"

"No, I didn't admit any such thing. You asked me if we'd had a quarrel and I said it had been more a difference of opinion. That's hardly an admission."

"But you did quarrel . . . did you not?"

"No . . . well, not really. It was all one-sided. I spent most of the time trying to pacify her."

"I see. Would you agree that she was angry with you?"

"No, not what I'd call angry. Impatient, yes, and also somewhat distressed."

"Why was she distressed?"

"I don't really know. It was all quite silly."

Something had happened to his voice. Quinn knew he would break very soon.

Inspector Elvin asked, "What was silly?"

"Oh, she'd got herself worked up over nothing at all. Told me she had to go away and think things over."

"By that you mean her relationship with you?"

It took a considerable effort before Parry managed to say, "Well, yes."

"Did she tell you how long she proposed to be away?"

"Only until the end of the week."

"Any mention of where she was going?"

"Not" — he stumbled over the words — "not at first."

There he had to get rid of something in his throat. When he'd swallowed several times, he said, "I'd better tell you the rest of it."

"It might be a good idea," Elvin said.

"Well, I asked her where she intended to go and she said she didn't care. When I insisted on her telling me because people would think it was very peculiar if I didn't know she said I could tell them she'd gone to Wood Lake."

"Did you believe she meant to go there?"

"Well . . . no."

"But you let other people believe it. In fact, you wanted them to think so, didn't you?"

"No, it was a matter of indifference to me. All I wanted was to avoid embarrassment."

"Why should you be embarrassed because your wife had gone away for a few days? Was it because you suspected that she had no intention of coming back?"

Michael Parry didn't answer. When Elvin prompted him he swallowed again and cleared his throat and mumbled, "I didn't really think she meant it. I told her she could stay away as long as she liked but she said she'd be home on Friday and I was to meet the eight-ten bus. That's gospel truth."

"Had she on that day or on a

347

previous occasion expressed any desire for a divorce?"

Michael's right hand slid over his left and took possession of it. He stared into the distance as he said, "Yes — once or twice."

"Why did she want to put an end to your marriage?"

"She said" — his faded blue eyes sought everywhere but found no escape — "she said there was nothing between us any more. All I wanted was my creature comforts . . ."

"What else did she say?"

"Nothing much. I knew she didn't really want us to break up. It was just — just a passing mood."

"You're saying, in effect, that you refused to consider the idea of divorce?"

"Yes. After all, we got on as well as most married couples — "

"On your wife's money, Mr. Parry? Is that what you mean?"

Michael Parry flushed a dull colour. "You've no right to talk like that. I wasn't referring to money."

"Then perhaps it's time we did refer to it. She provided the wherewithal for domestic and other expenses . . . did she not?"

"That's the way she wanted it. She was a wealthy woman . . . and she always said it made no difference which one of us paid the bills . . . and so on."

"By so on, you mean every penny that both of you needed for food, clothing, and shelter and also your own pocket money . . . don't you?"

There was nothing that Parry could say. With a drawn look on his face he turned to stare out of the window.

Now Quinn knew part of the truth. It wasn't pleasant to see a man like Michael stripped naked of all pretence. *. . . The poor devil depended on Adele to preserve his image. Life would've been intolerable if he'd thought people felt pity for him — pity and a measure of contempt because his wife had left him for another man. Probably he knew she was being unfaithful but* *he could turn a blind eye to that. What he wouldn't tolerate was public ridicule . . .*

Elvin clothed the thought in words. He said, "Your wife had a lover, Mr. Parry, hadn't she?"

Parry twisted round slowly. He had a beaten look.

"That's a lie . . . just a dirty lie."

"I'm afraid it isn't. All my information leads me to that one conclusion. And I'm of the opinion that you knew it . . . didn't you?"

"No. And I'm not going to let — "

"But you weren't meaning to do anything about it. So long as this other man kept your wife happy, you could pretend you didn't know. You wanted things to go on as they were. From your point of view it was a convenient arrangement all round . . . very convenient."

In a dry voice, Parry said, "Unless you've got proof of that I can make a lot of trouble for you. And don't think I won't."

"But you can't, Mr. Parry. It happens to be true. I have a witness to your wife's association with another man. I also know she was prepared to bribe you to divorce her. I'm referring, of course, to the will she'd made recently."

"Oh, are you? Well, that's not true for a start. She never made any will."

"But she did. I've spoken to Mr. Watling of Cockburn, Watling and Company, her solicitors. He was instructed by your wife to draw up a will and also draft an agreement in which she undertook to pay you the sum of £10,000 if you would divorce her."

With a look of growing awareness in his eyes, Parry asked, "When was all this done?"

"Last Thursday. She told Mr. Watling she'd return on Monday to sign the documents. Meanwhile she'd discuss the terms with you over the week-end."

"And you think" — a nerve twitched in one of Parry's eyelids — "you think she did talk to me about it. You just refuse to believe that I never heard from her after she left here last Monday."

Inspector Elvin said, "The facts make it difficult for me to believe anything you say. When I wish to check your movements yesterday I find no corroboration at all. Probably you can tell me the name of the barber in Poole: probably he can confirm that you went there for a haircut. But that accounts for only a short part of the morning . . . a very short part. How do I verify where you were between then and three-thirty in the afternoon?"

"I've told you over and over again. I had a few drinks in Poole, called at the Bird-in-Hand on my way home — "

"So you say. But there's no confirmation of your story . . . is there?"

Parry pushed back his chair and stood up. The twitch in his eyelid was very noticeable.

He said, "I don't have to provide

confirmation. It's your job to go looking for it."

Elvin shook his head. "You're mistaken, Mr. Parry. That isn't my job. But, as it happens, I did have inquiries made. So far I've drawn a complete blank. And I think that's because your story is a distortion of what you actually did yesterday morning."

"No, it isn't. I've told you exactly what I did from the time I left here to go to Poole. If you ask Mrs. Gregg — "

" — she'll say you left at eleven o'clock. And the barber will say you were there about eleven-thirty and left some time around twelve o'clock. I believe all that. It's what happened between midday and half-past two that I'm questioning."

With a raw look on his face, Parry turned to Quinn. "How do you convince a man you're telling the truth when he's already decided you're a liar?"

Quinn said, "Not by asking rhetorical

questions. If I were in your position I'd try absolute frankness, no matter how much embarrassment it caused me."

"Dammit, I have been frank! But he's got an idea in his head and nothing I say will make him budge from it."

"You're wrong," Elvin said. His voice held an underlying threat. "However, I'll tell you my idea and we'll see what Mr. Quinn thinks of it. All right?"

"Now, that's a rhetorical question if ever I heard one," Parry said. "Anybody would think I could stop you saying or doing what you like."

"Very well. Here's what I've had in mind ever since I spoke to your wife's solicitor this morning. I suspect that you drove from Poole to Salisbury where you met her at the station. On your way home she told you the terms of the will she'd asked Mr. Watling to draft . . ."

Parry stood listening with his mouth open. In his eyes, Quinn saw neither admission nor denial.

" . . . If she was on the train that gets in at twelve fifty-five you could've got back here by about a quarter to two. That would have allowed you time to give your wife a glass of drugged brandy, wait for the drug to take effect, and still be at the Bird-in-Hand before two-thirty. Do you understand what I'm saying?"

In a bewildered voice, Michael Parry said, "No, I don't. You've got me going round in circles. Didn't you tell me last night that she must've taken the stuff about half past three?"

"Estimates of this kind are never very reliable," Elvin said. "It's quite possible that Dr. Bossard was inaccurate by an hour — or even more — in arriving at the approximate time of your wife's death. If so, his estimate of the time the drug was administered would be equally wrong."

Parry felt for the chair behind him and sat down as though he were suddenly very tired. Then he looked up at the inspector and asked, "Do you believe this . . . really believe it?"

"Not altogether. But after making all due allowance I think it's a fair reconstruction of what may have taken place."

"Maybe it is. Maybe someone did meet Adele at Salisbury and bring her home. But I wasn't the one. I never saw her again after she left here last Monday afternoon."

His eyes lifted wearily to Quinn's face. "How about you? Do you agree with the official line?"

Quinn said, "No . . . but not because I think you're incapable of doing it. I just don't believe Dr. Bossard could've made that kind of mistake."

"He's only human — like the rest of us," Elvin said.

"Or even more so. Parry's wife got him to make a much more serious kind of mistake, didn't she?"

"You mustn't say things like that. If he heard you — "

"He could sue the pants off me," Quinn said. "Nobody could ever prove now that she was his mistress because she's dead. But all three of us know it's true . . . don't we?"

Michael Parry got half-way to his feet. Then he slumped back into his chair again.

In a mechanical voice, he said, "You expect me to pretend I didn't know. Well, you're wrong. I couldn't help knowing. She made no secret of it. In fact, she went out of her way to make sure I knew."

"Because she wanted you to divorce her," Quinn said.

"Yes. She needed sex like other people need to eat and drink . . . and yet it's funny — " He broke off with a little humourless laugh.

Inspector Elvin asked, "What's funny?"

"The way she worried about her reputation. You didn't know her so you can't appreciate how absurd it was. She'd sleep with a man after knowing him for five minutes but at heart she was middle-class respectability.

Fornicate three times a day with the milkman, the postman and the family doctor but don't let the neighbours find out or they'll talk." He laughed again.

"A doctor has even more reason to be afraid of people finding out," Quinn said.

Parry looked up, his eyes full of contempt. He said, "No, not Bossard. There was nothing for him to worry about. So long as a doctor isn't named as co-respondent he has no reason to be afraid. And Bossard knew I wouldn't divorce my wife."

"How did he know?"

"By using his own common sense. She's bound to have told him I was aware of what was going on . . . and yet I didn't do anything about it. I let my wife behave like a whore because I didn't want to give up the soft living she provided."

With a sick look on his face he stared up at Inspector Elvin. "You asked me to be frank. Well, that's the whole unabridged story of my life. If you go on asking questions I'll know it's because you enjoy seeing me crucify myself."

Elvin said, "I don't enjoy it, Mr. Parry, I don't enjoy it one little bit. But in my job I have to take the rough with the smooth. Good day to you."

12

NEIL FORD arrived back in time for the evening meal. He seemed to be in a more affable mood and exchanged a few words with Quinn as though there had been no unpleasantness between them.

Parry didn't join the others. He said he wanted to post his letters and so he'd take a walk down to the village. If he felt hungry he would have a bite to eat later.

Carole was subdued, Irene Ford talkative but vague. She kept harking back to the subject of Adele's death and how terrible it was for the family and what people must be saying . . . on and on as though it were a compulsion neurosis.

Eventually Neil Ford rounded on her. " . . . For God's sake, leave it alone, will you? We feel bad enough as it is without you making it worse. Anybody would think you got pleasure out of raking the whole thing up, over and over again."

She put a hand to her face as though he had struck her. She said, "How can you say that . . . to me of all people? You seem to forget I was the one — "

With tears in her eyes she got up from the table and half ran towards the staircase. Carole called after her but she didn't answer. As she went stumbling upstairs she was wailing " . . . Oh dear . . . oh dear . . . oh dear . . . "

Ford said, "Now I've done it. Each time it happens I swear I'll know better next time but I never learn."

He looked at Quinn. "I can guess what you're thinking so you needn't say it."

"You can't guess," Quinn said. "So I'll tell you. Maybe you were kind of rude, but she did go on a bit. I was getting tired of it myself."

Carole said, "Don't encourage him.

361

Irene's had a most distressing experience and she's not the kind of person who finds it easy to adjust. I think she should've gone home. After what's happened this is the last place she should be."

"Michael insisted on her staying," Ford said. "Asked me not to persuade her to leave. Seems he can't bear the thought of being here alone."

"I don't blame him," Quinn said.

Ford gave Carole a quick look. She asked, "Why do you say that?"

"Why shouldn't I? There's nothing clever about it. He needs company to keep the gremlins away. It's only natural."

"Depends on what type of gremlins he's scared of," Ford said.

A withdrawn look came into Carole's face. She said, "This is all wrong. Whatever Michael's faults and failings, we've no right to sit here and condemn him for something that's no more than a suspicion. There's been a lot of talk but no one can say definitely that Adele didn't commit suicide."

"I'm not saying it was anything else," Ford said. "But Quinn knows the police aren't satisfied. And I can tell you that's really what's upsetting Irene — not so much the fact that Michael might've done it, but what people are going to say if he did."

"Oh, that's absurd!"

"All right. Have it your own way. But I ought to know her by this time."

He gave Quinn a nod. In the same off-hand voice, he said, "Take my advice and don't get married. It leads to nothing but trouble . . . as you may have noticed ever since you got here. Now I'll go and see if I can console my wife before she works herself into a state of hysterics."

When he'd gone upstairs, Carole began clearing the table. Quinn said, "Can I give you a hand with the dishes?"

"No, thanks. It's no trouble at all. I'll put them in the dishwasher and they'll be ready to stack away by the time I get back."

"Going somewhere?"

"Yes, I thought I'd make my peace with Ariadne Wilkinson. I wasn't very nice to her last night. Will you be all right for a little while on your own?"

"Don't worry about me," Quinn said. "Have fun."

She disposed of the crockery and the cutlery. When she'd switched on the dishwasher she came out of the kitchen and asked, "Have you told anyone that Geoffrey Bossard is my husband? Neil Ford, for example?"

"Neither Neil Ford nor anyone else, for example."

"Shouldn't you have told the police?"

"Yes, but I didn't."

Her wide dark eyes studied Quinn reflectively. "Any special reason?"

"I don't see that I need one. The police aren't really interested in who's married to whom."

"You know that isn't true. They

364

want all the information they can get about everybody in this house."

"Maybe so. But in my opinion it would only be confusing the issue."

"What makes you say that?"

"Because I don't think Dr. Bossard killed Adele Parry," Quinn said. "That's what you wanted me to tell you, isn't it?"

She tucked her lower lip between her teeth while she stared past Quinn at the russet glow of the sunset. Then she said, "I've never been the least bit afraid that he had anything to do with it."

"But you know she must've been the woman he entertained at your cottage that night?"

With a look of defiance, Carole said, "Yes . . . but I don't believe it happened more than that once."

"You don't believe it because you don't want to believe it," Quinn said. "As I told you last night you're still in love with him. But you're too damn' stubborn to admit it. Why not put your pride in your pocket and give him the chance to make a fresh start?"

Quinn saw the conflict in her eyes. It lasted only a moment.

Then she smiled. As though she had at last seen the answer that had been there all the time, she said, "I think I will . . . Now that Adele is dead, perhaps we can begin again."

He watched her go outside, he heard the sound of her car starting up, he saw her drive past into the light of the dying sun. And he thought he knew where she was really going.

As he listened to the dwindling murmur of the engine, he told himself, "Well, that's that. Playing Cupid without even a bow and arrow. The lads back home would say you were out of your tiny mind. Must be getting senile."

Maybe he should get away from Elm Lodge and forget about Adele Parry. Maybe the truth would only do harm . . . unless the truth exonerated her husband . . . if he were innocent of her murder . . . if she had been murdered . . .

The phone rang. It was Inspector Elvin.

" . . . Thought you'd like to hear the results of the P.M. Analysis of the stomach contents reveals that she must've had a massive dose of pentobarbitone."

"That's what's in Pembrium, isn't it?"

"The same. Based on what they found, she'd swallowed anything up to forty grains. The minimum fatal dose is thirty grains . . . and what she got was taken in conjunction with brandy. The pathologist tells me what most of us know — that alcohol acts as a potentiator which increases the effect."

"Was it the same stuff in the bottom of that brandy glass?"

"Yes . . . but no partly-dissolved gelatine in the stomach as one would expect. Somebody's been just a little bit too clever."

"Which rules out Dr. Bossard," Quinn said.

"But of course. He'd know better than to leave any capsules in the glass to make it look like suicide. I've known all along you were barking up the wrong tree."

"What made you so sure?"

"Well, for one thing, police surgeons aren't in the habit of committing murder."

"Neither are they in the habit of committing adultery — but it's been known."

Elvin said, "Now you're being slick."

"All right. Tell me the rest."

"Not much more. Pembrium is supplied in one and a half grain yellow capsules which can be opened quite simply by pulling the two halves apart. The drug itself is a white, odourless, crystalline powder with a slightly bitter taste — a very slightly bitter taste."

"Too slight to be noticed in brandy?"

"If mixed with a little milk and sugar

it would probably not be detected by the average person. When you consider that forty grains is just about a rounded teaspoonful and that Pembrium is freely soluble in alcohol . . . well, it's too easy, isn't it?"

"As you say," Quinn said. "Go on."

"I found an empty bottle in the bedside cupboard with the label of a Blandford chemist. He checked the number on the label and confirmed that the bottle had contained Pembrium capsules — twenty-five of them. They'd been prescribed for Mrs. Parry by Dr. Bossard."

Quinn said, "Good old Dr. Bossard. Wherever we go we keep falling over him."

"Don't start all that again. He happens to have been her doctor and — "

" — the prescription just happens to have been for twenty-five capsules. Twenty-five times one and a half is thirty-seven and a half . . . which is near enough the quantity that your pathologist estimated. Right?"

Inspector Elvin said, "Your arithmetic is right but not your conclusions. A doctor's entitled to prescribe sleeping pills for one of his patients."

"This doctor also prescribed something else for this patient — but you can't get it on National Health."

"You're being slick again. No one can ever prove that their relationship wasn't perfectly ethical."

"Not now," Quinn said.

He remembered the smile on Carole's face. That could have been what she had meant.

" *. . . Now that Adele is dead, perhaps we can begin again.*"

The phone was saying " . . . This is what a bachelor doctor's always up against. He's an easy target for gossip while there are women like Miss Wilkinson around. Bossard should get himself a wife."

★ ★ ★

The sun went down and dusk settled in the elm trees. Quinn chain-smoked and thought about Michael Parry and wondered how long it took him to post a bundle of letters.

. . . Could be he's having a booze-up at the Bird-in-Hand. Hasn't had a drink all day so far as I've seen . . . or last night, either. Maybe he doesn't need the stuff any more. Maybe he only drank so as to forget what she and her money had made of him. Now he doesn't have to drink. Now that Adele is dead he's a new man. The world's a different place for many people now that Adele is dead . . .

It was growing dark when the phone rang again. As Quinn picked up the receiver he could hear music at the other end of the line.

Ariadne Wilkinson said, "Well, how about that? The very man I want — and don't take that the wrong way. You're not my type. I meant that it was you I wanted to speak to."

Her facetious gabble distracted and

irritated him. He said, "About what?"

"Oh, do I detect a certain lack of warmth?" she gave a high-pitched laugh. "We're not in a very good temper, are we?"

Quinn said, "Look, I don't want to appear rude but I'm expecting a very important phone call . . . so if there's anything you have to say would you make it as quick as you can?"

"Important . . . dear, dear. How do you know this phone call isn't important?"

"I don't. And I never will unless you get to the point."

"For a man who doesn't want to be rude" — now there was a touch of sarcasm in her deep, masculine voice — "you're doing pretty well. It would serve you right if I didn't tell you . . . hold on a minute while I turn the radio down. It's making a terrible row . . ."

The music in the background stopped abruptly. When she came back to the phone she went running on as though there had been no interruption.

" . . . Have you ever wondered why they call it incidental music when it's so loud you can hear nothing else but? You set the volumes at just the right level to hear speech comfortably and next thing you know it's making enough noise to bounce the pictures off the walls."

She laughed again. Then she asked, "Why didn't anyone tell me Adele must've been drugged before half past three in the afternoon? I thought she'd come home much later."

Quinn was in no mood to exchange gossip with someone like Ariadne Wilkinson. He said, "Does it make any difference what time she came home?"

"But, of course! Do you remember I asked you how you thought Michael would've felt if he'd found out what was going on behind his back?"

"Yes, but I don't see — "

"Because you don't know what I know . . . even though I've explained how I saw Dr. Bossard making his frequent visits to Elm Lodge."

"All right. So I don't know. But you can soon remedy that, can't you?"

"Ah, how about that? The man's not in such a hurry to hang up now . . . but he's a devil for demanding proof."

"I haven't got the foggiest idea what you're talking about," Quinn said.

"That's too bad. I'd be glad to put you in the picture . . . but I don't want to occupy your telephone when you're anxiously waiting for an important phone call . . . ha-ha."

Quinn said, "You've already occupied the telephone to no purpose."

"Not quite. I wasn't sure my information was correct about Adele being put to sleep before half past three. Now you've confirmed it."

"So?"

"So all I have to do is ask a couple of pertinent — or impertinent — questions and I'll have enough proof to sink a ship."

"Proof of what?"

"Oh, no. I'm going to teach you a lesson in good manners. Next time you won't be so abrupt with a lady."

"Now you're being silly," Quinn said.

"Not me."

She was laughing as her voice receded from the phone. "If you'd been more patient I'd have let you share my secret. So it's the well-known Mr. Quinn of Fleet Street who's silly . . ."

He tried to break in but he was too late. The line went dead before he managed to say a word.

★ ★ ★

At eleven o'clock he got tired of sitting alone in the big empty living-room and decided to go to bed. Carole had not yet returned. Michael Parry was still out posting his letters.

As Quinn went upstairs he heard voices talking in Mrs. Ford's bedroom. The house was very quiet and he caught an odd phrase now and again, a few words that made him tread cautiously as he approached their door. Then he heard the name Adele.

A moment later, Neil Ford said, "Don't raise your voice. Carole's gone out but that fellow Quinn's downstairs and he's got ears like an elephant. That's why I didn't like the idea of him staying here over the week-end. In his job he just loves to rake up dirt."

"But there wasn't anything wrong — really wrong — between you and her, was there?"

"No, of course there wasn't! How many times have you got to ask? I thought I'd explained the whole thing. Don't you trust me? Don't you know I wouldn't let you down?"

"Yes, dear, I do know. But it's come as a shock all the same . . . especially after what I've been through since yesterday. I wish you hadn't told me."

"What else could I do? You knew she'd made one or two phone calls and I was afraid you might let it out accidentally. That's all somebody like Quinn needs to hear. He's an expert at making a mountain out of a molehill."

In a snuffling voice, Irene Ford said, "But I didn't know she'd come to Ringwood several times and met you without me knowing. If only you'd told me — "

"It wasn't several times . . . just two occasions. And there was nothing to tell. At first I thought she just wanted to confide in me, to ask my advice as to what she should do about Michael, but when I discovered what she was really after I put a damn' quick stop to it. You don't think I'd let a woman like her make a fool of me, do you?"

"No, of course not. I wouldn't ever believe you could do a thing like that . . . so you don't need to reassure me. But I'm scared, Neil, terribly scared. What if they find out?"

Ford said, "There's nothing for them to find out — nothing at all. I keep telling you that."

"Yes, I know, dear. But supposing

somebody saw you and her together — "

"Nobody saw us. So long as we don't say anything the whole business can be forgotten."

"But you can't be sure. If they learn the kind of woman she was and then hear you'd been seen with her they might imagine — "

"How can they? For God's sake, how can they? Just tell me that."

"I don't know," Irene Ford said miserably. "I don't know how they discover such things. I've just heard they sometimes can. And I'm afraid. You've no idea how afraid. If they should find out — and please don't be cross with me, dear — what'll they do?"

"Nothing — absolutely nothing. I've told you that already. If someone poisoned Adele it wasn't me. And that's all the police are interested in."

"You're not — worried?"

"Not in the slightest . . . so long as we keep our mouths shut and you stop looking so damn' silly. You'll make

378

people suspect we have something to hide if you don't take a hold on yourself."

"I can't help it. I've never found it easy to pretend. And I'm upset, anyway. You might not care but I was fond of Adele. I know she had a thing about men . . . but she was like a sister to me. Now you've spoiled that by telling me she wanted you to . . . well, you know. If only you hadn't — "

There Irene began to weep. Neil Ford said, "If you're going to start that again, I'll leave you to get over it by yourself. One thing I can't stand is when you turn on the waterworks."

Footsteps stamped towards the door. Quinn had just time to duck into the bathroom before Neil Ford came out, pulled the door shut with a bang, and hurried downstairs.

★ ★ ★

Footsteps in the corridor roused Quinn as he was falling asleep — the clip-clop of a woman's high heels followed by a man's heavy tread. After a whispered "Good night . . . " they went into separate rooms.

He knew the woman was Carole and the man had walked like Neil Ford. That left Parry still absent. And Quinn's watch said the time was ten past twelve.

Of course, he might have dozed off without knowing it. He hadn't heard the sound of an engine . . . and yet Carole must have returned in the car. Possibly Michael Parry was already home in bed.

Vagrant thoughts took on larger-than-life substance as sleep clouded Quinn's mind again. He wondered how long Carole and Neil Ford had been talking together downstairs . . . and what they had talked about . . . and if the way Ford looked at Carole meant anything.

He was far from being a man's man but that didn't mean to say he couldn't be attractive to women. They had their own ideas of what they liked in the opposite sex.

. . . Even intelligent women have been known to get soppy over types that the average man can spot a mile off. And Carole is no exception. I could have been wrong. There might be something between her and Ford. Maybe it wasn't Bossard who broke up the marriage. Maybe she was the one who strayed off the straight and narrow while her husband was at sea. Maybe he only had an affair with Adele Parry because he felt that what was sauce for the goose . . .

Behind the old saying, Quinn caught a glimpse of another thought . . . leading to yet another . . . and another . . . like the mirror-image that loses definition as it shrinks into infinity.

Then the cloud grew darker in his mind and the procession of thoughts were footprints in the sand at the water's edge. He saw the tide flow in under the light of the moon to fill the footprints with molten silver . . . and when the sea rolled back it took the footprints and left the smooth expanse of beach untrodden again.

One thing only remained before he fell asleep. Ariadne Wilkinson was saying " . . . *I'll have enough proof to sink a ship.*"

13

H E slept late next morning. It was nearly ten o'clock when he went downstairs.

Irene Ford was in the living-room reading one of the Sunday papers. Her eyes looked tired.

She asked him what he would like for breakfast and protested weakly when he said he'd get something for himself. As he went into the kitchen her anaemic voice was still complaining.

" . . . Oh, you shouldn't really. I think it's a shame."

Then she said in a brighter tone, "Michael hasn't come down yet. I think he must've got to bed very late. I didn't hear him come in."

Quinn said, "Where's your husband? Is he still in bed, too?"

"Oh, no. He and Carole have gone out for a stroll. They said it was too nice a day to stay indoors . . . Are you sure I can't get anything for you? I feel I shouldn't be sitting here while you make your own breakfast. It doesn't seem right for a man to do that sort of thing . . . if you know what I mean."

He didn't bother to tell her that coffee and toast presented no problem. In any case she wouldn't have heard him above the rustling of the newspaper.

While he was pouring out his coffee the phone rang. Irene Ford said, "I wonder who that can be? If it's for Michael I suppose you'll have to go upstairs and waken him. I never like to . . . well, you know what I mean."

Through the open door, Quinn saw her pick up the receiver. She said, "Yes? . . . Oh, yes, I'm a lot better now, thank you . . . well, he's upset, naturally. You wouldn't expect him to be anything else . . . "

As she listened she gave a little wriggle and felt the neck of her dress. Quinn saw the suddenly altered look on her face.

384

Then she said, "I've no idea what you're talking about and I don't believe it, either . . . when? . . . No, it's not true."

The voice on the phone made scratching distant noises. Irene said, "You shouldn't say things like that. It's not right to talk about her now she's dead. Whatever she may have done, it's nobody's business — "

There the phone whispered again. When it stopped, she said, "Please, Ariadne, we've had enough trouble already . . . you're wrong . . . no one poisoned her. I've thought about it ever since Friday night and I'm sure she did it herself . . . no, it isn't true."

She listened, her hand fumbling with the neck of her dress as though it were tight. Then she said, "I don't know. But whatever reason he had I'm sure it was all quite proper . . . Michael wouldn't do a thing like that . . . no . . . no, he's still in bed."

Moments later, the nervous, frightened look on her face changed. In a voice that Quinn had never heard her use before, she said, "I don't understand why you should want to make trouble. If you'd only let well alone . . . all right, if you insist . . . then I think you're a horrible person. Michael's never done you any harm and you've no reason — "

Quinn heard the phone click. With her mouth open, Irene turned to look at him.

"She's hung up. I was in the middle of talking to her and she hung up. I've never met such a nasty woman in all my life — not really."

"What was it all about?"

"Something I'd never have thought possible. She's got the cheek to say Adele was a friend of hers and yet she comes out with the most filthy suggestions. Tells me Dr. Bossard was Adele's lover and he used to come here often . . . and eventually Michael found out — "

" — and killed her," Quinn said.

Irene Ford put down the receiver.

With a wriggle of her bony shoulders, she said, "Yes. That's what she says must've happened. Isn't it outrageous? Wants me to believe she's got proof, too."

"What kind of proof?"

"According to her, she saw Michael returning home quite a bit before half past three on Friday and so he'd have had time to drug Adele. Do you know what she means?"

"Yes . . . but I don't necessarily believe it. When you said ' . . . if you insist,' what had she asked you to do?"

"Wants me to tell Michael she's coming here this afternoon with Dr. Bossard so as to bring the whole thing out into the open. Why she wants to do this to Michael, I just don't know — not really. Perhaps it makes her feel important . . . or perhaps she was jealous of Adele all the time . . . if you know what I mean."

Quinn said, "Only too well. There's

no stopping a woman like Ariadne Wilkinson once she gets started."

Irene wriggled again. The old nebulous, fearful look was back in her eyes.

"I wish I knew what to do. Even if Adele was carrying-on with Dr. Bossard it wasn't his fault. He's a bachelor and she was very beautiful . . . and I can see how he'd be tempted . . . especially if she wouldn't leave him alone. Now it'll all come out and he'll be ruined because he'll have to give evidence . . . won't he?"

"If Michael Parry is tried for the murder of his wife," Quinn said.

She touched the phone, drew her hand away, and shivered. "Are you going to tell Michael what she's threatening to do?"

"Why not? It's only fair to warn him."

"Do you think" — she faltered and her eyes lifted reluctantly to Quinn's face — "do you think he did it — really?"

"I'm not a judge and jury," Quinn said.

He told himself she didn't care a brass button for Michael Parry. The fear he could see in her eyes was for her husband.

. . . Might be a good idea if Elvin checked up on Neil Ford's whereabouts on Friday afternoon. Maybe he picked her up at Salisbury and brought her home. Maybe she'd finished with Bossard and had dug her claws into Ford, instead . . . and he wanted to be free because he'd got someone new. And that's where I came in . . .

Carole . . . She'd had the time and the opportunity. But not to protect her ex-husband. Ford was now the best bet. Either he'd done it himself . . . or Carole had done it for him. And if Ariadne Wilkinson could be persuaded to tell a lie in the cause of justice, the right one might be bluffed into an admission of guilt.

Irene Ford said, "You're hiding something from me . . . aren't you?"

In the sunlight from the long panoramic window she looked cold.

"Only a passing thought," Quinn said.

"Won't you tell me?"

"It's not worth the telling. Maybe I'll explain later. Meantime, you go and do some sunbathing until Carole and your husband get back."

"What about you?"

Quinn said, "I'm going to finish my breakfast. Then I'll rouse Michael and give him the glad news that he can expect visitors this afternoon."

★ ★ ★

Dr. Bossard's housekeeper took the call. She told Miss Wilkinson that the doctor was upstairs but she would go and fetch him if it were urgent. Miss Wilkinson said it was very urgent.

The housekeeper was present when Dr. Bossard spoke on the telephone. She heard him say he would do his best to call on Miss Wilkinson at twelve-thirty, but he might be a little late as he had another visit to make. His housekeeper also heard him tell Miss Wilkinson to do nothing hasty until he got there.

★ ★ ★

Ten yards short of the gate he backed off the road and reversed into a cart track overgrown with tufts of grass and weeds and straggling hedges. When he was as close to the nearside as possible, he got out and collected his medical bag from the front passenger seat and made sure he had a pad of prescription forms in his pocket.

With the bag pulling at his arm he trudged along the narrow road to Rose Cottage. The wicket gate was unlatched. He pushed it open with his knee and walked heavily up the tiled path and through a rustic arch smothered in flowers which screened the front door from the sun.

There was nothing to be heard

inside the cottage. All around him lay the quiet of the countryside on a hot summer's day interwoven with the grumbling drone of a bee, the chirping of crickets in a cornfield across Northwood Lane, the far-off barking of a dog up on the hillside. Overlaying the sounds that he knew so well he could hear a car engine idling at a fast speed somewhere behind the house.

When he had tugged at the old-fashioned bell pull without result he rapped on the door. After he had waited another ten seconds he rapped again. Then he tried the knob.

The door opened. He saw an empty hall, a table with a vase of red roses, a doorway through which sunlight spilled from a window at the back of the house.

He took a step inside and called out, "Miss Wilkinson! Are you there, Miss Wilkinson?"

The house was as silent as though it had been unoccupied for a long time.

There was only the bubbling noise of a car exhaust, muffled and yet amplified behind closed doors.

He looked in another room, found it also empty, and glanced at his watch. It was just after twelve-thirty. As he stood listening, all he could hear was the persistent murmur of a car.

His bag was heavy and he realised he had no need to carry it from room to room. He placed it on a chair, massaged his fingers, and again called out, "Are you there, Miss Wilkinson?"

His voice seemed to linger in the stillness. If she had been anywhere in the cottage she would have been bound to hear him.

He told himself he had spent enough time. With the noise of the car growing louder and louder inside his head he went into the tiny sunlit kitchen and opened the back door.

A cinder path cut through the well-tended vegetable garden, turned at right-angles past an apple tree in blossom, and ended outside a brick garage. From there the cart track wound its way between high, overgrown hedges to Northwood Lane.

He could see his own car at the foot of the track, its rear bumper flashing in the sun, when he reached the garage. There was no sound from Northwood Lane, no sound from anywhere except the drumming of a car exhaust behind the double doors of the garage.

The doors were locked. With his mouth close to the leading edge, he shouted, "Are you in there, Miss Wilkinson? This is Dr. Bossard. Open the door."

For half a minute he stood listening to the rhythmic beat of the exhaust, his mind filled with the knowledge that he would get no answer. Then he sprinted round to the rear of the garage.

There were two windows. He had to make a cowl with his linked hands to shut out the reflection of the sky before he was able to see inside.

The glass was dirty and his own reflection kept getting in the way but he could see the radiator grill and the head-lamps of Miss Wilkinson's Morris Oxford, a glimpse of the windscreen. The bonnet was raised and a piece of yellow cloth lay on one of the front wings. Every few seconds the vibration of the idling engine caused the cloth to tremble as though it were fluttering in a current of air.

Against the left-hand wall of the garage stood a lawn mower. Near it the grass box rested end up on top of a wooden crate with compartments for bottles. Above the mower some garden tools hung from nails driven into the brickwork.

He leaned nearer and cupped his hands more closely around his eyes. Now he got a view of something else. Between the offside front wheel of the car and the wall a woman lay huddled on the floor, her head resting on the roller of the lawnmower.

She was a plumpish, fair-haired woman dressed in blue jeans and a yellow sweater. Her eyes were shut, her mouth was a gaping hole in her discoloured face.

That much he saw in the few seconds that he stood looking down at her from the dusty window. Then he ran round to the front of the garage.

There was nothing at hand to force the door. After he had tried to get his fingertips under the moulding alongside the lock he went hurrying down the track to his car.

All he found in the boot was the starting handle, the jack, and a spare fan belt. He never carried any tools. In the event of a breakdown he wouldn't have known what to do with them.

What he did know right then was that the end of the starting handle would be too thick to get between the leading edge of the garage doors — but he had to do something. So he ran back and made a dozen attempts to lever the handle into the narrow gap.

It was hopeless. He struggled with it for a couple of minutes, battering at the edge of the door until the moulding was chipped and scarred, and then he threw the handle on the ground and set off at a run down the track to Northwood Lane.

The nearest house was a quarter of a mile from Rose Cottage. He got into his car, fumbled in every pocket for the ignition key, and then at last bumped and jolted his way out of the cart track.

That was when he caught sight of Quinn less than a hundred yards from the cottage. Bossard scrambled from the car and shouted, "I need your help! Hurry, man, hurry!"

Quinn broke into a run. As he reached the car, he asked, "What's the trouble? Why all the excitement?"

"Miss Wilkinson asked me to call at half-past twelve. When I got here I found her lying on the garage floor . . . and the engine of her car is running. Can't get the door open. Tried using my starting handle but it won't work."

"Aren't there any windows?"

"Yes, but they're fitted with wired glass. Take a long time to get in that way. Maybe between us we can force the door."

"What kind of tools have you got?"

"Only this thing and a jack. But there's no time to waste and we must try."

Quinn said, "All right, I'll take the jack. Let's go."

As they ran side by side, Bossard asked, "What're you doing here, anyway?"

"I was going to call on Miss Wilkinson, too."

"Why?"

"She phoned Elm Lodge this morning and in view of what she said to Mrs. Ford I thought I'd like to chat with her."

"What did she say?"

"Something to the effect that she knew who killed Adele Parry."

Dr. Bossard slowed momentarily and took a deep breath. "Did she, indeed? Now that is interesting."

They reached the garage. Quinn said, "Let me have a go . . . "

He used the jack as a hammer and smashed blow after blow at the strip of moulding close to the lock until part of the wood tore off and left a space wide enough to take the end of the starting handle. Then he said, "Stick the handle in there, Doctor, and I'll bash it farther in so as to give us plenty of leverage . . . that's right."

Two or three blows were enough. Bossard took hold with both hands and set himself.

He said, "Stand back out of the way in case this thing flies open suddenly."

Quinn moved aside as the door creaked and groaned. Bossard used every ounce of his strength in one tremendous final effort — an effort that brought the sweat out on his face. He saw the gap widen . . . the edge of the door bulge outwards . . . the wood begin to split vertically . . .

Then the tongue of the lock broke free with a report like a pistol shot and the door sprang open. It flung him back, his arms upraised to protect himself, and he'd have toppled over if Quinn hadn't caught hold of him.

Quinn said, "We'd better open the other side and let some of the fumes out."

As he unfastened the top and bottom bolts, he added, "Don't go rushing in yet. Give it a few seconds for the air to clear."

Dr. Bossard said, "We can't afford the time. Take a good breath and cover your nose and mouth with your handkerchief. While you're switching off the engine I'll drag her out. And, for heaven's sake, don't loiter."

He waited outside until Quinn was reaching into the car for the ignition key. Then he rushed past him to the spot where Miss Wilkinson lay sprawled on the floor beside the lawnmower.

He heard the drumming noise of the engine stop. With the stench of burned oil stinging his eyes, he got his hands under her armpits, lifted her clear of the mower, and dragged her backwards to the doorway, her feet scraping on the concrete.

When he stumbled outside, Quinn took her by the legs and they carried her over to a rectangle of lawn behind the garage. Bossard said, "While I'm attending to her you get on the phone and dial 999. Tell them I want an ambulance here as quickly as possible . . . oh, and emphasise that they're to bring both oxygen and carbon dioxide. Got that?"

Quinn said, "Sure, I'll tell them. You carry on."

He trotted along the cinder path and went in by the back door of the cottage. As Dr. Bossard began artificial respiration he told himself it was a waste of time . . . but he had to go through the motions.

She had no pulse and her colour was bad. Another case of a stupid person who'd started the engine of her car while the garage doors were shut. That, more or less, was what the

Coroner would say — unless it came out that she'd said she knew who had poisoned Adele Parry. Then he might ask some more questions . . . which could be embarrassing.

. . . Not that it will make much difference in the end. Everybody knows she wallowed in malicious gossip whether it had any basis in fact or not. She was a mean woman all her life. Now she looks mean even in death. I doubt if anyone will shed a tear. And a few people with something to hide will feel a lot easier in mind . . .

Quinn came back. He said, "Ambulance is on its way. How's she doing?"

"Too early to say yet. In a case like this you just keep on working and hope for the best."

"If you get tired, show me what to do and I'll take over for a while."

"That shouldn't be necessary," Bossard said. "I hope the ambulance will be here before then. But thanks all the same."

As he rocked to and fro, compressing

Miss Wilkinson's chest in a regular rhythm, he added, "If you want something to do, take a look in the garage and see if you can find any reason for her being in there . . . but don't touch anything. Just look around."

"O.K."

"And make sure the air's fit to breathe. Swing the doors backwards and forwards to get rid of the carbon monoxide. No need to go rushing in — unless you fancy getting what she got."

Quinn looked down at Ariadne Wilkinson's blotched and lifeless face. It could have been an accident . . . but for someone it might be a very fortunate accident.

. . . Even if she didn't realise the danger of letting the engine run in an enclosed place without ventilation, why were the garage doors shut, anyway? It's a hot day — a damned hot day. Assuming she actually was messing about with the car, why should she

have locked herself in? You'd imagine she'd want all the fresh air she could get . . .

"No, I don't," Quinn said. "I can think of better ways of dying. And if you ask me she's had her chips."

The ambulance arrived fifteen minutes later. Miss Wilkinson still showed no sign of response.

When they had taken her away, Dr. Bossard asked, "Have you found anything that explains how this happened?"

Quinn said, "Well, it could be she was checking the oil in the automatic transmission. The long dipstick had been taken out and wiped clean and there was an empty oil-can standing on the battery with the cap off."

"Is it the kind of thing a woman would do?"

"If she was interested in the mechanical side of her car — yes. Not that you have to be clever. You set the lever on the steering column in position P and let the engine idle fairly fast for several minutes to warm up. Then you check the dipstick and top up as required. That's the whole job."

"How do you come to be so knowledgeable?"

"I'm not. Just interested. How long would it take for her to be overcome by the fumes?"

"In a closed garage, not long. Five or six minutes might've been enough. She'd almost certainly not realise what was happening until it was too late."

"But, if she'd left the doors open, she'd have been all right?"

"Probably. The exhaust gets away and so there's no dangerous build-up of carbon monoxide."

Quinn said, "Wonder why she locked herself in? On a cold day you'd expect it, but not on a day like this."

"Maybe she did it from force of habit," Bossard said. "Women sometimes feel nervous unless the door's locked. And this place is fairly isolated."

"Yes, that's true."

While Bossard watched him Quinn walked over to the garage door and studied the lock. It was hanging loose.

When at last he looked round, he said, "Yes, it might've been that."

"Might've been what?"

"She could've got locked in accidentally, if the door had swung shut, because it's a spring lock. Not that she couldn't have got out again without any trouble . . . but she might not have bothered if she was busy with the car."

"That's probably the answer," Bossard said. "However, it's not our problem. A Coroner's jury will decide . . . If you want to go, don't wait for me. I'll have to stay here until the police arrive."

Quinn said, "Then I'll be off. May see you later."

He'd got as far as the wicket gate when he stopped and looked back. "There's just one thing . . . "

"What's that?"

"Well, it would take a fair gust of wind to swing that door shut and there hasn't even been the slightest breeze all

406

morning. So either she did it herself because she liked the hot stink of oil and petrol in a stifling garage . . . or someone else shut it. What do you think?"

With a look of disapproval, Dr. Bossard said, "I think you should leave this sort of thing to people who are more qualified. And didn't you yourself say she was checking the oil in the automatic transmission of her car?"

"I said she could have been," Quinn said. "I didn't say she was. If she's dead her death will have come as a merciful release — for several people in and around Castle Lammering."

Bossard shook his head. "That's a wild allegation. You're suggesting — "

"No, I'm not. I'm making a plain statement of fact."

"You shouldn't listen to gossip."

"What's happened to her isn't gossip. It's a very convenient accident."

"There's no evidence to show it was anything more than that."

Very hastily, Bossard went on. "And

don't twist my words. I didn't mean it was convenient. From all I've seen she was overcome by exhaust fumes. Perhaps she realised her danger and tried to get out but hadn't enough strength to do so. Carbon monoxide causes extreme muscular weakness. When she fell she struck her head on the lawnmower . . . and that finished any chance she might've had of escape."

Quinn said, "That's your version. I'll admit it's very plausible, too."

He opened the wicket gate and went out. When he'd fastened the latch he looked back again.

"Now I'll tell you mine. Ariadne Wilkinson knew too much. What was worse, she talked too much. So she had an accident that stopped her talking any more. Simple, Doctor, isn't it?"

Dr. Bossard shook his head again. In a tone of dismissal, he said, "That doesn't mean it's necessarily true."

"You're entitled to your own opinion," Quinn said. "But I'm sticking to mine. I always prefer a simple explanation."

14

HE got back to the house at half-past one. Carole Stewart was alone in the living-room.

She said, "You're just in time. I was about to have lunch."

"Where's everybody else?"

"Well, Irene told me Michael's gone to the Bird-in-Hand for a drink . . . so we won't see him until after they're shut. I've only just got in myself."

"Enjoy your walk?"

With her mouth drawn in, Carole said, "No. I should've known better than to go out with Mister Neil Ford. His idea of a walk is to get behind the nearest hedge with an obliging female."

Quinn said, "I could say it's your own fault . . . but I won't. What did you do?"

"I gave him a smack across the face

that he won't forget in a hurry. Then I went for a walk by myself until I'd cooled off. If I'd come straight back here I'd have been tempted to tell Irene exactly what I thought of her precious husband."

"You might be doing her a favour if you did. What time was it when you left Ford?"

"Oh, I don't know. Twelve o'clock, perhaps."

"Any idea where he went?"

"No . . . and I don't care, either. When he started pawing me I could have killed him."

"You seem to have been unlucky with the men you've met recently," Quinn said. "You told me you didn't like being pawed when I kissed you at Charlie Hinchcliffe's party."

She looked uncomfortable. "That was different. I only meant it as a figure of speech."

"Good job, too. If you'd taken a hefty swipe at me I'd have been out for a week. I felt dizzy enough that night, as it was. And, talking about being dizzy, where's precious husband's wife?"

After a moment's thought, Carole said, "Oh, you mean Irene. She's gone out."

"Where did she go?"

"To find Neil. I think she guessed there was something wrong when I came back alone. I hadn't been here five minutes before she suddenly decided she needed some exercise. I heard her say it was time for lunch and she'd walk down to meet him . . . but you know the vague way she rambles from one thing to another."

Quinn said, "Yes, I know. Did she tell you what time Michael went out?"

"Before twelve . . . I think. She mentioned something about him having to wait for the pub to open."

"Funny how I didn't see him. After I'd wandered around for a while I called in at the Bird-in-Hand after twelve o'clock . . . and I didn't leave until almost twelve-thirty. But Michael never showed up while I was there. Maybe he didn't actually say he was going for a drink but Irene took it for granted."

A little frown narrowed Carole's eyes. She said, "It's possible . . . Why all these questions, anyway? Has Inspector Elvin asked you to keep a check on everybody's movements?"

"No, this is entirely my own idea," Quinn said. "Nevertheless, when he hears the news, he'll want to know where you all were this morning between twelve o'clock and half-past."

"What news?"

"About Miss Wilkinson. After I left the Bird-in-Hand I decided to call on her. When I got there I found Dr. Bossard trying to break into the garage. He asked me to help him force the door because she was locked inside and the engine of her car was running."

Carole put a hand to her mouth. In a thin voice, she said, "Oh, no . . . "

Quinn said, "I'm afraid it was oh yes.

We got her out eventually, phoned for an ambulance, and she was taken to hospital. Not that anybody could do much for her. I'm quite sure she was already dead when we forced open the garage door."

After a long silence, Carole asked, "Why do you say the inspector will want to know where we were between twelve and half past?"

There was a look of horror in her eyes — a look that Quinn couldn't believe was assumed. He said, "Because I'd say she must've been lying in the garage at least half an hour. She'd been hit over the head and locked in the garage no later than twelve o'clock, in my opinion."

"So that means you think — "

"Yes, I do. I think she was murdered by one of three people — the one who killed Adele Parry. It's a question of choosing between Mrs. Parry's husband, her doctor and her latest lover. Has anyone told you that Miss Wilkinson phoned early on this morning and said she knew who poisoned Adele?"

Carole said, "No." She sounded as though she had something in her throat.

"Well, I was having breakfast in the kitchen when she spoke to Mrs. Ford. The gist of it was that she'd be coming here this afternoon with some kind of proof. I passed that on to Michael . . . and I've no doubt Mrs. Ford told her husband when he came back after you smacked his face."

"But he wasn't in the house — "

"He could've been and gone. And if he's the one, we know where he went."

In the same difficult voice, Carole asked, "Did you mean Neil when you talked about Adele's latest lover?"

"Yes. I heard him trying to explain to his wife that he'd been the victim of a designing female and just managed to get away from her with his chastity intact."

A car changed gear at the foot of

414

the long climb up from the village. Carole walked to the window and stood looking out, her sleek dark hair glistening in the sunlight, her pretty hands clasped tightly together.

Quinn still thought she was a cute little girl. Pity that things couldn't have been different. Now she would have to work out her own salvation.

With her back towards him, Carole said, "If you suspect it was Neil, why drag anybody else into it? Michael, for example, has gone through a lot and — "

"Michael, for example, doesn't mean two hoots to you," Quinn said. "All you're concerned about is dear Geoffrey. You'll do anything to protect him, won't you?"

She swung round. "Well, after all, he is my husband."

"Taken you long enough to think of that . . . hasn't it?"

"Perhaps. But I know now. Whatever's happened doesn't matter. I intend to stand by him."

Quinn said, "Three hearty British cheers . . . With Adele Parry dead, he doesn't need your wifely support. Michael can't sue for divorce and anyone who dared suggest that Dr. Bossard's relationship with his late patient wasn't strictly ethical would risk an action for criminal slander. So he's in the clear. Not a breath of suspicion attached to him . . . now that Ariadne Wilkinson's had her mouth shut, too."

With contempt in her eyes, Carole said, "I wish I hadn't felt sorry for you that night at the party. Everything you say is an insinuation. Why are you so anxious to make trouble for him?"

"Someone killed Miss Wilkinson. And it's as likely to have been your Dr. Bossard as anybody else."

"How? You told me she must've been lying in the garage for at least half an hour. If he'd only just got there — "

"That's his story," Quinn said. "Who saw him arrive? Who's to say he hasn't been hanging around since before twelve o'clock . . . or that this wasn't his second visit to Rose Cottage?"

The car reached the top of the rise. As it rounded the elm trees, Carole said, "How does anyone know you weren't paying a second visit? If it could be shown that you had a motive . . . oh, this is absurd! I'd better watch out or you'll make me as bad as you are and — "

She broke off as the car pulled up outside. Then she asked, "Why are you looking like that? What did I say?"

Quinn said, "You've just made me realise something. The obvious motive isn't always the real one."

"Is that supposed to be a profound remark?"

"More profound than you know." As the door-bell chimed, he added, "They say 'When in doubt, ask a policeman.' So now's your chance. That's Inspector Elvin at the door. He's got Sergeant Taylor with him and there's a uniformed driver in the car . . . so I'd say this is no social call . . . "

Elvin came in briskly, gave Quinn a nod, and said good afternoon to Carole Stewart. " . . . I suppose you've heard about Miss Wilkinson?"

"Yes, Mr. Quinn told me."

"I see . . . You've already met Sergeant Taylor, haven't you? No? Well, he's here to assist me."

Sergeant Taylor mumbled some greeting, twiddled his hat, and then stared up at the ceiling, his big heavy feet impassive. Under the point of his chin there was a trace of dried blood where he had cut himself shaving.

Carole asked, "Any possibility it might've been an accident?"

"Oh, there's always that possibility — always." Elvin looked at Quinn. "But the doctor tells me you don't think so . . . m-m-m?"

"No. And I'll go on not thinking so until we know where Parry, Ford and Bossard were from some time before twelve o'clock until twelve-thirty."

Inspector Elvin pondered for a moment, his head tilted as though he were listening for any sound from upstairs. Then he said, "I see . . . Well, that shouldn't be very difficult. Dr. Bossard will be along shortly and we'll see what he has to say. Meantime, let's ask Mr. Parry and Mr. Ford . . . shall we?"

"They're not here," Quinn said.

"Indeed? When are they expected back? Do you know, Miss Stewart?"

Carole said, "All I can tell you is that Michael is supposed to have gone to the Bird-in-Hand and Mr. Ford went out for a walk."

"How long ago?"

"Just after half past nine."

The inspector looked at his watch. "Nearly two o'clock . . . Four hours is a lot of walking on a hot day. Of course, he may be another one who's sampling the wine of the country. Do you think that's likely?"

"I've no idea," Carole said.

"Then shall we ask his wife?"

"She's not here, either. She went out about half an hour ago."

"Indeed? Do you know where?"

"To see if there was any sign of her husband. She wanted to get lunch over and — "

"Don't try to cover up the truth," Quinn said. "You know she's gone to play hell with him because he got fresh with you when you were out together."

Carole said angrily, "That's the last time I'll tell you anything! What happened between Neil Ford and me is no concern of the police and I don't want it discussed."

Inspector Elvin bobbed his head in agreement. "You're quite right, Miss Stewart. It is a personal matter . . . and I can assure you I have more important things to discuss with Mr. Ford — much more important things. However, there is one question I think only you can answer . . . if you don't mind?"

"Not at all. What is it?"

420

"Just this: what time did you leave Mr. Ford — and where?"

She glanced at Quinn, her eyes still angry. Then she said, "It was before twelve o'clock. He asked me if I'd like to call in at the Bird-in-Hand for an iced lager and that's where we were going when" — she made an impatient gesture — "when he acted silly."

"I see . . . And you left him there and then?"

"Of course."

"Yes, I can understand. Where were you when this happened?"

"The other side of the village."

"How far from Miss Wilkinson's cottage in Northwood Lane?"

Carole gave Quinn another fleeting look. She said, "Just a few minutes' walk."

"You haven't seen him since you parted company?"

"No."

"Did you come straight back here?"

"No, I was very annoyed and I didn't want Mrs. Ford to see me looking

421

upset in case she guessed her husband had been making a fool of himself."

"I see . . . Were you anywhere near Northwood Lane after you left Mr. Ford?"

Carole head went back. In a stiff voice, she said, "I don't know what you mean by that, Inspector, but if you're suggesting — "

"I'm not suggesting anything," Elvin said. "The purpose of my question was to ascertain if you, perhaps, saw Mr. Ford in the neighbourhood of Northwood Lane . . . or going in that direction."

"I've no idea where he went."

Inspector Elvin stroked his silver hair and made a puckered mouth while he thought. Then he said, "Very well. Seems there's only one thing to do. I'll wait and see what Mr. Neil Ford has to say for himself."

15

IT wasn't a long wait. From his place at the window Quinn saw Michael Parry and Mr. and Mrs. Ford come in sight beyond the elm trees. They were talking together and appeared to be on very good terms. He wondered how Neil Ford had managed to persuade his wife that Carole's return alone had had an innocent explanation.

They came past the trees, the two men on either side of Irene Ford. Quinn heard her giggle at something her husband said.

Then one of them saw the police car parked outside the door and the talk stopped abruptly. With Michael walking ahead of the others they passed the window and entered the porch.

He used his key. When he came in he looked at Elvin and asked, "What is it this time?"

423

"In the light of certain information I have just received I require to ask further questions. That is why I'm here."

"Well, I have no further answers. I've said all I intend to say."

"You're under a misapprehension," Elvin said. "I haven't come to question you again."

He nodded to Neil Ford and gave Irene a smile that made her wriggle with embarrassment. "Let me introduce myself. I'm Detective-Inspector Elvin of the Blandford C.I.D . . . and my colleague is Sergeant Taylor. We are investigating the death of Mrs. Adele Parry."

Ford said, "I didn't know there was anything to investigate."

"Oh, but there is — a very great deal. And I think you can help us in our inquiries."

"Why me?" He turned on Quinn and asked in a bristling voice, "What have you been saying?"

Quinn now understood many things

that he should have seen long ago. It was no use blaming himself, too late for regret. If he had used his head, if he had listened to Ariadne Wilkinson instead of being impatient with her she wouldn't have had to die.

In a moment of time that seemed endless he could hear himself telling Dr. Bossard " . . . *I always prefer a simple explanation.*"

And now it was easy to explain why the light had been on in the nursery — so very easy. The whole thing hinged on that apparent trifle . . . and the kind of woman Adele Parry had been. Mrs. Gregg had told him. So had Irene Ford and Miss Wilkinson. But he had been too stupid to see the obvious.

. . . They served it up to you on a plate and you never saw it. Better not tell anyone or they'll know you for the dolt you are. You got bogged down with motives: first Michael Parry; then Dr. Bossard; and last night Ford added himself to the list.

Jealousy . . . fear . . . hatred . . . that's what the three of them represent . . .

The funny thing was that Ariadne Wilkinson couldn't have known. But she had held the key.

He stared back at Neil Ford and said, "I haven't been saying anything about you . . . but don't push your luck. You could be in worse trouble than — "

"I'm not in any trouble. Just keep your nose out of my affairs — that's all."

Inspector Elvin said, "I think it would be better, Mr. Ford, if you and I had a private conversation. Is there a room we can use where we won't be interrupted?"

"That isn't necessary," Ford said. "Whatever you want to talk about you can discuss it with me right here."

"In front of all these people?"

"Why not? I've got nothing to hide."

Elvin shrugged. "As you wish. I just thought you might not like Mr. Parry and your wife to learn of your

426

relationship with Mrs. Parry."

Ford's neck bulged over his collar. In a suppressed voice, he said, "This is outrageous! There was nothing between Mrs. Parry and me that anyone couldn't — "

"My information leads me to believe that you were her lover," Elvin said.

Irene Ford closed her eyes and made a choking noise. "Oh dear . . . oh dear . . . oh dear . . . oh dear . . . it's not true, it's just not true."

Elvin said, "I'm afraid it is. I tried to avoid causing you this embarrassment but your husband wouldn't let me. If you would prefer not to hear any more there is no reason why you should stay."

She didn't seem to hear. Her eyes slowly opened and she pointed a finger at her husband.

"You told me you'd only met her once or twice. Soon as you realised what she had in mind you refused to see her any more. You swore you'd never been unfaithful to me. And all the time you were lying . . . "

Michael Parry sat down and put his face in his hands. Carole looked at Quinn and then turned away. Sergeant Taylor stopped twiddling with his hat. Now he was watching Ford.

With his womanish mouth distorted, Ford said, "I didn't lie. Why should you believe a thing like that without asking him to give you proof? Go on! Ask him to prove it."

Irene dropped her hand. Like a mechanical model she jerked her head round to look at Inspector Elvin.

"Can you — can you prove it?"

"No, I can't. But only for one reason."

Ford said, "Oh, very clever. What is the reason?" His flaring anger seemed to have burned itself out.

"You know it as well as I do," Elvin said. "After Mrs. Parry died there could never be anything but circumstantial evidence that you'd had an immoral association with her — evidence which would show that Mrs. Parry had been visited by you on numerous occasions when you had no proper motive for being here."

"That's another lie."

"No, Mr. Ford, it isn't. You were seen visiting this house many times in the past — "

"Who saw me? Go on. Who was this witness?"

Quinn could hear a car on the road up from the village — a car travelling fast. Inspector Elvin must have heard it, too. He glanced at the window and paused for a moment as though listening while the sound came nearer.

Then he said, "Miss Wilkinson saw you. From her cottage there is a good view of the drive in front of this house. That is why she was attacked this morning and left in the garage with the engine of her car running."

Michael Parry's head jerked up as if it had been pulled by a string. Irene looked like a woman who was about to faint. Neil Ford seemed to have had all the breath driven out of him.

Carole looked at Quinn and he saw a question in her eyes. Before she could speak, Ford said, "You must be mad. I was nowhere near there. I've never been to her cottage. Why should I want to kill her, anyway, even if she did see me visiting Mrs. Parry . . . once or twice?"

"For the best of all motives," Elvin said. "Suppose her evidence could prove that you were responsible for Mrs. Parry's death?"

The car swung round the clump of trees and crunched its way to the porch, gravel spurting from its rear tyres and brakes squealing as it came to a halt. Dr. Bossard got out. As he hurried into the porch, Sergeant Taylor went to let him in.

And all the time, Ford stood open-mouthed, his eyes filled with confusion. At last, he said, "Maybe I'm the one who's going mad. You can't be serious. You can't really believe I killed Adele. What proof have you got? How can you say a monstrous thing like that?"

"I can prove you were here, in this house, last Friday afternoon," Elvin said.

"You're a liar! I was in Ringwood all day."

"Suppose I ask you to produce proof of that?"

Neil Ford had no opportunity to answer. In a dry, difficult voice, his wife said, "I'm his proof. He was with me all day on Friday."

She moved her thin shoulders nervously and swallowed several times. Then she repeated, " . . . all day." When she saw everybody looking at her she shrank in on herself and the light of dour determination came into her eyes.

Inspector Elvin asked, "Are you willing to swear to that, Mrs. Ford?"

She swallowed again. She said, "Yes . . . yes, I am."

He turned to Neil Ford. "Well, now, you've heard your wife say you were together all day on Friday. If she makes a written statement to that effect, and it is not true, she will be guilty of perjury. I don't need to tell you the consequences, do I?"

Ford looked at his wife and said, "You didn't have to say that . . . but thanks. It's more than I deserve. From now on I'll make up for everything . . . you wait and see."

With infinite weariness in her face, she murmured, "I only want to go home and never see this house again. Whatever you did I don't blame you. It was Adele's fault . . . it was all her fault."

Quinn told himself that was what Irene Ford believed, that was how she would rationalise the whole affair. No one could be more self-centred than a stupid woman. Now she had her husband again. Now the threat to her narrow little world had been removed. Now everything was all right.

As Ford put his arm round her and turned to the staircase, Inspector Elvin said, "Not yet. We're still a long way from settling this matter."

Ford let go of his wife and asked, "What else is there to talk about?"

"Quite a lot. To start with, you haven't yet confirmed that what your wife said is true."

"Don't be ridiculous. Do you expect me to deny it and make a liar of her?"

"No, I don't expect that. But I still want you to confirm that you and your wife were together all day Friday — especially between the hours of one and four p.m. in the afternoon."

Without any hesitation, Ford said, "All right . . . if that's all you want. We were together the whole of Friday — morning, afternoon and evening. Can we go now?"

"No, I'm afraid you can't. What do you do for a living, Mr. Ford?"

"That hardly seems relevant and I don't — "

"You can take it from me that it is relevant — very relevant. Please answer my question."

In a tone of artificial good humour, Ford said, "Very well. Anything to oblige. I deal in antiques."

"What kind of premises?"

"I have a shop in Ringwood. The address is 24 Castle Street and if you are interested — "

"Wasn't your shop open for business on Friday?"

"Yes, of course. We're open six days a week . . . and the answer to your next question is that my wife helps me to run the business. She understands antiques almost as well as I do and that's why she's there all the time."

"Any other assistance?"

"Only part-time. I employ a lady on Saturdays so that my wife can do the week-end shopping . . . and also if we want a few days off. Got all you need now?"

Inspector Elvin said, "So far as Friday is concerned — yes. Let's turn to the events of this morning. I understand you went for a walk with Miss Stewart. Is that right?"

"Yes. We left the house" — Ford gave Carole a wary look — "between nine-thirty and ten."

"And were in each other's company until — what time would you say?"

"Until just before I met Mr. Parry in the Bird-in-Hand."

"When was that?"

"I don't know," Ford said irritably. "On a Sunday I don't keep looking at my watch every five minutes."

"No, of course not. But surely you can give me some approximate idea?"

While Ford thought of an answer, Dr. Bossard skirted the room to where Carole was standing. She looked up and smiled and Quinn saw her take Bossard's hand. Then she turned to watch Neil Ford again.

He took as long as he could before at last he said, "It would be about twelve o'clock. Mr. Parry and I had a couple of drinks and we were coming out when we met my wife. She'd come looking for me . . . so we persuaded her to have a drink, too, and went back in again. That's why we got home so late."

Inspector Elvin looked at Parry and asked, "Were you already in the Bird-in-Hand before Mr. Ford arrived?"

A change had slowly come into Michael's face. He pushed himself to his feet and said, "Yes." He sounded as if something was struggling for expression.

"What time was it, Mr. Parry?"

"Well after half-past twelve."

"Are you sure of that?"

"Quite sure. I can't say to within a minute but — "

"You're mistaken," Ford said roughly. "It was nowhere near that time."

Michael Parry looked at Quinn and said, "You know when it was. I saw you leaving as I got there. You didn't see me . . . but I'm right, am I not?"

Quinn said, "Yes, you're right."

Without taking his eyes off Neil Ford, he added, "I can bear out what Mr. Parry says, Inspector. When I left the Bird-in-Hand it was close enough to twelve-thirty . . . and neither he nor Ford were there yet."

Elvin nodded. He said, "Evidently, Mr. Ford, you're the one who's mistaken. So let's check the measure of your mistake."

He glanced at Carole. "Do you agree, Miss Stewart, that Mr. Ford was in your company until twelve o'clock?"

She shook her head. Then she said in a small voice, "No, it was earlier than that. Not much . . . but earlier."

"How much earlier?"

"About ten to or a quarter to twelve."

"And you left him — where?"

"The other side of the village."

"How long would you say it takes to get from there to Miss Wilkinson's cottage in Northwood Lane?"

"About" — she gave Neil Ford a fleeting look — "about ten minutes."

He'd been listening with the air of a man who didn't fully understand what was happening. Now he said in a ragged tone, "It would also take ten minutes to get to the Bird-in-Hand . . . but I was wrong and I admit it. I didn't go straight to the pub. I took a walk first."

Inspector Elvin said, "And you didn't arrive at the Bird-in-Hand until some time after twelve-thirty?"

"Probably — probably not."

"So there is a period of at least forty minutes to be accounted for?"

"I've told you what I did. I went for a walk."

"Are you seriously asking me to believe that?"

"Why not? Is there a law against it?"

"No. But you and Miss Stewart had been walking since before ten o'clock. I'd have thought — "

"What you'd have thought doesn't interest me," Ford said. "Neither, for that matter, does all this talk about where I was and when and for how long. I'm telling you once and for all that I was nowhere near Miss

Wilkinson's cottage this morning or any morning. If you want to find the person who attacked her you'd better look elsewhere."

Elvin said, "I'd be more impressed by your attitude, Mr. Ford, if you could provide something in the way of evidence to support what you say. For example, did you meet anyone or see anyone who could corroborate that you were some distance from Northwood Lane at, say, twelve-fifteen?"

Neil Ford moved uncomfortably. "I don't think you've any right to go on questioning me like this. Unless you intend to make some charge I've nothing more to say."

"I see. Then you leave me no alternative but to — "

Inspector Elvin got no further. Irene said, "I can corroborate what my husband says. I was with him at a quarter past twelve."

A growing look of confusion darkened Michael's pale blue eyes. As he was about to speak, Elvin said, "Oh, no,

Mrs. Ford. Not this time. It won't work twice."

"But it's true. When it got to near twelve o'clock and he wasn't back yet I went looking for him."

"Did you know which direction he and Miss Stewart had taken?

Irene wriggled and took a long time to answer. Eventually, she said, "No . . . not really . . . but I had a fair idea. I guessed it would be" — she made an aimless gesture that could have meant anything or nothing — "that way."

"And you found him without too much trouble?"

"Oh, yes."

"What did you do after that?"

"We talked for a little while . . . if you know what I mean."

"And then?"

Once again she needed time to think. "I came back here to" — she gave Carole a fleeting look — "to fix up lunch."

"Were you here when Miss Stewart returned?"

"Oh, yes, she'll tell you herself — "

"Whatever she has to tell me doesn't require any prompting by you," Elvin said.

As Neil Ford opened his mouth in protest, the inspector stuck out a long forefinger. "And that goes for you, too, Mr. Ford. I don't want you to interfere from now on. Your wife chose to involve herself in this affair and I am, therefore, entitled to ask her any questions I consider necessary — any questions at all."

His manner changed as he turned to Carole. "Now, Miss Stewart. Was Mrs. Ford in the house when you came back?"

"Yes."

"What time was that?"

"Almost half-past one."

"Did she go out soon afterwards?"

"Within two or three minutes."

"Thank you." His eyes flitted to Irene's thin, anxious face. "All right, Mrs. Ford, let me see if I've got this in the correct order. You went out at twelve o'clock to find your husband: you found him some time prior to twelve-fifteen, spent a little while talking to him, and then returned to Elm Lodge: when Miss Stewart came back at about one-thirty you went out almost immediately, again to find your husband. Is that an accurate summary of your movements this morning?"

Irene looked down and tugged at her skirt. She said, "Yes . . . but the way you put it sounds funny . . . if you know what I mean."

"It sounds funny because it is funny," Elvin said. He pointed to Michael. "You, Mr. Parry, would seem to have been the only other person in this house. Miss Stewart and Mr. Ford had gone out . . . so had Mr. Quinn. That left you and Mrs. Ford alone. When did you go out?"

"About" — Michael brushed up the ends of his straggly fair moustache — "about half-past eleven. I told Mrs. Ford I was going to the Bird-in-Hand . . . " He paused, his eyes shifting from Irene to Carole and then back to Inspector Elvin's face. He still seemed to be trying to come to grips with something which eluded him.

Elvin prompted, "Yes, Mr. Parry? Go on."

"Well, I didn't actually leave right away. There was no hurry to get down to the Bird-in-Hand because it doesn't open until twelve on a Sunday. So I thought I'd fill in the time by taking a look at my car. She hasn't been running too well recently and I had an idea the lead to the coil hadn't been screwed in properly when they fitted a new radio last week. As it happens that wasn't the trouble . . ." He paused again.

"You can spare us the technicalities," Elvin said. "From what you're saying I gather that you spent some time in the garage. What happened while you were in there?"

"I saw Mrs. Ford leave the house. I'd have called after her but she seemed to be in a hurry. Never thought anything of it then and it's only now when I've heard her say she didn't leave until nearly twelve that I'm beginning to wonder."

"What time would it actually be?"

"Not five minutes after I'd gone into the garage — twenty to twelve at the latest."

Irene tugged at her skirt and wriggled when she saw everybody watching her. Then she stared at nothing, her mouth set in stubborn lines.

Inspector Elvin said, "Well, Mrs. Ford, don't you think you've been very foolish?"

She glanced at her husband, caught sight of the look in his eyes, and turned away. She said, "Anybody can make a mistake . . . and I still say it wasn't far off twelve. Not that it matters. You're trying to make out my husband was in Northwood Lane at a quarter past twelve . . . and it's not true. I was with him then and I'm willing to swear he never went anywhere near that woman's cottage."

Quinn knew the end was not far off. She'd go on fighting but the façade of her existence had already begun to crumble.

Elvin said, "It's no use, Mrs. Ford. Don't keep on trying to act as his alibi. You were not with him at a quarter past twelve and you may as well admit it."

With her face set in lines of bitter obstinacy, she said, "I won't — I won't admit it. You can't make me change my mind. I was with him . . . I was."

"You couldn't have been. Someone saw him at that time — and he was alone. I have a witness who will say you were not with your husband at twelve-fifteen."

Irene did a little wriggle but said nothing. In a bemused voice, Neil Ford asked, "Who — who's supposed to have seen me?"

"There's no supposition about it," Elvin said. "Dr. Bossard was on his way to visit a patient when he passed you walking in the direction of the

Bird-in-Hand. Isn't that so, Doctor?"

Bossard said, "Yes." He didn't sound very pleased.

"But if" — Ford stumbled and began again — "if you knew I hadn't been in Northwood Lane why did you try to make out that I killed Miss Wilkinson?"

Inspector Elvin smiled. He said, "You jumped to conclusions — unfounded conclusions. I didn't say you killed her. I didn't say anyone killed her. Actually, Miss Wilkinson isn't dead — far from it."

His eyes shifted from Ford to Irene and then settled on Michael Parry. "You kept doing your best to attract my attention while Mrs. Ford was rather foolishly trying to provide her husband with an alibi that he didn't need. When eventually I asked you what happened here after everybody but you and Mrs. Ford had gone out you said you had told her you were going to the Bird-in-Hand . . . but instead you went into the garage and while there — "

"I've explained all that," Michael said. He looked bewildered and guilty.

" — while there you saw Mrs. Ford leaving the house, some time between twenty-five to and twenty minutes to twelve. If that's true . . . "

He glanced at Irene. "Is it, Mrs. Ford?"

In a tone little more than a whisper, she said, "Yes . . . I think so."

"Then there's one thing you've succeeded in doing, Mr. Parry, that you may not have realised. You've put yourself in a position where no one can say what you were doing from that time on until you arrived at the Bird-in-Hand a little after twelve-thirty. Would you like to account for that period of close on an hour?"

Sudden anger drove the guilty look from Michael's face. He said, "No, I wouldn't. I don't know what's going on here . . . but you've shoved me around long enough. So far as I'm concerned — "

"You still say you spent the time tinkering with your car until you went

447

to the Bird-in-Hand?"

"Yes, I do . . . for a very good reason. It happens to be the truth."

Inspector Elvin said, "There's a saying: 'Great is truth and shall prevail.' You may be glad to know that I believe you — without qualification."

"I'm neither glad nor sorry. For your information, I couldn't care less."

With a little nod, Elvin said, "Perhaps I don't blame you."

He looked at Irene and his voice changed. "Well, Mrs. Ford? I said you'd been very foolish, didn't I? You were so anxious to provide your husband with an alibi, you didn't think you might need one yourself. And now it's too late. I won't bother to ask you where you were around twelve o'clock to-day — I know."

She stared at him as though waiting for him to go on, as though he hadn't finished saying all that had to be said. When he remained silent, she began to tremble, her hands plucking at her skirt, her eyes sick with terror.

Carole turned away and put her face against Bossard. Quinn saw Sergeant Taylor come a step nearer. Like a man talking to himself, Michael Parry murmured, "I don't believe it . . . no, I don't believe it."

In a voice he couldn't control, Neil Ford asked, "What the hell are you talking about? What is all this?"

Inspector Elvin said, "Kindly remain quiet. I told you not to interfere." His eyes hadn't left Irene's face.

Then he went on, "Well, Mrs. Ford. You thought there was no hope for Miss Wilkinson, didn't you? You thought she'd be dead before she was found . . . and so she'd never be able to reveal that she saw your husband's car in front of this house last Friday afternoon. She assumed it had been one of his usual visits until she learned that Mrs. Parry must've been given a dose of poison at or about that time."

Neil Ford said huskily, "Oh, my God! I never guessed — "

He caught hold of Irene and forced

her to look at him. "You pretended you didn't know about Adele and me. And all the time . . . " He choked down the rest.

When he released her she didn't move. She was still staring at Elvin as if hypnotised.

He said, "Oh, yes, Mr. Ford, your wife knew all right. What finally drove her to kill Mrs. Parry is something that only she can explain. I'd say, however, that she probably made that decision during a phone call she received from Adele Parry on Friday morning . . . "

Quinn saw Dr. Bossard whisper something to Carole. She nodded and they walked towards the door. As they went outside, Elvin's voice ran on.

" . . . The switchboard operator who'd put through the call was off duty yesterday. When she came back this morning and heard the news she gave the hotel manager certain information that he passed on to me. It seems the operator cut in on the conversation, thinking it was finished, and overheard your wife arranging to meet Mrs. Parry at Salisbury . . . "

Slowly and heavily, Michael began walking to the foot of the staircase. He didn't look back.

" . . . It gave me something to go on . . . but it wasn't proof. For that I needed Miss Wilkinson. And as soon as I heard what had happened to her I knew there could be only one thing she'd seen last Friday that made it vital to stop her talking."

Irene Ford was trembling again, her face tormented like the face of a woman wracked with pain. Twice she tried to speak but the words refused to come out.

Then the inner struggle exhausted itself and she became quite still. Her eyes were no longer afraid.

In a calm, resigned voice, she said, "I don't care what you do now. Nothing matters any more. Adele had everything. She was rich and beautiful. Between her looks and her money she could have whatever she wanted. The whole world was hers — but she was going to steal my husband. I couldn't let her do it. She deserved to die and I'm glad I killed her."

Neil Ford had been staring at her as though he had never seen her before. Now he said, "Be quiet . . . for God's sake, be quiet! If you keep your mouth shut, they don't stand a chance of proving . . . " He ran out of breath and couldn't go on.

She turned to look at him, her hands fondling each other like creatures which possessed a life of their own. She said, "You don't care what happens to me . . . not really. Adele wasn't the first. There have been other women . . . but you always came back to me. That's where she was different. She thought she could bribe me to let you go . . . like she was going to bribe Michael."

"But I wouldn't — " He broke off again.

"You wouldn't have left me?" She shook her head. "I wonder . . . "

452

With a touch of colour in her pallid cheeks, she went on, "I didn't do it just because of you, Neil. I hated her. She was the kind of woman I've always despised . . . and don't try to stop me. I may as well admit the whole thing and get it over and done with. Even if I don't, Ariadne can tell them all they want to know."

Inspector Elvin cleared his throat and said, "I'm afraid she can't. That was merely subterfuge on my part. Miss Wilkinson is dead."

Irene stared at him, her eyes filled with indignation. She said, "You cheated me. That isn't fair. You had no right to tell lies — not really."

"Perhaps we'll discuss that some other time," Elvin said. "Right now you are not obliged to say any more. If, however, you choose to make a statement, it is my duty to warn you that anything you say . . . "

16

THE inquest on Adele Parry took place Monday morning. It lasted three-quarters of an hour and the coroner returned his verdict just after a quarter to twelve.

Then Quinn asked someone, "Is there a pub round here where the beer isn't luke warm?"

He was told to try the Wheatsheaf. " . . . It's along there to your left. You can't miss it."

Quinn said, "If I do there must be something wrong with my homing instinct . . . "

The lounge of the Wheatsheaf had a half-moon bar, a quiet atmosphere, and a barmaid who knew how to pull a good pint of bitter. He was thinking of ordering a second when Inspector Elvin came in and joined him.

Elvin looked at the empty glass and asked, "Can I buy you another?"

"That's the best invitation I've had so far to-day," Quinn said. "You've arrived just in time. I'll be glad to drink your health."

"My pleasure. I owe you more than just a beer."

"Well, if you feel that way you can go on buying them until the debt's paid off."

"No, I'm serious," Elvin said. "You've been most helpful."

Quinn waited until the barmaid had served them. When she went away, he said, "I think you're right. My humble efforts did help to speed the course of justice. Incidentally, I don't mind drinking beer with you but I wouldn't sit down to a game of poker."

"I never play cards," Elvin said.

His silver hair was immaculate, his lean face remote and thoughtful as ever. He wore a tie in keeping with his discreet grey suit.

Quinn said, "Maybe you don't. But

you know how to work a very slick bluff. Even I fell for that story about Miss Wilkinson."

Inspector Elvin looked down as though admiring the shine on his well-polished shoes. With a faint smile, he said, "You fell for something a lot more important."

"Did I?"

"Yes. Dr. Bossard didn't see Ford walking by himself in the direction of the Bird-in-Hand. If I hadn't persuaded the doctor to tell a little white lie I'd never have proved that Mrs. Ford wasn't with her husband around twelve o'clock yesterday."

In the recesses of Quinn's mind, Ariadne Wilkinson was talking again like a voice out of the far distant past. " . . . *I'm going to teach you a lesson in good manners. Next time you won't be so abrupt with a lady.*"

He said, "Now you mention it, I did wonder about that. Of course, it shouldn't have been necessary. If I'd been a little more civil to Miss

Wilkinson on the phone that business at Rose Cottage would never have happened."

"You appear to be a man with a conscience," Elvin said. "Take my advice and don't let it get out of hand. Some things are destined to happen. I think it was Shakespeare who wrote: *'There's a divinity that shapes our ends, rough-hew them how we will.'* Remember it?"

Quinn said, "I remember another saying . . . but it doesn't always seem to apply: *'Be sure your sin will find you out.'* In Bossard's case he's managed to get away with it."

"You shouldn't say that. We still can't prove there was anything wrong in his relationship with Adele Parry."

"Why can't we? His wife threw him out because she discovered . . . oh, I forgot. You don't know he's married, do you?"

Elvin played with his glass and smiled. He said, "Yes, I do. Sorry to appear omniscient. I can assure you

457

I'm not. But I have known for some time that Dr. Bossard had a wife in the background. This weekend I made inquiries and learned that she was Miss Stewart."

"And so now they'll live happily ever after," Quinn said. The taste had gone out of his bitter.

Very gently, Elvin asked, "Jealous?"

As though that one-word question acted as a catalyst for all his conflicting emotions, Quinn felt suddenly better. When he'd taken a long drink, he said, "Yes, I am . . . or, at least, I was. They say that confession is good for the soul, don't they?"

"I wouldn't know about that," Elvin said. "But I hope it brings some good to Mrs. Ford." He was no longer smiling.

"How much has she told you?"

"Just about everything. She had a showdown with Mrs. Parry who offered her a substantial amount of money if she'd divorce her husband. Mrs. Ford pretended to agree, they sealed it with a drink which she doped with Pembrium, and then she helped Mrs. Parry to take her case upstairs. There the drug began to take effect . . . but by that time it was long after three o'clock."

"And Michael might come home and find his wife before she was dead . . . so she had to be carted into the nursery," Quinn said.

"Yes. The first plan to leave her in the bedroom with a brandy glass by her side had to be cancelled. Soon as Mrs. Parry was unconscious, Irene Ford removed her shoes — so as to avoid making scratches on the parquet floor — and dragged her into the nursery where things were made to look once again like a case of suicide."

"Those shoes ought to have put me on the right lines much sooner," Quinn said. "Standing them neatly side by side under the foot of the bed was the kind of thing that a woman would be most likely to do."

"Particularly a woman like Irene Ford. After talking to her last night

I came away with the impression that she's got an almost pathological love of tidiness."

"Next to her love for Neil Ford," Quinn said.

Inspector Elvin put down his glass and slid both hands into his jacket pockets, thumbs outside. He said, "I'm not sure I'd call that love in the accepted sense — more pride of possession. Until she met him she'd considered herself one of those women who seem born to be old maids . . . as they used to be called. After he married her she never ceased to marvel at her good luck."

"Which enabled him to go off on the side whenever he fancied a bit of fresh," Quinn said.

With a distasteful look, Elvin said, "I don't admire your choice of expression . . . but that, broadly speaking, was the situation between them — "

"Before he got on intimate terms with the rich and beautiful Adele Parry. That wench must've had an insatiable appetite for that there . . . to coin a euphemism."

"You mean a vulgarism," Elvin said.

Quinn finished his pint and rapped on the bar. When the girl looked round he gave her a nod and held up two fingers.

She said, "If that means you want the same again I'll attend to you as soon as I can. If it's meant to be a rude gesture I'll have you thrown out . . . and that can be arranged much quicker."

When she turned to speak to a man at the other end of the bar, Quinn said, "Somehow there's always one wherever I go . . . You didn't need to be told why the light was on in the nursery, did you?"

"No . . . but I had to ask all the same." A smile touched Elvin's tight-skinned face. "When did you guess the answer?"

"As soon as I realised that lights are only switched on if it's dark — not while the sun is shining. It wasn't dark when Miss Stewart and I arrived at the house: it wasn't dark when Michael left to go to Blandford. But it got dark shortly before Mrs. Ford screamed like a banshee and threw a faint at the top of the stairs. So I guessed that she'd put the light on to provide herself with an excuse for going into the nursery."

"She also needed a light to make sure that Mrs. Parry was dead."

"Yes. And if you want my opinion the scream that she let out was no fake. I'd say she got one helluva turn."

Inspector Elvin said, "It's difficult to go on hating somebody who's dead . . . even if you hated the person enough to cause her death."

The barmaid brought them two more beers and Quinn paid her. When she went away, he said, "Instead of philosophising, you might give some thought to my problem. Where do I go from here?"

"Not too far. We'll need you on Wednesday."

"Why?"

"You'll have to give evidence at the other inquest."

"And then the rest of my so-called holiday is my own?"

"Of course. You can go where you like and do what you want."

"Thanks. There's one thing I won't do."

"What's that?"

"You won't catch me going to a party without a personal invitation," Quinn said. "And it'll have to be in writing."

THE END

A FOOT IN THE GRAVE
Bruce Marshall

About to be imprisoned and tortured in Buenos Aires, John Smith escapes, only to become involved in an aeroplane hijacking.

DEAD TROUBLE
Martin Carroll

Trespassing brought Jennifer Denning more than she bargained for. She was totally unprepared for the violence which was to lie in her path.

HOURS TO KILL
Ursula Curtiss

Margaret went to New Mexico to look after her sick sister's rented house and felt a sharp edge of fear when the absent landlady arrived.

THE DEATH OF ABBE DIDIER
Richard Grayson

Inspector Gautier of the Sûreté investigates three crimes which are strangely connected.

NIGHTMARE TIME
Hugh Pentecost

Have the missing major and his wife met with foul play somewhere in the Beaumont Hotel, or is their disappearance a carefully planned step in an act of treason?

BLOOD WILL OUT
Margaret Carr

Why was the manor house so oddly familiar to Elinor Howard? Who would have guessed that a Sunday School outing could lead to murder?

THE DRACULA MURDERS
Philip Daniels

The Horror Ball was interrupted by a spectral figure who warned the merrymakers they were tampering with the unknown.

THE LADIES
OF LAMBTON GREEN
Liza Shepherd

Why did murdered Robin Colquhoun's picture pose such a threat to the ladies of Lambton Green?

CARNABY
AND THE GAOLBREAKERS
Peter N. Walker

Detective Sergeant James Aloysius Carnaby-King is sent to prison as bait. When he joins in an escape he is thrown headfirst into a vicious murder hunt.

MUD IN HIS EYE
Gerald Hammond

The harbourmaster's body is found mangled beneath Major Smyle's yacht. What is the sinister significance of the illicit oysters?

THE SCAVENGERS
Bill Knox

Among the masses of struggling fish in the *Tecta*'s nets was a larger, darker, ominously motionless form . . . the body of a skin diver.

DEATH IN ARCADY
Stella Phillips

Detective Inspector Matthew Furnival works unofficially with the local police when a brutal murder takes place in a caravan camp.

STORM CENTRE
Douglas Clark

Detective Chief Superintendent Masters, temporarily lecturing in a police staff college, finds there's more to the job than a few weeks relaxation in a rural setting.

THE MANUSCRIPT MURDERS
Roy Harley Lewis

Antiquarian bookseller Matthew Coll, acquires a rare 16th century manuscript. But when the Dutch professor who had discovered the journal is murdered, Coll begins to doubt its authenticity.

SHARENDEL
Margaret Carr

Ruth didn't want all that money. And she didn't want Aunt Cass to die. But at Sharendel things looked different. She began to wonder if she had a split personality.

MURDER TO BURN
Laurie Mantell

Sergeants Steven Arrow and Lance Brendon, of the New Zealand police force, come upon a woman's body in the water. When the dead woman is identified they begin to realise that they are investigating a complex fraud.

YOU CAN HELP ME
Maisie Birmingham

Whilst running the Citizens' Advice Bureau, Kate Weatherley is attacked with no apparent motive. Then the body of one of her clients is found in her room.

DAGGERS DRAWN
Margaret Carr

Stacey Manston was the kind of girl who could take most things in her stride, but three murders were something different . . .